What people are saying about …

JILTED

"In *Jilted*, Varina Denman brings Trapp, Texas, to life through her vivid descriptions, memorable characters, and seamless prose. Readers will be enthralled from the first page to the last in this touching conclusion to the Mended Hearts series. The power of love to heal and restore hearts and lives that are broken shines through this story. Well done!"

Carrie Turansky, award-winning author of
A Refuge at Highland Hall and *Shine Like the Dawn*

"Varina Denman has the storytelling gift. I am confident that if Trapp, Texas, were a real town, I would recognize it the instant I arrived thanks to Denman's vivid imagery, her compelling writing, and her believable and thoroughly lovable characters. A delightful and satisfying ending to the Mended Hearts series, *Jilted* handles topics such as clinical depression and PICS (post-incarceration syndrome) with understanding, humor, and hope."

Terrie Todd, author of *The Silver Suitcase*

"In *Jilted*, Varina Denman captures the grace and sweetness of a second-chance love set in a little town that affords few second chances. Forgiveness, healing, and truth braid together well in this satisfying conclusion to the Mended Hearts series."

Connilyn Cossette, author of
Counted with the Stars

"With her skillful ability to pull readers, slowly but surely, deep into the hearts of her small-town characters, Varina Denman proves to be an author worth paying attention to! Fans of Robin Lee Hatcher's newest contemporaries will absolutely love Denman's Mended Hearts series."

Dawn Crandall, award-winning author
of *The Hesitant Heiress, The Bound Heart,* and *The Captive Imposter*

JILTED

A NOVEL

VARINA DENMAN

David C Cook®

transforming lives together

JILTED
Published by David C Cook
4050 Lee Vance View
Colorado Springs, CO 80918 U.S.A.

David C Cook U.K., Kingsway Communications
Eastbourne, East Sussex BN23 6NT, England

The graphic circle C logo is a registered trademark of David C Cook.

LCCN 2016934346
ISBN 978-1-4347-0838-0
eISBN 978-0-7814-1487-6

© 2016 Varina Denman
Published in association with the literary agency of The Blythe Daniel
Agency, Inc., P.O. Box 64197, Colorado Springs, CO 80962-4197

The Team: Ingrid Beck, Jamie Chavez, Nick Lee, Jennifer
Lonas, Helen Macdonald, Susan Murdock
Cover Design: Amy Konyndyk
Cover Photo: Getty Images, iStockphoto

Printed in the United States of America
First Edition 2016

1 2 3 4 5 6 7 8 9 10

032416

For those who go it alone

Two are better than one, because they have a good return for their labor: If either of them falls down, one can help the other up. But pity anyone who falls and has no one to help them up.

Ecclesiastes 4:9–10

CHAPTER ONE

My daughter, Ruthie, always called me a glass-is-half-empty kind of person, but she was wrong. Not only was my glass half empty, but a tiny crack shot diagonally from a chip on the rim, and something bread-like hovered in the murky liquid. But I was in the process of tossing that damaged tumbler and getting a brand-new one. Even though I would never be a Susie Sunshine, I was determined to stop hiding inside myself. But it wasn't proving easy.

Today I sat in my hatchback on the side of Highway 84, sizzling like bacon in the afternoon sunshine. I did this a lot. Sometimes I turned off at the lake and stared at the rippling water, but most times, like today, I drove all the way to the wind fields to gaze at the turbines—white needles against a blue sky. I reached across the seat and cranked down the window on the passenger side to allow a breeze in. Ninety-four degrees in September, but it could have been worse. Last week we were still in triple digits.

As a pickup truck sped past, my little silver car rocked gently and I almost ducked, but it was only Old Man Guthrie. His index finger made a slow salute in greeting, but I did nothing in response. My typical hello. My friend Clyde Felton called me distant, but really I was just tired. Tired of waving. Tired of pretending. Tired of trying.

I focused my gaze on the jagged pastureland beyond the pavement and hoped nobody else would interrupt my thoughts. Then again, I sometimes wished God had provided an on/off switch so we women could shut down our brains when the memories started echoing.

For me, those memories were men. Ruthie may have insisted that my glass was half empty, but I liked to think it was filled up fine until the men in my life started throwing rocks at it for sport. Over the years I had gradually trained myself to shy away from males, other than the men in my family. And Clyde. Even Old Man Guthrie knew better than to stop and check on me, thank goodness. If he had, I would've been forced to explain why a grown woman was sitting in her car on the side of the highway, staring at the wind turbines. I smiled.

Those windmills, marching across the Caprock like evenly spaced tin soldiers, stretched for miles south of town and settled my nerves like a dose of Valium. Not that I'd had any Valium lately, but one doesn't quickly forget.

Depression almost killed me.

Twice.

I beat the demon both times and lived to tell the tale, but even now it threatened to rear its ugly head. *The nerve.* I had trampled it, but still the sadness haunted me like a villain hiding just beyond the glow of streetlights. Waiting.

So I took to fighting it with a spotlight. They say an ounce of prevention is worth more, so whenever I felt the beast slithering through my heart, I would make a mental escape to protect my happy thoughts.

This was one of those days.

I inhaled ninety-four-degree oxygen until my chest couldn't expand any more, and then I released it back into the hatchback as the muscles in my neck relaxed. Sure, I was a mild recluse, but at least I got out of my house now. I bought my own groceries and went to Panther football games and smiled at people. Sort of. I even ate dinner with Ruthie and her preacher-husband occasionally. I was beating the demon. I was.

I squinted at the nearest turbine, watching its slow-motion arms slice the sun as it cast moving shadows over the hood of my car. The hazy grayness slipped along my skin, then sailed, distorted, to the far side of the highway, where it slid across the pavement before looping back to slap me again.

Round and round and round. The wind fields were a temporary escape from life and the beast. From people. From my hometown. I snickered. I never got very far from Trapp, so I suppose that as much as I disdained the place, I still didn't want to leave it behind.

Flashing lights caught my eye from way down the road, and I leaned forward with my arms along the steering wheel and my chin on my wrists. The West Texas landscape lay so flat that I could watch the car approach from halfway to Snyder. It seemed to crawl along at a snail's pace before finally coming close enough for me to hear the whine of the siren. A highway patrolman. He barely slowed before turning on the lake road.

I rested my head against the seat and smiled at the predictability. This happened every so often. A group of fishermen would hole up in a cabin, get drunk, and then turn stupid. Last year a couple of them actually fired shotguns into the water, thinking they would shoot the fish, since they weren't biting.

Yes, Trapp was predictable. Quaint. Simple.

Narrow-minded.

Clearly my daughter was right. I was—and always would be—a glass-is-half-empty kind of girl, but at times, when I stared at the gentle windmills, I wondered if I could be happy again—truly happy, not just faking it—and deep inside, I felt a glimmer of hope.

The moan of another siren swelled on the breeze, and I located a patrolman in my rearview mirror. And through the front windshield, I saw what looked like a fire truck silently making its way closer. This was *not* predictable.

A lone highway patrolman was to be expected, along with the game warden, but not emergency vehicles from two towns. I turned in the seat as an ambulance sped past, and I covered my ears to block the screeching wails.

As I started the car, curiosity niggled at my brain, but I didn't follow them. Instead, I took a last glance at the towering sentinels that brought me such solace, and then I did a U-turn and headed back to Trapp. I was scheduled to work at the diner, and it wouldn't do for me to be late. Besides, the news of whatever was happening at the lake would probably beat me back to town.

CHAPTER TWO

Clyde Felton pulled into a parking spot in front of Dixie's Diner, turned off his headlights, and swung open the door of his old sedan. But then he hesitated. Maybe he wouldn't eat at the diner after all. He could whip up a quick meal at home, run through the shower, and be in bed an hour earlier than usual.

As he hoisted himself to his feet, a hot gust pushed a smattering of sand across the brick pavement, and the familiar stench of manure crept past his shoulders. More than once he'd heard strangers gripe about the odor of the feedlot when they'd stop on their way through town, but it didn't bother Clyde. He'd smelled worse. The outdoorsy scent of too many cows in too small an area hardly compared to the stench of human waste in a cell block.

Trapp, Texas, with its foul smells, outdated buildings, and unsurprising people, was home, and that's where his good memories lay. Memories before prison. Memories of freedom and happiness and friends.

But one of those friends had him all bent out of shape. He peered through the front windows of the diner, where Lynda

Turner stood behind the counter frowning at an order slip. The problem had started Tuesday when Clyde went to the diner for lunch. As usual he took a seat at the counter, and that's when he noticed it.

Lynda had been waiting on a fellow Clyde had never seen—probably a rig worker on his way through town—but the stranger wasn't the one who'd stirred Clyde's dander. It was Lynda. She'd been promoted to cook months ago, so she spent most of her time back in the kitchen, but that day she'd been out in the dining room waiting tables again. And she was smiling. When she poured the stranger a cup of coffee, the man let his eyes travel over her brown work uniform as a red hue crept up Lynda's neck. Then he handed her his card.

Even now, two days later, Clyde's insides tightened when he considered the obvious explanation. He was jealous, and the absurdity of it made him chuckle. Not only did he not need a woman in his life, but Lynda, as fiery as cayenne pepper, had never looked at him as anything more than a friend. Or worse, a brother. The two of them had been through too much life together to go messing with things, but Tuesday was different. Tuesday he felt drawn to her in a way he hadn't been drawn to a woman in a long, long time.

He shoved away from the car, took two long strides, and pushed open the door of the diner, stooping slightly so as not to bump his head.

Lynda now stood at her usual post in the kitchen, and when she noticed him through the pass-through window, he thought she might have rolled her eyes. But that was just Lynda.

"Hey, Lyn." He lowered himself to a stool at the counter and reached for a menu, but instead of opening it, he tapped it against the Formica. "I'll take pork chops, I guess."

"With carrots and corn bread. I know." Then she really did roll her eyes.

Every time he came in, he ordered the same thing, knowing she would razz him about it. They had a comfortable routine. He lifted his eyes from the menu, now open on the bar in front of him. Her long hair was pulled back in a messy ball, same as always, and some of it was falling around her neck, same as always. Even though she concentrated on her work, if Clyde looked closely enough, he could see that the corners of her mouth teased upward as she hummed an old Eagles melody. Dang, she was pretty.

Clearly, other men in town thought so too. Clyde noticed them. They would talk to her, try to get her attention, sometimes ask her out … but she wouldn't have it. She hardly seemed to notice and never, ever blushed.

That's what had been different on Tuesday.

She brought out his plate, and when she plopped it on the counter, the meat was still sizzling. "Dixie gave you an extra chop. I think she has a crush."

Clyde grunted. "Sure she does." The owner of the diner was at least twenty-five years older than him and a happily married great-grandmother.

Lynda reached under the counter for a saltshaker. "How are things at the Dairy Queen?"

"Same."

"Burned anything lately?"

"Naw."

She refilled his tea glass even though it was almost full, and then she said, "This afternoon I saw emergency vehicles out on Highway 84. You heard anything about it?"

He sliced his corn bread with his fork, then smeared half-melted butter over it. "Could've been an accident on the wind fields."

"Holy cow, I didn't think about that." She stared unseeingly toward the door, seeming to replay in her mind whatever she had seen earlier. "No, it was closer to the lake."

"That's good."

"Why do those idiots work on the turbines?"

This probably wouldn't be a good time to tell her that Troy Sanders had been hounding him to apply for a job. "Somebody's got to do it."

She rolled her eyes again.

"It ain't that dangerous, Lyn. Besides, they make decent money."

"Climbing three hundred feet straight up isn't dangerous?"

He took a drink of his tea, then set his glass down gently. "Not all wind techs climb."

"But they all want to."

It was his turn to speak. Taking turns was the way it was done, but he scooped a forkful of carrots into his mouth to avoid it. For crying out loud, he knew Lynda better than he knew anyone else in town—anyone left, at least—but since Tuesday, he felt a twinge of nervousness every time he talked to her.

"Well," she said, "if those emergency vehicles weren't out there for a turbine worker, I figure it was the Tarron boys dynamite fishing. They're home on leave, but the game warden'll catch them sooner or later."

Over the warm scent of his food, Clyde noted a hint of perfume, and he wondered if Lynda had always smelled like that. Sort of fruity. "You been sitting on the side of the road again?" he asked.

She squirted a spray bottle, then wiped the counter with a cup towel. Her shoulders inched up, then down, almost imperceptibly.

Right then Clyde thanked God for the chunk of pork chop he was able to shove in his mouth, masking his smile. If Lynda had noticed, she would have thought he was making fun of her for choosing such a strange location to pass the time, and he never would have been able to explain that he simply found her very ... interesting. And likable.

Nobody thought of Lynda as likable.

The woman rarely smiled, and when she did, it seemed forced. She didn't make friends easily. Even her family got fed up with her mood swings. But beneath those sharpened porcupine quills lay the soft fur of a bunny. A cottontail, not a jackrabbit.

A waitress slapped an order on the counter next to Clyde's plate, and Lynda picked it up. "Duty calls," she said through a sigh.

As he finished his meal, Clyde watched her through the pass-through window as she moved around the kitchen. In twenty minutes, he would be home in bed, and if tonight was anything like the past two nights, he would be lying awake for a while, trying to make sense of the jumble in his head.

He sucked on a piece of crushed ice, then chomped it between his teeth. "Hey, Lyn," he called. "Saturday I'm helping Troy and Pamela clean up that dumpy shop they bought. Want to tag along?"

She stood in front of the grill, side by side with Dixie. "Might as well." Her gaze never left her work as she flipped chicken breasts.

Dixie, however, raised an eyebrow and winked.

Clyde busied himself digging through his wallet. He and Lynda had already discussed helping their old friends get their used bookstore set up, so there was no reason for the Christmas-morning excitement coursing through his veins. None that he cared to admit anyway. He tossed the money on the counter.

The cowbell over the door clanked near his ear as he ducked his way to the street, where the breeze still blew from the direction of the feedlot. After more than twenty years of turbulence, his life had finally become peaceful, and he knew he should leave well enough alone. He already had everything he needed.

Everything he deserved.

For just a few seconds, he stood in front of the glass door, telling himself to forget about Lynda and her cottontail fur, but he couldn't stop himself from glancing back into the restaurant. Just once.

CHAPTER THREE

"Lynda, that man wants you."

I pressed my lips together and scowled at Dixie, ending the conversation before it started. Clyde Felton may have fancied me when we were teenagers, but I had never returned the sentiment, and Dixie knew it. Besides, a lot had happened since then. Through the front window, I scrutinized Clyde's back as he stood on the sidewalk blocking the doorway with his bulky frame. His blond hair was tied at the base of his neck, and when he looked up and down the street, the short ponytail brushed across his back. He glanced over his shoulder, and his gaze flitted to mine before he stepped to his faded sedan.

I set two plates on the ledge above the grill and slammed my palm against the bell. Clyde didn't have the gumption to get a decent job, much less chase after a woman. Not that I'd given him reason to.

Dixie reached for a tomato, then motioned to the dining room with her paring knife. "Here comes Ruthie. Take a break if you want."

"Fifteen minutes?"

"Ten. I expect a rush just before closing time when the city council meeting lets out."

My daughter perched on the same stool Clyde had been on five minutes earlier, but unlike him, she immediately started swiveling back and forth. She may have been twenty-two years old, but daily she proved she didn't have to act like it.

"Pie?" I asked as I scooped ice into two glasses, then filled them with tea.

"French fries." She hopped off the stool and peered into the kitchen. "You hear that, Dixie?"

"Got it, sweetie."

Ruthie stepped to the nearest table, snatched a bottle of ketchup, and then returned to her perch. "How long you been here, Momma?"

"Since three."

"Things were quiet at the grocery store tonight, so Gene let me leave early."

"Lucky." I wrinkled my nose at Dixie, then walked around the counter and set the glasses on the Formica. When I eased onto the stool next to Ruthie, the muscles in my thighs gently reminded me I'd been standing for six hours.

Dixie brought a plate of fries. "I was just telling your mother she should date more." She crossed her arms and ignored my frown.

"I've been telling her that for years," Ruthie said. "You see how she listens."

Ruthie thought she knew everything. She had found the man of her dreams, fallen for him like a bag of cement, and was now living her happily ever after. It was nauseating. "I've got no need for it," I said.

"I think you should date." Lonnie Lombard, the high school ag teacher, sat at a booth near the restroom, chewing with his mouth open and giving me a suggestive smile.

I smirked.

"You're all wrong for her, Lonnie," Ruthie said.

He straightened. "I'm a fine specimen of masculinity."

"It's true you are, but Momma likes men with hair."

His jaw fell open, and he ran a palm over his slick head. "Bald is beautiful. Or hadn't you heard?"

"Yes, I got that memo, but Momma never did."

Dixie crooned softly, "I was thinking of someone with blond hair. In a ponytail."

A slow breath labored through my lungs as it made its way from my pride to my lips, and I cocked my head toward Dixie. "Could you give it a rest?"

She hummed a melodic *yes* as she returned to the kitchen.

Ruthie continued to banter with Lonnie, but I ignored them and sipped my drink, wishing I were better at chitchat.

Once he was gone, Ruthie turned her attention back to me. "Sunday is the birthday party," she said.

"Yes …" I already knew where she was headed, and it had nothing to do with a birthday party for my nephew's baby. Now that Ruthie was married to the preacher, most of her sentences began with the words *Sunday* or *Wednesday*. At least when I was around.

"If you came to worship with us, we could all go to the park together."

"I'll meet you there."

"Girl," Dixie called from the kitchen, "your momma ain't ever going back to that church. You might as well give it up."

I decided to give Dixie a better gift for Christmas this year.

Ruthie didn't say anything else, but she didn't have to. Her eyebrows shot up as she squirted ketchup.

That was Ruthie—*Ruth Ann*, as I called her. Hoby and I named her after our mothers, but she was Ruthie to everyone else in town—spunky, straightforward, invasive. It was enough to drive a well-balanced, emotionally healthy person over the edge, and I had never been described in such positive terms. But she meant well. I knew she did. She wanted me to be as happy as she was, and she hadn't yet realized that happiness could evaporate like mist in a single afternoon.

I pulled the band from my hair, fingered the loose strands back in place, and then reworked the bun on top of my head.

The bell above the door clanked, and when I saw Neil Blaylock, I automatically clenched my jaw, but just slightly. Dixie's cousin stepped into the restaurant, and his raised chin and sweeping gaze seemed to judge the worth of each person in the room—two elderly women, a family of four, a teenager in the corner ... and Ruthie and me. After his instantaneous analysis, he turned and held the door for his daughter.

Fawn, with her willowy legs and curly blonde hair, still looked out of place pushing a baby stroller. She bumped past chairs to make her way to the table behind us. "I finished my economics paper, Ruthie."

My daughter swiveled on her stool. "Stop bragging."

"I'm not bragging. I'm rejoicing."

"Same thing, and it's ugly."

The two girls couldn't have been more different—Ruthie in worn jeans and her work shirt from the United grocery store, and Fawn wearing a pale-pink mini-sundress complete with matching nail polish—but they complemented each other in ways that went unseen.

Neil's boots scraped across the linoleum as he wandered toward us, and I wondered if the man had to buy new footwear every month just from wearing holes in the soles. The action, coupled with his straight-backed posture, created an air of confidence that most people found intimidating.

I knew better.

Neil Blaylock was a deceitful coward, but even though the townspeople could see through him, they acted as if he were a celebrity because he had enough money and power to buy their respect. *Welcome to Trapp, Texas.*

I toyed with the idea of escaping back to the kitchen.

Fawn maneuvered the stroller between her chair and Ruthie's stool, and Neil took the chair opposite her. He mumbled a greeting to Ruthie and me before turning in his seat so we were looking at the side of his face. Cold, but even so, his behavior had drastically warmed since Fawn married JohnScott, my nephew. Apparently Neil lowered himself to our status in order to appease his daughter. Whatever.

"Bummer, Nathan's asleep." Ruthie poked the toddler in the stomach. "Can I wake him up?"

"No way. He's probably down for the night."

"Fawn, you want a sandwich?" I asked.

Her eyes smiled. "That would be great, Lynda."

I may have been lousy at conversation, but at least I remembered my customers' favorite orders. Fawn was easy—chicken salad—and I would have added a side of well-cooked green beans for her baby had he been awake. Normally Fawn would have him in her arms, talking to him, tickling his neck, laughing. Happy, happy, happy.

I let the waitress take Neil's order.

"Ruthie, can you babysit tomorrow?" Fawn asked.

I walked into the kitchen, but if I stayed close to the window to fix the sandwich, I could still plainly hear the rest of the conversation.

"Mother and Dad have a meeting at the same time as my business math exam."

"Sorry," Ruthie said, "but I'm scheduled to work then, and Dodd will be writing his sermon."

An extended silence prompted me to look up and notice that both girls were gazing at me with eyebrows raised. "I'm working the day shift," I said quickly, "so I can go to the football game tomorrow night."

Neil squirmed in his seat as though joining the discussion caused him physical pain. "Your mother can pick Nathan up after the meeting, but it'll be a good hour after you leave for class." At least the man was trying to be social. Thanks to Fawn, Neil had spent the past year attempting to undo some of the hurt he had caused—and I was glad for it—but it would be a while before I could sit next to him in Dixie's Diner and shoot the breeze. Ruthie, on the other hand, shoved fries into her mouth and chattered merrily to Neil and Fawn and anyone else in the restaurant who looked her way.

She scooted over one stool to lean toward the next table where the two elderly women were just finishing peach cobbler. "How are you ladies today?"

The closer of the two laid down her fork. "Not too good since we went to the quilting bee over at Sophie Snodgrass's place. Should've stayed home."

"What happened?" Ruthie tilted her head, and even though she sat with her back to me, I could tell she made eye contact with Fawn. The two of them secretly called the old sisters *Blue* and *Gray*, and even though the nicknames made perfect sense because of their hair colors, I always feared Ruthie would accidentally slip someday and say the names aloud.

The gray-haired woman clucked her tongue. "We're getting too old for news like this, but we can't give up our quilting." She pointed a crooked finger as she looked from Ruthie to Fawn to Neil. "Something happened out at the lake today."

"Dad was telling me about that," Fawn said. "He heard it at the city council meeting."

Neil shifted in his chair again, but Gray raised her voice and spoke before he could open his mouth. "We heard it all from the police chief's wife. Biggest thing that's happened here since—" Her eyes shifted from Neil to me, and her face wadded as though she had just remembered a distasteful joke.

"Since a long time ago, Sister," Blue chimed in.

Gray's lips puckered slightly. "Anyhoo, the chief's still out there doing what he can to help the sheriff's posse, but he called Clara Belle on his cellular telephone so she wouldn't be too worried if she heard something about it on the radio or television."

"Radio or television?" Ruthie glanced at me to see if I was listening.

"I don't think there'll be any media out there," Neil said. "From what I heard—"

"You'll never believe what they found," Blue interrupted. "Over on the south side of the lake, not a quarter mile from Rock Creek, a couple hikers were skipping stones on the water—"

"I think folks ought not to skip rocks like that," Gray said slowly. "Could fill up the lake eventually, don't you think?"

"Or at least make it too shallow for boats. I've never been out to Lake Alan Henry, but I've heard it's a little low."

"Don't leave us hanging," Ruthie blurted. "What did they find?"

"Oh, Land sakes." Gray waved her palm. "They found bones!"

Ruthie, Fawn, and I stared at her blankly while Neil peered toward the back corner of the dining room.

"So?" Fawn asked.

Blue's hand swept the air. "*Human* bones!"

I started wiping down my work surface, but I stayed close to the window, as did Dixie. Blue and Gray were the town's most notorious gossips, and couldn't always be trusted, but Neil had just come from the council meeting, and he wasn't disputing the rumor.

Ruthie asked the question I was thinking. "How do they know they're human?"

"One of them was a *pelvic bone*," Blue bragged. "The other was a thigh bone, also known as a *femur*."

It occurred to me the sisters might not truly be sorry they had been at Sophie's quilting bee.

Ruthie rested her chin on a fist. "Maybe it's another Native American skeleton like the one they found five years ago. Remember? The anthropologists could even tell the woman was bowlegged from riding a horse."

Gray ignored her. "They're calling in the *Texas Rangers*." She emphasized the last words as if that tidbit of information put her back in the center of the conversation.

"Dad, what did you hear?" Fawn asked.

"Ruthie could be right." He shrugged. "There'll be a hubbub for a few days, and then everybody will forget about it. Even if it's not another Indian, I imagine they won't be able to identify the body from only two bones."

A cold chill shivered down my arms and legs, just like when I watched crime scene investigation shows.

Blue and Gray teetered to the cash register, and I met them there. "That'll be seven dollars and five cents."

"I think I've got a nickel." Gray handed me a ten-dollar bill, then set her handbag on the counter so she could rummage through it, looking for her coin purse. She tucked her chin. "Sister? You think our convict had anything to do with those bones?"

"Might at that," Blue said.

Six feet down the counter, Ruthie crossed her arms, and as I glanced at Fawn, I knew she had heard the accusation as well. My nephew's wife smiled as she chewed her sandwich, but her eyes were dull and lifeless.

For as long as he lived, Clyde Felton would be suspected of any crime that happened in our little town, be it bones found at the lake or a candy bar stolen from the United grocery. He was the town's *ex-convict* after all, and it would take a lifetime to live it down, whether he deserved the sentence or not.

I jabbed the cash register to open the money drawer and quickly pulled out three dollars. "Forget about the nickel."

"Now, Lynda, aren't you a sweet girl." Blue fiddled with the toothpick dispenser next to the cash register, then followed Gray.

As the women shuffled through the door, I remembered Clyde standing on the sidewalk. He had looked back at me one last time before he left, and even though his eyes only met mine for a split second, in them I could see anticipation. And hope. And something else.

Another chill skittered down my thighs. Good Lord, Dixie was right.

Clyde Felton wanted me.

Even now.

CHAPTER FOUR

Clyde wasn't sure how he had gotten himself in this fix. When Fawn called and asked if he could babysit Nathan, he had thought she was joking. Now he stood in his living room looking down at the little guy, who watched him with suspicious eyes. It seemed to Clyde that the child had heard all the rumors in town and was contemplating whether or not they were true.

After lowering himself to the edge of the couch, Clyde leaned forward with his elbows on his knees and waited for Nathan to do something. The toddler sat on his bottom in the middle of the rug, waiting as well. It was a standoff.

"Well," Clyde said too loudly, "what do you usually do to pass the time?"

Nathan giggled.

"You think that's funny?"

The baby clapped his chubby hands.

"Have you heard the one about the convict who caught the measles? … He broke out."

Nathan's laughter came from deep in his chest, and Clyde chuckled.

"Okay, how about this one? A murderer, a rapist, and a drug dealer are in the same car. Who's driving?" Clyde paused for effect, but Nathan had become mesmerized by the lamp on the end table. He held his palms in the air as if he were about to push against a brick wall, then slammed them against the rug and took off crawling.

Clyde laughed at Nathan's determination, then mumbled, "A cop, that's who." But when the child used the table leg to pull himself into a standing position, Clyde wasn't prepared.

Just before Nathan jerked the lamp cord, he squealed happily as though he were telling a joke of his own. When the lamp toppled with a crash, Nathan stared wide-eyed at the exposed lightbulb. "Uh-oh." His voice tremored like a startled doorbell, and then he whimpered.

Clyde reached for the lamp but hesitated, wondering if he should pick up the baby first. The dilemma momentarily paralyzed him in the middle of the floor until his gaze met Nathan's. The child's eyes begged for deliverance while the electrical cord still dangled from his tightly closed fist.

"Aw, now. It ain't that bad."

Nathan's chin quivered as Clyde put one palm on the baby's stomach and another on his rump and lifted him into a sitting position with his back hugged firmly against Clyde's chest.

"Come on up here. Things are always better at a high altitude."

Nathan's head bumped Clyde's shoulder as he turned to peer at him.

"It'll be all right now." Clyde walked to the back window, thinking Fawn was crazy to trust him with her baby. Even though she had been to his trailer house several times before, this morning her gaze had skimmed across the tattered furniture and lingered on the hole in the wall by the front door.

"It'll only be for an hour or so," she had said. "Mother can pick him up when she gets out of her meeting."

But her words hadn't eased Clyde's concern. Instead, his insides tightened at the thought of Susan coming to his house. They hadn't been alone together since before Clyde went to prison, and he sure as heck didn't want to be alone with her now.

His gaze lingered on Nathan's black curls, and he shook his head. Even without the worry of Susan, Clyde clearly wasn't fit for the task of babysitting. For crying out loud, the lamp almost landed on the kid's head.

An outdated phone hung on the wall by the dinky kitchen table, and it jangled loudly, causing Nathan to startle. Clyde shifted until his wide palm covered Nathan's stomach, and he held the child firmly while Nathan gently kicked his feet.

Clyde raised the phone to his ear. "Yeah?"

"How's he doing?" It was Fawn, checking up on him. She hadn't been gone thirty minutes.

"Not too bad."

The baby closed his palm around the corkscrew phone cord and shoved it in his mouth. He frowned at the taste, pulled the cord out to inspect it, and then jerked his arm, sending the cord into frenzied arcs. "Mama!"

"I hear him. What's he doing?"

Clyde looked down at Nathan to see the child's face change from pink to dark red. The baby's lips pressed together as if he were choking on a softball, and panic shot through Clyde like a dose of adrenalin, but just as quickly his fear evaporated.

"He might be filling his britches at the moment."

"Bless your heart. Mother should be there in fifteen minutes. Save it for her."

An image of Susan Blaylock changing a crappy diaper in her high heels flitted across Clyde's mind.

"I know what you're thinking," Fawn said, "but you'd be surprised what that woman can do under pressure."

"If you say so."

"Thanks again for watching him. I made it to class with time to spare, but I better go. The exam is starting soon. Oh, and …"—the hesitation in her voice caused Clyde to press the phone tighter against his ear—"Dad may be with Mother when she comes by."

"Right." Clyde supposed he should have muttered more than one word, but he laid the phone on its cradle and cautiously returned his palm to Nathan's bottom.

There was no love lost between Neil and Clyde, but the fact that the man didn't trust his wife—or Clyde—for something as harmless as babysitting duties made him grit his teeth.

Nathan kicked Clyde in the hip, and Clyde realized he had been standing motionless at the back door. He moved numbly into the living room and laid the toddler on the couch. "You and me need to talk." Clyde sat and pulled the diaper bag toward him. "Why'd you go and poop your pants?"

"Poo." Nathan's lips formed a circle around two tiny teeth, and then he scrunched his nose and giggled.

"I don't see the fun in it, kid." Clyde fumbled with the bag, unzipping and zipping compartments. He had seen Fawn do this enough to know that the wipes were in the white plastic box.

A light tap on the front door set off a chain reaction of mixed emotions, and Clyde stood. Apparently the Blaylocks had hurried. *No problem.* They just needed the baby. They hadn't come to deliver a sentence or dredge up the past or cause problems. Besides, now he wouldn't have to change the diaper. He should be glad.

He pulled Nathan into a sitting position on the low couch before he opened the door.

Susan stood in front of him in a sequined blouse with her smile pulled so widely across her face that her teeth reminded Clyde of a denture commercial. His nerves ricocheted up and down his spine like red sand in a dust devil because he realized she didn't want to be standing in front of his house any more than he wanted her there.

"Hey, Susan."

"Clyde."

Neil stood behind her with his cell phone pressed against his cheek and his elbow stuck out. His other hand rested at his waist with his thumb behind his shiny belt buckle. He didn't look at Clyde or even acknowledge the door had been opened. "Where are they now, Hector?" Neil grunted in disgust. "Are you at least keeping the things locked up somewhere?"

Clyde held the door open and motioned them inside. "I'll get his bag." He offered no other comment, and Susan offered nothing in return.

Nathan, joyously oblivious to the tension that snapped like distant firecrackers on a clear night, appeared to be doing the wave at a Panther football game.

Susan took a cautious step into the house, but her husband turned his back as he continued his phone conversation. "I'm no investigator," Neil said, "but if the bones have no DNA left on them anyway, why would you keep up the search? Seems like a waste of time and money."

Susan's lips pressed against each other, forming a thin, hard crack. "On the phone with the sheriff."

Clyde bent to retrieve the items he had pulled from the bag—a thermometer, a blanket, and a small bottle of baby shampoo—and he shoved them into the diaper bag. When he turned to bid Susan a speedy exit, her head was cocked to the side as she inspected the fallen lamp, still shining brightly.

"Everything go all right?" she asked.

"Just a little mishap." Clyde righted the lamp. "No harm done."

"And what happened here?" She pointed to the hole in the wall.

"That was already there. The little tyke didn't damage the house yet."

Her sigh held traces of a laugh, but then she glanced over her shoulder at Neil just as he dropped his phone in his shirt pocket.

"Thanks for tending to our little man." Neil leaned against the doorframe and smiled as broadly—and artificially—as Susan had, but then he dropped his voice. "We should get out of the man's way, Susan. I'm sure he has plenty to keep him busy." He strolled toward the street, leaving Susan to carry Nathan and all his equipment.

"Kid's muddy," Clyde admitted to her. "I didn't change him."

Her gaze bounced from her grandson to the curb. "I'll change him at the house." She pulled the diaper bag over one shoulder and bent to pick up Nathan, who was cruising around the room, using furniture to keep his balance.

"Aw ..." Clyde didn't know how to finish his thought. Neil and Susan's ranch was thirty minutes from town, and even though Clyde didn't know a lot about diapers, he was fairly certain half an hour was too long to leave the kid in a nasty one.

Susan said nothing else, and Clyde shut the door as soon as her heels cleared the threshold.

He shivered. The memories flooding his brain were as unwanted as they were haunting. Susan reminded him of his mistakes and regrets, but he figured he could ignore the memories and steer clear of his past. *Their* past.

He peeked out the front window to watch as she stuffed the kid into a car seat, and he expected Neil to greet Nathan with the syrupy smile he reserved for his grandson, but he hardly looked at the child. The rancher crouched in the driver's seat of his fancy pickup, and for a second, Clyde thought Neil was biting his fingernails. But that couldn't be. Neil Blaylock didn't bite his nails. He didn't crouch in his truck. He didn't ignore his grandson.

Clyde wished he had spoken to him. To both of them. He let the curtain flutter back down, then bent to retrieve a toy car from the floor. He should have said something to clear the air, to make all the awkwardness go away, to erase the pain he had caused for two decades. Once again, guilt washed over him like moonlight, and he reminded himself for the thousandth time that he had an obligation to the Blaylocks.

He owed them an apology.

CHAPTER FIVE

"Lynda, I don't see why you're in such a god-awful hurry. The game doesn't start for an hour."

As my sister pulled into the school parking lot, gravel crunched beneath the tires, producing a sleepy baritone of pops beneath the backseat floorboard. Velma drove her Chevy with the same forceful control she used when she drove the tractor, and at approximately the same speed.

"I ain't in a hurry to get to the game. Just to get moving."

With his index finger, Ansel made a slow arc over the dash and pointed to a parking area near the entrance gate of the stadium. My brother-in-law never wasted his breath if a simple gesture would suffice.

"I see it." Velma swatted his hand. "There's only five cars in the lot. I figure I can manage a parking spot for an ornery old man."

"Never know," Ansel crooned.

He sat directly in front of me, and even though I couldn't see his face, I heard a smile in his voice. He pushed his door open, and when it moaned, I found it oddly appropriate. Ansel was only seventy, but his body had weakened in the past few years until he moved like a ninety-year-old. As he climbed from the car, he slowly raised a wooden toothpick and clamped it between his teeth. Undoubtedly he carried a stash of chewing tobacco in his shirt pocket for when the toothpick wasn't enough.

"He any better?" I whispered to Velma as we followed him.

"Not a bit. And don't worry about being quiet. His hearing aids don't pick up anything behind his back."

We paused as Ansel pulled his wallet from the hip pocket of his Wranglers. With his thumb and forefinger, he withdrew two bills from between the folds of leather and calmly handed them to the Booster Club mother manning the gate.

"What does the doctor say?" I asked Velma.

"More tests and more money."

"But he'll be all right?"

She hefted her stadium seat to her other hand. "Doc Perkins says Ansel's too hardheaded to be down for long, and he should know. They've been friends since grade school."

"When will you hear something?"

"Next week sometime, but I wouldn't put it past the old doc to push the tests through quicker. He's just as anxious as we are."

I followed her into the stadium, but Ansel veered to the right, away from the bleachers and toward the fence by the concession stand. He would lean his elbows on the top rail, chew his toothpick, and nod his head to every male who passed him. By the time the game started, at least three accomplices would join him, and he wouldn't make it into the stands until close to halftime.

Velma and I climbed up the ramp and made our way to the fifty-yard line, where we had our pick of seats. "Is JohnScott still helping on the farm?"

"He tries, but football season don't leave much time."

I nodded. As head coach of the high school football team and part-time farmer-rancher on the side, my nephew worked harder than any man I knew, but there were only so many hours in the day. "I suppose Sundays are off limits."

"Sure enough. JohnScott generally spends Sundays with Fawn and Nathan." JohnScott was Velma's baby, and as the youngest of nine children and the only son, he was somewhat of a pet. I knew it had been hard on Velma when he married and settled down, even though she loved Fawn as much as one of her own daughters.

As I sat down, my gaze drifted to the end zone, where a few brawny players stretched on the field. Ansel leaned on the fence near them, looking shriveled in comparison. "I can't help worrying."

"JohnScott says God will work things out."

I rolled my eyes, but Velma didn't pay me any mind. The two of us settled into a comfortable silence and watched the crowd gather, and when Velma noticed Ruthie and Fawn climbing toward us, she gave a satisfied chuckle.

"Momma, you want a bite?" Ruthie sat down holding an oversize soft pretzel toward me so I could pinch off a piece with my fingers.

We still had ten minutes before kickoff, and Nathan held our undivided attention. I would never admit it aloud, but I enjoyed seeing Fawn and that rascally boy of hers as much as I enjoyed seeing Ruthie. Who would have thought I would ever willingly spend time with a Blaylock? Especially Fawn. But she was a Pickett now—as good as family.

"Ruth Ann, where's Dodd?" I pointed my pinky. "He's not at his usual post near your elbow."

"He's praying with JohnScott and the team."

"Of course." I blinked hard to keep from rolling my eyes again. Clyde had been making fun of me so much lately, I was trying to cut back. I bit my lip instead.

Fawn held Cheerios in her palm. "Dodd's bound and determined to get everybody in town into the church building one way or another."

Velma wagged her head back and forth. "He's got his work cut out for him with Ansel."

"And Momma," Ruthie said.

I had packed a Dr Pepper in my bag, intending to save it for halftime, but to slow the conversation, I reached for it now and twisted off the cap. "Church is not for me," I mumbled into the bottle as I took a swig.

"It could be, though," Ruthie said.

I frowned at the field, where four players waited for the coin toss, but I didn't answer. Ruthie and I had beat that discussion so firmly into the ground, even wild devil's claw wouldn't grow in the trampled soil.

"Okay." She sighed. "I'll drop the subject."

Nathan was sitting calmly on Fawn's lap, but without warning, he lunged for Ruthie, and the two girls became a tangle of arms as they transferred him from one lap to the other. He faced Ruthie with one tennis shoe on each side of her hips, and with his pudgy hands, he explored her face.

Babies were cute and all, but I didn't see how people could stand all that touching with spit-sticky hands. It had been so long since I mothered Ruthie, I barely remembered the mechanics of it, but Hoby had been a natural. I sipped my Dr Pepper and let the too-warm carbonation burn the back of my throat. Sometimes it had seemed that Hoby wanted our baby girl even more than he wanted me.

Nathan's hands tangled in Ruthie's hair, and she patiently pried his fingers loose.

"Here's a safe topic," she said. "The bones found out at the lake."

I wrinkled my nose. "Why does everybody keep talking about that?"

"You can't be serious. It's a dead body, for goodness' sake."

"My dad's tired of hearing about it, too," Fawn said. "Told me and Mother to hush up."

"It's not a dead body," I said. "It's a couple of bones. A wild animal could've carried them from miles away."

"Actually," Ruthie said, "the news reported that wild animals wouldn't have dragged them very far. They said the rest of the body is most likely within fifty feet or so."

"It's like *CSI*," Fawn said, "only not as gross."

Velma sniffed. "*CSI* is the most disgusting show I've ever seen."

"And guess what?" Ruthie said. "I heard there's a crime scene investigation team looking for the rest of the body, so it really is like the TV show."

Velma's eyes strayed from the kickoff long enough to peer at Ruthie. "Who told you that?"

"Dixie Edison."

The fans around us briefly went into a flurry as the Panthers gained thirty yards in the first six seconds of the game, but when the sound level waned, Ruthie leaned over me and nudged Velma's shoulder.

"Know what else Dixie told me?" She paused for a millisecond. "She thinks Clyde Felton has the hots for Momma."

"For crying out loud, Ruth Ann." I glanced around to see if anyone had heard, but apparently the crowd was too worked up to pay attention to gossip.

Velma peered at Ruthie as though the girl had become an encyclopedia of knowledge. "You don't say."

"I do."

I shook my head and blurted the first thing that popped into my head. "Dixie shouldn't be pairing anyone up with a convict." I instantly regretted my words.

"*Ex*-convict," Fawn mumbled. "You sound like Blue and Gray."

"I felt like slapping those old women," Ruthie said. "Why would they insinuate that Clyde had anything to do with that dead body?"

"Once a jailbird, always a jailbird. In their eyes," Velma said.

"But he didn't deserve to go to prison in the first place," Ruthie countered.

"I'm not saying he did," my sister said. "But people around here remember the prison sentence longer than they remember the details of the thing."

Their comments rubbed a soft spot behind my lungs. "All they remember is that Clyde broke the law."

Fawn frowned.

"But he and Susan loved each other," Ruthie said. "Once upon a time."

"Aw, Ruth Ann," I said softly, "if he cared enough about Fawn's momma to have sex with her, he should've cared enough not to."

Ruthie's face pinched, and I knew I had said the wrong thing again. I tilted my head from side to side, stretching my neck muscles. The two girls didn't mind pushing Clyde into my life—but they strongly disapproved of me pointing out that he had been convicted of statutory rape.

I looked at Fawn and exhaled. "Sorry to talk about your daddy that way, but both you girls might as well look at the big picture. Clyde and I have a lot of baggage in our past, and you fancying us together is absurd."

"Momma …" Ruthie stared at me, screaming with her eyes. "Fawn doesn't call Clyde *Daddy*."

"It's all right." Fawn dug through Nathan's diaper bag. "I know Clyde's not without fault, but he's not a bad person either. He made one unwise decision that affected the rest of his life."

"There were five of us whose lives went into a tailspin," I corrected her. "Not that I put the responsibility entirely on him. Clyde and your momma just set it all in motion."

We fell into a stiff silence, broken only by Nathan's giggles, but when the Panthers ran for a touchdown, we stood and cheered with the rest of the fans, our squabble temporarily forgotten.

I glanced toward the dark end of the field, on the far side of the track, to the pastureland where the scoreboard rose beyond the goalposts. If I remembered correctly, the property belonged to Wilmer

Justice, who currently had it planted in cotton. Clyde's sedan was parked just over the fence.

He watched all the games from there. Most people thought he was legally forbidden to set foot on school property, since he was a registered sex offender, but really, he just didn't want to cause trouble.

Thin strands of barbed wire separated him from the festivities, and he sat on the hood of his car. He had one foot on the bumper, and he was sipping something from a can. If it turned out to be a beer, I'd lay into him, but I would be surprised if it was. He had all but sworn off alcohol, saying he had too much to lose.

He stood and craned his neck as the Panthers blocked the opposing team's drive, and when the Panthers thwarted them on the three-yard line, Clyde punched his fist in the air.

I envied him, alone on the other side of the fence, even though he had told me more than once he'd rather sit in the stands with Fawn and Nathan. But I knew that from his perch on the hood of his car, the announcer, the band, and the noise from the crowd would all be muted, and he wouldn't be able to hear the snide remarks or see the looks on people's faces.

Suddenly a shiver of anticipation vibrated through my core, and I was surprised to realize I wouldn't mind sitting over there. Where it was peaceful. I wouldn't mind sitting with Clyde. In fact, I might prefer sitting with him over just about anyone.

Even Ruthie.

Even Velma.

Even anybody.

But I couldn't do that.

CHAPTER SIX

When Clyde and Lynda arrived at Troy and Pamela Sanders's junk shop on Saturday morning, Clyde only hesitated a second before stepping aside to hold the door for her. "After you, Lyn."

She paused as though surprised by the pungent scent of a stink-bug, then rolled her eyes. Just like Clyde knew she would.

Troy and Pam had purchased the store and all its contents with the intention of sprucing up the place and turning it into a used bookshop. *More power to them.* The building, which had once been a post office, still held rows of copper-plated mailboxes, as well as the USPS emblem on the side wall, but the nostalgia ended there. The previous business owners had filled the place with garage-sale trash and called it a flea market, when it was actually nothing more than a front for drug deals.

At least Troy and Pam had gotten it cheap.

"Felton!" Troy stood behind a cluttered counter, spreading his arms wide. "Welcome to the Trapp Door, our town's first-ever used bookstore and secondhand novelty shop."

"The Trapp Door?" Clyde stepped over a box filled with scented candles.

"Pam came up with the name." Troy grinned with his mouth open slightly. "You know … all those PO boxes on the back wall … and all those tiny little doors. You get it?"

"I got it." Clyde glanced at Lynda, worried she would feel out of place. Even though she had been friends with Troy and Pam for years, Clyde sensed they hadn't done much socializing since Lynda left the church. However, he knew for a fact that Pam made a point to talk to Lynda at the diner.

Lynda picked up a Mr. Potato Head toy that had several empty holes where parts were missing. "I can't believe you paid money for this stuff, Troy."

"Aw, you know." Troy's grin was cemented on his face. "Gives Pam something to keep her busy. Now that Emily's away at college, the wife gets awful lonely during the day when I'm at work."

Lynda's gaze slid from a stack of coffee mugs to a basket of pot-pourri. "Keep her busy so she won't think about you risking your life every day?"

Clyde considered the fact that Lynda needed a spanking, but he looked over her head and made eye contact with Troy. More than once his friend had voiced his concern about his dangerous job, but he always tagged on a few excuses.

"Now, Lynda." Troy came around the counter and cast puppy eyes down at her. "Wind techs make a good living, and Pam knows that."

"Wind techs are crazy fools." Her right eyebrow coiled like a leather whip intended to pop sense into Troy, but her gaze shifted to Clyde at the last second, just in time for him to feel the sting as well.

Troy slapped Clyde on the back and laughed loudly. "That goes without saying, don't it?"

Lynda looked back and forth between the two men, but then she shook her head and smiled. "I'm not going to argue with you. I came here to work."

"Alrighty, then! Clyde already has your assignment—should you choose to accept it—so if y'all don't mind, I'll leave you in charge of the place while I run to Home Depot in Lubbock. Pam wants more shelving."

"You sure you trust us with your inventory?" Clyde reached for a gaudy piece of costume jewelry.

"If you steal anything, I'll know where to find you."

***

Fifteen minutes later, Clyde and Lynda were settled at a table in the back room, surrounded by boxes of books, and Clyde was trying to find the courage to ask Lynda out on a date. Or maybe not a *date*. That sounded all formal and stuffy, and Clyde didn't really do formal and stuffy. But he knew in a strange way that she had become the missing link that connected the past to the future, and he felt it all the way down in his bones.

Lynda held an old book in her hands and slumped back in a metal folding chair. "I can't believe you talked me into working in this dusty closet. Your ex-girlfriend is the one who donates her time to worthy causes, not that this shop rates as a charity cause."

Suddenly Clyde was back in the cell block, with catcalls and taunts being hurled through the air like knives. He pulled another box toward him and picked through the titles. "Don't call her that, Lyn."

She flipped the book over and glanced at the back cover, and judging from the way her chin puckered, Clyde thought she might have been sorry she said it. She blew on the spine of the book, and a gray puff of dust floated away from her. She gave him a quizzical look. "So you've been helping Troy and Pam for a while now?"

"A couple Saturdays."

She continued to study him, scrutinize him, frown.

Like a prison guard.

He shifted the remaining books in the box, picking them up one at a time, reading the titles, forcing his gaze away from her. Not really wanting to talk.

She sighed. "Okay, so the drill is to pick out *the good books*." She made quote marks with her fingers. "Then vacuum them, wipe them, and sort them." She raised her eyebrows. "That right?"

"Yep, that's it." She was deliberately being a toot, and he had no idea why. Women didn't make a lick of sense to him.

Not that he had been around many in his lifetime.

He rested his forearms on his knees and reached for a roll of paper towels, swinging his hair out of his eyes.

"Why do you let your hair grow long? It used to be short all the time."

She was full of questions today, and it made him wonder. "Because I can."

"Could you give me more than three words? Please?"

He straightened and met her gaze, then shrugged one shoulder. "They kept my hair short in prison, but now I do what I want." He didn't mention that Trapp's barber looked down on him, and the only other option was Sophie's Style Station, an estrogen-infused hovel Clyde didn't dare set foot in. He supposed he could go to the little barber shop in Snyder, but he'd probably scare that old man to death. "Besides, Lubbock's too far anyway," he added, figuring Lynda would understand the rest without his going to the trouble of speaking it.

"You know what I think?" She wiped a paper towel across a book cover. "I think they used to decide when you got your hair cut, and now you can't figure it out on your own."

"I like it long." Okay, maybe he didn't—he wasn't sure—but he didn't see the need to burden her with his problems. Truth was, she was dead on target. He had trouble making decisions, but Dodd Cunningham was helping him work through all that. Clyde enjoyed his early morning coffee meet-ups with the preacher, even though Lynda's son-in-law seemed to think Clyde needed professional counseling.

"Whatever you say." The corner of her mouth curled into that spunky smile of hers, and then she ducked her head. "I like it long, too, I guess."

Her words sounded careless, as though they weren't important, as though she hadn't just tossed him a thread of hope to cling to. He grasped at the confidence it gave him, all the while hoping she wouldn't cause his heart to unravel like his grandmother's old crocheted afghan.

"That's a good one." He pointed to the book she was wiping.

"So …" She narrowed her eyes. "You read?"

"Sure."

"Since when?"

"Prison."

She leaned her elbows on the table and tilted her head. And stared.

A lot of people stared at him. Now that the rumor mill had spread the truth about him and Susan, things were different, but many citizens still treated him like he had the plague. Children pointed and women scurried away. Men crossed their arms and planted both feet on the ground, but he had gotten used to that.

Lynda's stare felt different though, because her eyes didn't scour him like the others', and he didn't have the urge to run away and hide. Instead, when Lynda looked at him, he wanted to look back at her. And hang around and listen to her talk.

"Have you read any of these?" Like a salesgirl, she swept her slender hand through the air above the stacks.

"I figure I have."

"What does that mean?" She moved the Dustbuster so she could look through the paperbacks beneath it.

"The books in the prison library didn't have covers." He picked up a novel with a white stallion on the front. Swirling, dark clouds surrounded the horse, and red breath shot from its nostrils. The name didn't sound familiar to Clyde, but he knew he would have remembered that picture if he had seen it before. He tossed the book onto the table. "I can remember the well-known titles, but the covers won't look familiar."

"So the books were all old or something?"

"Some were. Some weren't."

"Then why no covers?"

Clyde rubbed the side of his thumb against his shoulder, not sure what he should tell her, not sure he wanted her to know that much about him.

He let his gaze wander over the pile of paperbacks until he located one that clearly wouldn't pass Pam's morality code. He reached for it and tore off the front cover.

Lynda made a little sound but didn't say anything. She watched silently as he folded the thick paper in half, then in half again. Moving quickly, he rolled the remaining shape into a cylinder and held it tight in his fist. A hard, sharp, pencil-like rod.

Her mouth fell open. "They used books as weapons?"

"They used everything as weapons."

Her brown eyes looked sadly from the tip of the rod to his fist, and she shivered. "You've done that before."

Clyde unrolled the paper, then tossed it in the trash can. "Twenty years, Lynda." He hadn't survived that long without learning a few tricks, but he should probably keep the rest to himself.

"The Clyde I remember from years ago was a gentle giant." She snickered. "Unless you were on the football field, and then it was 'Annie get your gun,' but *this* ... this is new. I'm trying to imagine you using a homemade knife, but my brain can't get around the notion."

Great. The last thing he wanted was for her to picture him defending himself in prison.

She hugged a stack of books to her chest and rose, placing them one at a time on the shelf behind her. "Sometimes I think we don't even know each other anymore. Not really."

"We've known each other since fifth grade."

"But we had a twenty-year gap in our friendship. And things change." She looked at him over her shoulder. "Sounds like you have a lot of secrets."

"Making a shiv out of a piece of paper ain't exactly a secret." He reached for the minivacuum.

"But I bet you've got more." She looked at him straight on then, crossing her arms.

He hated it when she challenged him, which was often. He hated when she pushed him for information about the past or the future or even the present. But more than anything, he hated the way he couldn't open up to her, even though he wanted nothing more than for her to know him, really know him, inside and out.

Honestly, he didn't have many secrets left, other than being a closet bookaholic. But still, fear swept across him like a searchlight, because he longed to ask her one simple question. A question that could make or break him for the rest of his life. *Would you still like me if you knew my secrets?* He couldn't be sure how she would answer that question, but he could be sure of one thing. The feelings he had for Lynda Turner wouldn't go away on their own.

He lifted his chin and shrugged. "Everybody has secrets, Lyn." He flipped the switch on the Dustbuster and let its soft hum mask the ear-piercing beating of his heart.

CHAPTER SEVEN

After you, Lyn.

Those words echoed in my ears. That silly convict had actually held the door open for me, and he never held doors. The action, coupled with his comment about secrets, left me wondering what he was up to.

No, that's not right. I figured what he was up to.

I just wasn't sure I was ready for it.

We had worked for two hours, and even though I tried not to enjoy it, in the end I admitted to Clyde that I sort of liked the smell of the books. Most people would have said I was strange, but Clyde didn't. Instead, he opened *To Kill a Mockingbird*, sniffed its yellowed parchment, and slowly nodded.

When I got back home, I drank a glass of chocolate milk—comfort food—changed into a clean T-shirt and an old pair of cut-off blue jeans—comfort clothes—and then stood on my back porch and let the sunshine soak into my skin—vitamin D. But in spite of the food and the clothes and the sunshine, in spite of the undeniable tingle I always got when I knew a man noticed me, in spite of all that … I could still feel my mood slipping.

My proverbial cup was half empty.

I wandered through the house, ending up in my bedroom without ever deciding to go there. As I lowered myself to the edge of the bed, I scrutinized the plaster on the wall. The Sheetrock had been painted so many times, the texture was nearly invisible, but I knew it was there beneath layer upon layer of semigloss. My hand reached out, and my finger traced a small chip in the paint. An oval.

Clyde Felton wanted me. He had all but told me so, though not with words. *After you, Lyn* didn't exactly count as a declaration of romantic intent, but his actions spoke louder than his deep voice ever could. Not only had he pulled me out of my daily routine, but he had helped me reach outside myself by taking me to the Trapp Door.

My hands lay clenched in my lap, and I willed them to stay that way. I tried to force my mind away from painful memories, but on days like today—days when life tempted me with happiness—the past wouldn't leave me be. Like narcotics that numb the senses, my memories prevented me from feeling anything good, and I was addicted to that numbness as hopelessly as a junkie is addicted to crack.

Still staring at the wall, I pulled open the drawer of the bedside table and felt around for the letters. This time they were all the way at the back, pressed flat against the cheap wood and buried beneath tissues and ChapStick and long-forgotten odds and ends. Apparently it had been a while.

I slid one letter from an envelope, and the page fell open, the creases behaving like well-oiled hinges to reveal the scratchy writing. This letter had kidnapped my sanity for more than two decades.

Its mate was younger, though—less than twenty years old. I hated those letters. Despised them. Whenever I touched the paper, my heart flared with anger—not just any anger but the rage produced by rejection, jealousy, and injustice. I ought to hide them in the metal firebox under my bed where they belonged. Where they would leave me be.

My palms jerked as though I had been bitten by red ants, and the papers fluttered to the worn carpet. Scooting back on the bed, I lay down and curled into a ball. I had made it two weeks between spells, so that was good. I called them spells. Ruthie had always referred to them as *episodes*, but now that she was taking a college psychology course, she had all kinds of new terms she threw around. Like *clinical depression, mood disorder*, and *long-term treatment*. The girl thought she knew everything.

I curled tighter, wrapping my arms around my knees and tucking my head in an effort to disappear. To be less significant. To become a smaller target for life's arrows. My forehead pressed against my knees until it hurt, and I thanked the Lord I wasn't scheduled to work.

Yes, occasionally I thanked the Lord, but only for things like my work schedule. I would check in with Him, usually during a spell, but I wasn't too sure He had much patience with me. Ruthie certainly didn't, and she and the Big Man were BFFs now.

Today my thoughts blared through the room like a stinking-mean cheerleader with a megaphone, telling me not to consider Clyde because he would probably leave me, too. Besides, I would never be worthy of him. Ironic, but true. Clyde may have been a convicted rapist, but at least he could function in society without taking routine trips to the funny farm.

I sighed. Hoby had known a thing or two about clinical depression, mood disorders, and long-term treatment. My husband could put Ruthie's psychology notes to shame, since he had lived through everything in her textbook. He left me all those years ago, yet his memory met me in this bedroom every time I had a spell.

I thought we had been happy together.

Until he drove away in his wrecker and left us. We had argued that day, and he stormed out of the house saying he needed to tow Izzy Arellano's Buick to the shop and get started on it, but he never came back.

Not even for Ruthie.

I buried my face in the pillow, then laced my fingers between my toes and held tight. I did not cry. Right after Hoby left, I stifled my tears for months, until my sadness was replaced by hatred. That lasted several years but eventually gave way to apathy. Now the sum total of all my feelings only amounted to a swell of bitterness every so often.

But I wouldn't allow myself to wallow. Not for long anyway. I'd give it an hour or so, and then I'd get up, splash cool water on my face, and eat a quart of Rocky Road.

***

"Momma, Sophie Snodgrass told me Clara Belle Covington saw you at Troy and Pamela's junk shop with Clyde."

"Yeah, so?" I nestled my feet between two couch cushions and pointed the remote at the television, blacking out a rerun of *CSI*. "She's not the chief of police. Her husband is."

"So, what were you doing?"

The pitch of her voice rose near the end of her sentence, and I tried not to grit my teeth. Ruthie had this theory about pulling me out of my *episodes* by reacting dramatically to every *single* thing that came up in conversation. I rested my elbow on the arm of the couch and leaned my chin on a fist.

"Dusting books," I said slowly, attempting to tamp down her spirit to an appropriate level of boredom.

"Admit it. He's interested in you."

A thread on the hem of my shorts, one among many, fell slightly longer than the others in the fringe, and I fingered it, pulled it, snapped it off. "What if he is?"

"What if he is?" Her mouth fell open as though I had just confessed to capital murder. "Good grief, Momma, you've been alone for years. Don't you think it's time?"

I chewed a tiny spot on the inside of my cheek and wished Ruthie would leave. I needed to go curl up in bed awhile longer so I could think. And remember. And forget. I felt my shoulders begin to droop, but I jerked them back up with a reviving intake of air. "I'm doing fine, Ruth Ann."

"You could do better."

Irritation niggled at me just like it did whenever a huge family came into the diner five minutes before closing time. "I'm holding down a job," I argued.

"Why aren't you working today?"

"Day off."

She tilted her head to the side as though considering how to cast the next round of the debate. "Well, you don't socialize with anyone you're not related to. You could go out with your old friends."

A flash of anger exploded between my eyes, and I blinked hard before answering her. "I'm getting out of the house now, Ruth Ann. I talk and smile and visit with people, but as far as my *old friends* are concerned, I have no desire to spend time with them." I lifted my palms, then let them fall back to the couch cushions. "You see what it gets me? I help Pam with a few books, and in less than three hours, you're over here grilling me about it. I don't need this."

I expected her to lash out at me sarcastically, as was our habit, but instead, she glanced out the window, watching Corky Ledbetter pass by on the street pulling a red wagon filled with her two youngest children. When Ruthie looked back at me, I was surprised to see sadness in her eyes. Typically Ruthie showed about as much emotion as I did.

She smiled, but her gaze bounced between the coffee table and my left shoulder. "I want to have a baby, Momma. Dodd and I are making plans."

A tiny hum sounded in my ears as if a favorite song was stuck in my head, filling my thoughts so thoroughly, I couldn't make sense of her words. I forced my lips into a smile, and once they were there, it felt right. "That's wonderful," I mouthed silently.

"We've been praying that you would be happy." Her gaze briefly returned to the coffee table.

"Yes." My voice didn't sound like my voice. I could hear the difference, but I couldn't clear my throat, much less conjure up more words to say to her. I tried again. "Yes, Ruth Ann."

She half giggled, half sighed—a frantic sound. "So you see why I'm worried about you staying well."

I dug my toes deeper into the couch, and they pressed painfully against an exposed metal spring. Actually, I didn't see what she meant. I didn't see at all.

"What if a baby changes things, Momma? I'll be really busy with work and school, and I might need some help. I might need *you*. With our family's medical history"—her eyes locked with mine—"I'm scared I might get postpartum depression."

The humming in my ears popped into silence, and suddenly I was powerfully aware of my surroundings. The afternoon sunlight streaming through the window seemed brighter than a moment before, and the hard lines of the television and furniture became clearer, more shiny, more polished. "I'll be here, Ruth Ann."

Robotically I unfolded my legs and stood, walked across the room, and patted her arm, as close to a hug as we ever got. My lips were still curved, and judging from the way her shoulders relaxed, I must have come across all right.

Babies weren't bad. Dodd would provide for her, and his mother and brother would be obnoxiously supportive, but what if she really did need me? Could I be there for her? Could I battle the megaphone voices in my head and keep myself out of the dark pit?

My new cell phone chimed in the back pocket of my shorts, startling me. I would never get used to the thing, but right then, I was thankful for the distraction. The screen showed it was Velma, and my anxiety instantly settled. My sister knew about babies and pregnancy. She knew about daughters and sons-in-law and being a grandmother. She knew about me and the god-awful trouble I had with living life.

Lifting the phone to my ear, I concentrated on keeping my voice even. "You'll never guess what Ruth Ann just told me." I gave Ruthie another feeble smile and waited for Velma's response. Knowing my sister, she would guess Ruthie's plans and immediately start coaching both of us.

But only heavy breathing came from her end of the line, and my gaze wandered back to the window, where I noticed a small rain cloud peeking from behind the roof of the house across the street. "Velma?"

I once heard a mountain lion's call in the darkness, and that sound came back to me when Velma spoke. Wild. Desperate. Instinctive. She cried out my name, long and low, and the sound of her despair sent a thousand doubts sailing through my already mangled thoughts.

"I'll be right there," I said. "Whatever's happened, I'm on my way."

I punched off the phone and backed away from Ruthie.

CHAPTER EIGHT

Strangely enough, Clyde liked his job. He stood alone in the kitchen of the Dairy Queen, stirring a vat of orange-brown chili. His responsibilities were mundane and predictable, mirroring his life. Troy had been urging him to apply for a wind-tech position, but honestly, Clyde wasn't interested in risking his life for the betterment of the community. And just this morning, Lynda had seemed dead set against the notion. Not that he had talked to her about it. Maybe Troy's wife had let the cat out of the bag, or maybe Lynda had read his mind. Either scenario was believable.

As he finished an order of chili dogs and set it on a red plastic tray, he saw Lynda through the front windows getting out of her car. He wiped a drip of chili from his work surface, but instead of starting the next order, he watched her for a second. A rain shower had left water in every pothole in the parking lot, and as she sidestepped and hopped, her long hair blew across her face. Lord, she was pretty. And tough. And aloof.

And fragile.

When she entered the restaurant, she gave a curt greeting to the front-end workers, then came around the counter to lean against the door of the walk-in freezer. "What time you get off?"

"Twenty minutes." He picked up a knife to chop onions, but before he made a cut, he pulled a wooden match from the pocket of his apron and stuck it between his teeth. He had read once that the chemicals in the match head kept the onion from burning your eyes. He figured Lynda would make fun of him, or at least ask him about it, but she only stared at the back of the ice-cream machine and rubbed her lips against each other. Something was up.

"Ruthie wants to make me a grandmother." She laughed, but there was no trace of humor in her eyes, and Clyde knew something else was wrong. Lynda may not have been keen on being a grandmother, but he had seen her with Nathan enough times to know that she wasn't completely against it. "A granny," she mumbled.

A soft ache nudged Clyde's stomach, and he slowly lifted his head, not wanting her to notice he was watching her. "You don't say."

When she nodded, her hair shifted across her shoulders. She had changed clothes since this morning at the bookstore, and now she wore old shorts and a tank top with her usual black Converse sneakers, looking more like a teenager than a granny. Clyde went back to slicing.

"And Ansel's dying." Her voice quavered, and the rattle in her throat, in her confidence, in her heart made Clyde's hands shake.

Lynda's parents had died in an auto accident when she was fourteen, so Ansel was the closest thing she had to a daddy. If he died, it would be one more person abandoning her. Clyde swiped the diced onions into a plastic bin, still gripping the knife. He wanted to stab something, but he forced himself to calm down. "That right?"

"He's got some kind of advanced cancer." She held her hands tightly at her waist, one palm gripping the opposite thumb. "Velma said he might not live six months."

Clyde wanted to go to her, unclench her hands, and give her a hug. But touching wasn't something they did. "That's not long."

"Nathan won't even remember him," she snapped.

Clyde pictured Ansel sitting in his recliner holding newborn Nathan in one arm and the remote control in the opposite hand. Now that the baby was older, Nathan would cruise around the recliner, jabbering nonstop, and Ansel would shoot the breeze as though Nathan were one of his buddies down at the feed store.

"Fawn has pictures." It was a silly thing to say. He desperately wanted to make things bearable for her, but what could he do? Lynda would never stand for it if he walked over there and … *what?* … let her cry on his shoulder?

She was too stiff and independent for that.

He blinked hard. Actually Lynda was as needy as Nathan had been when Fawn brought him home from the hospital. As needy as Dodd and Ruthie's baby would be. But Lynda didn't need *him*.

"Velma said she'll take care of Ansel at the house for a while, but pretty soon he won't be able to get around, and something else will have to happen." Lynda's eyes bored into Clyde's for a count of five, and then she looked away, this time to the back door leading out to the parking lot.

Probably she wanted to run out that door, to escape the unpleasant details. *Something else would have to happen.* Did she mean he would be in a nursing home? "Could be a while," he said.

"Yeah." She took a few steps to stand in front of the corkboard by the door. It was covered with announcements and old Dairy Queen sales pages. She had her back to him, with her head tilted to the side as she read a crooked note, but then she froze. Not moving, probably not reading, maybe not breathing.

"Velma will get through it." His statement wasn't enough. It wasn't even what he wanted to say. He wanted to tell her that *she* would get through it, that she could survive this just as she survived everything else, that this didn't have to set her back. He wanted to remind her to keep living. He wanted to walk up behind her, wrap his arms around her, and shelter her from everything life might hurl her way.

"Yep, Velma's a trooper," Lynda mumbled.

An order came back, and Clyde tossed two chicken-fried steaks in oil. Lynda still hadn't moved.

He shouldn't do it. Probably she wouldn't want him to, but he stepped toward the bulletin board and paused for a second as he stood behind her. She was so short he felt like an ogre about to pet a hummingbird, so instead of touching her, he carefully bent at the waist and tilted his head to gaze at her cheek.

Her eyes were closed, and her lips were pressed into a tight line. She was holding herself together, but barely.

Clyde laid his palm on her shoulder, afraid his touch might crumble her concentration, but she only inhaled, then exhaled, then opened her eyes.

Slowly she turned her head to peer at him, first at his hand on her shoulder, then into his eyes, and in one fluid movement, she spun on her heel and buried her face in his chest.

Clyde straightened quickly, then held his breath. His hands were on each of her shoulders, and he squeezed slightly, not knowing if he should hug her outright. Her arms were still crossed over her chest, and as she leaned into him, he could feel the warmth of her breath through his shirt. She didn't seem to be crying.

He lifted one hand to touch the top of her head, but she took a half step back and wiped her nose. "I'm all right." Her words tumbled over each other. "Sorry to get all emotional. I'm just fed up with things happening to me. Or I guess this isn't really happening to me. It's happening to Ansel. And to Velma. And … Nathan and everybody."

"I reckon you can claim it, too, Lyn."

Turning away from him, she stepped to the back door, causing a wave of regret to wash over Clyde, as if he held a lottery ticket that was one digit short of the jackpot.

She tilted her head toward the parking lot. "I'll wait for you out here."

When she pulled the metal door open, a flash of afternoon sun shot into the kitchen, and Clyde squinted, but just as quickly, the door closed behind her, leaving him blinded from the brightness and alone with his thoughts.

He fled back to his vat of hot oil and removed the well-done steaks, trying to figure out what had just happened. His heart ached for Ansel's family like it hadn't ached since his grandpappy died, but in spite of the gloom of Lynda's news, a tiny glimmer of hope cast a ray of sunshine in the darkness. Because Lynda was waiting for him in the parking lot.

CHAPTER NINE

"Want to go see the windmills, Lyn?"

Lyn.

Sometime over the past two years, Clyde had started calling me that, but sometime over the past two days, I had decided I didn't mind. "Where's your car?" I asked.

"Broke down again. Can I drive yours?"

The question seemed bold, but I was tired. "Sure." The two of us settled into my hatchback and rode silently through town, past the city-limit sign and twenty miles down Highway 84. He took me farther than I had come on Thursday—almost to Roscoe—and as the terrain opened up into endless cotton fields, my mind became less cluttered.

When he pulled to the side of the road, my head rested against the seat, and I let my gaze wander along the edge of the Caprock. I inhaled deeply, and when the breath released from my lungs, a tiny bit of my tension relaxed. "Not everybody has an addiction to wind turbines," I said.

"There's worse things to be hooked on, believe me."

I twisted my neck to look at him. "Do you think there's a twelve-step program?"

"If there is, you're somewhere around number seven."

"You sound like Ruth Ann."

"She's a good girl."

I leaned forward and rested my elbows on my knees. "I can't believe she wants to be a momma."

The windmills rotated in slow motion, mocking my heart, which spun as frantically as a child's pinwheel. Maybe my sanity would be torn to shreds like a plastic-and-foil toy thrashed by the gusts.

"It was bound to happen."

Irritation blossomed like a flowering thistle, but snapping at Clyde wouldn't change Ruthie. "I wouldn't mind her having a baby if it didn't mean I had to be a grandmother."

"I'm a grandpappy." Clyde's enormous frame shrugged as though he were trying to make himself look smaller than he was. "Is that bad?"

"No." I said the word too forcefully but didn't back down. "It's not against the rules for men to get old and gray and wrinkled." I yanked the rearview mirror around so I could look at my reflection. "Think how many movies have a man in his sixties courting a woman in her twenties. You never see it the other way round. Ever."

"You're not sixty."

"I might as well be."

"You want to be with a kid?" His eyebrows bounced playfully, but I didn't feel the humor.

I popped open the door and climbed out of the car. Even though I had no reason to be upset with him, anger had become a familiar blanket I habitually wrapped myself in. I bundled my hair and held it at one shoulder to keep the wind from slapping it against my face. I stared at the windmills traveling across the land and noticed a frozen turbine unaffected by the currents. A slight movement at the top caused me to squint and refocus, barely able to make out two men working high in the air, two gray dots on the head of a needle.

After a few minutes, Clyde appeared quietly beside me, leaning against the car with his arms crossed over his chest.

"I'm not mad at you." I pouted the half apology. "I'm mad at Ansel." Even though it wasn't Ansel's fault the cancer was taking him, any more than it was Ruthie's fault I was getting older.

Clyde nodded but said nothing. There was nothing to say to such an absurd notion.

Yet still I wanted to break something.

"Let's walk." Clyde pushed himself away from the car and stepped to the front bumper. When I didn't follow him, he started down the highway without me.

After a few seconds of indignation, I caught up and matched his turtle pace.

"I'll keep it slow," he drawled, "since you're so much older than me."

When I swatted his shoulder, my hand stung. "I'm only a few months older. Besides, you're the one who's a grandparent."

He glanced at me, and his lip curled. "Your hand okay?"

"If your muscles weren't so dang hard, it would be fine."

"Can't be helped. My doctor has me drinking Ensure."

My sour mood dissolved amid his light banter, and I laughed softly before my humor died. "Ansel drinks Ensure. A lot of good it did him."

Two cars sped past, and we moved closer to the muddy ditch, walking half on, half off the pavement. We continued in silence while the sun slid behind the Caprock and the turbines transformed into silhouettes against the orange-gold sky. In another hour, they would be hidden by darkness, yet even in the thickness of night, they would continue their endless toil. Suddenly I was weary. I was as small and inadequate and overwhelmed as a child, and I felt myself yearning to hold Clyde's hand, remembering a day when I was tiny, walking through the pasture with my daddy on our way to Picnic Hollow. His palms were large, and as was our habit, I wrapped my chubby fist around his index finger, holding on tightly as I tripped along beside him. I felt secure that day, knowing he would protect me from varmints and cacti and whatever else we came up against in the pasture.

Clyde cleared his throat softly. "Ansel doesn't want to leave."

"I know." I didn't have to ask what he meant. It was no secret I hadn't adjusted to Hoby's exit very gracefully.

As our shoes shuffled across the gravel on the side of Highway 84, I realized Clyde's strength felt safe, and I toyed with the idea of slipping my hand in his. But that was impossible. My memories wouldn't allow me to release the shadows from the past. The doubts.

"I was just thinking about Picnic Hollow," I said. "Remember when we used to go there back in high school?"

"I forgot about that place. Think it's still there?" His gaze slid across the horizon, where somewhere in the distance, a tiny bluff, covered with carvings from past generations, lay nestled between crags and boulders.

Another car zoomed past us as I snickered. "Where else would it be?"

"Could be underwater." He frowned. "I ain't been out there since they built the lake."

"I didn't think about that." I shut my mouth then, figuring I had said enough for a while, and I followed Clyde's gaze, wondering if Picnic Hollow had been relocated to the bottom of Lake Alan Henry.

That would've been a shame. My family had gone there many times when I was young, hiking through the ravines and down the riverbed, across to the sandstone cavity, whose walls were weathered smooth. Generations of people had hiked there with picnic lunches, spent the day in the cool shadows, and carved their names into the soft rock before making the slow trek home.

Back in the day, I had allowed a boyfriend or two to take me there. Clyde and I had even been there at the same time once, though I had been with Neil, and he had been with Susan.

Clyde stopped walking. "Neil acted strange yesterday."

So Clyde was thinking about that double date, too. "How so?"

"He seemed … antsy."

I didn't answer.

The words *Neil* and *antsy* didn't belong in the same sentence, and I certainly didn't care why Clyde had perceived him to be nervous. I had enough worries without adding *antsy Neil* to them.

Clyde started walking again, even slower. "You think the high school kids still go out there after the homecoming game?"

"Ruth Ann never mentioned it when she was in school. Neither did JohnScott." A short sigh cut from my throat. "It's on private property."

He was silent for a while, and when he answered, he sounded hesitant, almost as if he were asking a question. "We should go look for it sometime."

I crossed my arms to protect myself from whatever he might be insinuating, but when peace settled across my shoulders, I dropped my hands back to my sides. "Maybe."

The low rumble of a car coming to a slow stop beside us caused my mood to collapse like a wad of tinfoil.

It was the blue- and gray-haired sisters.

"You having car trouble, Lynda?" Blue rode in the passenger seat and leaned her head out the window, but she was so small, her bluish hair touched the door lock.

I bent to look in at them. "Just getting a little exercise."

Gray braced one hand on the seat so she could lean across and scowl at Clyde, but her skin smoothed when she shifted her gaze to me. "You sure everything's all right, hon?"

Blue didn't wait for me to answer her sister's question. "What you doing exercising on the highway?"

"Sounds suspicious to me." Gray muttered the words, but they were loud enough that Clyde and I could easily hear them.

"Actually, we came out here to look at the windmills." I fluttered my hand, indicating the army surrounding us, but the two women only stared at me.

Gray's eyes scrunched until they were nothing more than a tangle of wrinkles. "Why would you do *that*? Those things are eyesores."

"It's peaceful out here." Clyde shifted his weight, and his boot ground a pebble into the asphalt.

Both women startled when he spoke, and Gray's foot slipped off the brake, causing the car to jerk forward before she caught herself.

He bobbed his head politely. "We'll see you ladies back in town, I'm sure."

When he turned his back and continued strolling down the highway, I followed him. "Thanks for stopping to check," I called over my shoulder.

As the sisters' car eased away from us, the passenger window slowly slid up again, and my worries cranked up from the pit of my stomach to my throat. "I can't believe Blue and Gray saw us together."

Clyde glanced down as though he might find his clothes covered with soot.

"I mean, I don't mind walking with you …" Or maybe I did. I scrambled to finish my explanation. "They just tend to blow things out of proportion."

He squinted at the taillights fifty yards down the road. "You call them Blue and Gray?"

"Ruth Ann does. She can never remember their names, and neither can I."

"Hmm." Clyde's face was expressionless. "I don't have a problem remembering their names. The older one—Gray as you call her— her name is Algerita. Algerita Parker. And the younger one …" He chuckled. "You know what I mean. Younger than Algerita, but not young. Her name is O'Della."

"No wonder I can never remember."

"Tricky ones, for sure."

The taillights shrunk to tiny red dots. "How is it that you know their names? Do you talk to them?"

"Can't say I've ever talked to them—until today." He shrugged, looking smaller than normal once again. "But they talk about me so much, they're on my mind pretty often."

I stared at the spot where the Parker sisters' lights had disappeared, and the gentle giants on either side of the highway no longer comforted me. I stopped walking, and when Clyde looked back at me, I tilted my head toward the hatchback.

His eyes turned to slits. "You're not going to hide in your house."

"It's tempting."

"Lyn, you don't know what they're going to tell people."

My eyes blinked slowly, and in the momentary blackness, I felt the all-too-familiar dread of truth. "It doesn't matter, Clyde. They saw us together, and they'll make up the rest."

CHAPTER TEN

Clyde wondered if he would always attend worship alone. As he slipped through the double doors of the Trapp church building and stood in the tiny foyer, he could hear Dodd Cunningham teaching a Bible lesson behind a hollow door. Good man, Ruthie's husband. After Fawn and JohnScott had married, Dodd encouraged Clyde to come back to the small congregation, and somehow the young preacher had smoothed things over enough that the congregants tolerated his presence. Mostly.

When the bathroom door opened and Corky Ledbetter clambered through, pulling a small child by the hand, the entry shrank around Clyde.

He bobbed his head. "Ma'am."

"Morning, Clyde." She took three quick steps, then slowed. "So … you and Lynda Turner?" She smiled. "Y'all are a good match."

Clyde's back straightened, but just then a bell rattled, sounding as if it were mounted inside the wall. The thin paneling vibrated, producing a squawking hum that signaled the end of

Bible class. The door to Dodd's classroom opened, and congregants began filtering past Clyde, so he shuffled to a corner, feeling huge in the tight space.

Lee Roy Goodnight hobbled toward him, leaning heavily on a wooden cane, and stopped in front of Clyde to shake his hand.

"That grandson of yours is getting big."

"He is." Clyde's pride swelled not only because of Lee Roy's mention of Nathan but also because the old man had no qualms about referring to him as Clyde's grandson.

"Walking yet?" he asked.

"Just."

"Twelve months old. Right on time." Lee Roy wiped the corners of his mouth with his thumb and index finger.

"Cyde!" Nathan's baby voice rang from the hallway.

They turned to see Fawn coming toward them with Nathan in her arms and two bags hanging from her shoulder.

Lee Roy chuckled. "You have a good week, son. Keep enjoying that boy."

"Will do, Lee Roy. You have a good one, too."

"Cyde!" Nathan kicked his feet against Fawn's hips as though trying to propel himself out of his mother's arms.

She smiled. "He can almost say your name."

"Mm-hmm." Clyde didn't trust his voice to speak. He had gone twenty years without seeing a small person, and now there was one screaming his name.

"He's not going to calm down until you hold him," Fawn said.

Clyde reached for Nathan, resting one palm beneath the boy's rump and the other behind his back.

"You coming to the birthday party this afternoon?" she asked.

"Wouldn't miss it."

"It'll be hot as blazes at the park, but that seemed like the best option."

A mental image flashed across his mind—Neil Blaylock and him in the same living room—and he grunted. "I see what you mean."

Nathan stretched his hand toward a lock of Clyde's hair.

"No," Fawn said firmly.

"Aw, he ain't hurting nothing. People say I'm hardheaded." The child yanked a lock of hair back and forth, but Clyde only smiled. "Go back with your momma now."

"Sit with us today?" Fawn asked.

"Better not, but thanks."

A spicy scent overpowered the cramped space, and Clyde knew Susan was near even before he saw her. He frowned, running memories through the movie projector in his mind, but he couldn't remember her smelling that strong when they were young.

Her bracelets jangled as she patted Nathan and greeted Fawn, but Clyde kept his eyes trained on a tumbleweed rolling down the front sidewalk.

Two years ago, when Clyde returned to Trapp, Susan had been as cold as a norther blowing in from Colorado, but back then, Neil had been sitting on the pew next to her. Like two stone pillars, the Blaylocks had reigned from the second pew, the faultless church elder and his pious wife. When Neil stopped attending worship, Susan had been forced to thaw, but only slightly.

Now she and Clyde would greet each other real quick-like, just enough to show they were acting like Christians, but not enough for church members to make up crazy stories about them.

Fawn watched as her mother pranced away from them. "Did everything go all right when they picked up Nathan Friday?"

"I guess so." Clyde didn't bother mentioning Neil's peculiar behavior to Fawn, but she brought it up herself.

"Dad's been stressed lately."

Clyde wondered what sort of things would stress Neil Blaylock.

"Mother thinks it's a midlife crisis." She shrugged. "Here comes JohnScott."

"Hey there, Clyde." Fawn's husband approached with a cluster of teenagers, hung back to let them pass, then shook Clyde's hand.

"Good game Friday night," Clyde offered. Every person in town greeted the coach with one of two greetings, depending on stats, but Clyde didn't bother to get creative. "We at home again this week?"

"Yep." JohnScott grinned. "One more home game, and then we head to Tahoka."

The four of them went through the double wooden doors together, but Fawn continued down the aisle to sit near her mother while JohnScott settled next to Clyde on the back pew. Clyde knew the coach would sit with him until a moment before the service started.

"Sorry to hear about your dad," Clyde said softly. "Ansel's one of my favorites."

"He's everybody's favorite." JohnScott's eyes drooped.

"You all right?"

"Not really."

Clyde nodded. "Might take a while yet."

"You hear about those bones out at the lake?" JohnScott seemed to shake the gloom from his thoughts, and Clyde went along with it.

"I'm not deaf, right?"

"Last I heard, they're definitely human remains, but they don't know who it is."

Clyde lifted an eyebrow. "What do you think?"

"Aw …" JohnScott ran the tip of his tongue across his lips. "I'm figuring it to be a lost Boy Scout mauled by a mountain lion, but nobody ever reported him missing because he was such a toot in the first place."

"You think?"

"What about you?" JohnScott asked. "What's your take on it?"

Clyde rubbed the back of his index finger along the bottom of his chin. "Skydiving expedition gone bad?"

"And … why didn't anyone ever report him missing?"

"They did, but the wind carried him for miles."

JohnScott opened his mouth in a wide grin. "Maybe it's the same kid. Jumped from an airplane, then got mauled by a mountain lion."

"It could happen."

Fawn's husband pulled a dry washcloth from his pocket and dabbed a blob of moist cookie crumbs on Clyde's shoulder. "I see you held Nathan this morning."

"Sure enough."

The coach smiled, then joined Fawn and Susan near the front.

Clyde stared at the backs of their heads, wondering, remembering, thinking about the past. Life had turned out to be a strange, unpredictable storm, but he had long since determined to ride it out. Fawn's curly ponytail fell across the back of the pew, and Clyde marveled at her beauty, then studied Susan's puffy, blonde hairdo. He quickly compared her looks to other women in the congregation, but none of them had the same large mass.

For the hundredth time since coming home, he wondered what he had ever seen in her. No, that wasn't quite right. What he had seen in her twenty-two years ago was now gone. She'd been sweet and innocent back then, but now she was hard and brittle, and he cursed himself, realizing he was at least part of the reason she had changed.

He stood with the congregation and hummed along with "I'll Fly Away." When he was locked up, he had enjoyed booming the hymns, but here in this place, it didn't seem acceptable.

Like a bird from prison bars has flown …

He felt a slap on his back, and Troy and Pamela Sanders scooted past to the pew in front of him, coming in late from whatever Sunday school class Pamela had volunteered to teach.

Troy leaned toward him and whispered loudly, "There's a task force coming in tomorrow to rappel down the rotors. You should come and watch."

"Aw, now … I don't know, Troy."

"Sure," Pamela said, not bothering to whisper. "You can wait on the ground and catch them when they fall to their deaths." But then her frowning eyebrows lifted into soft arcs. "I heard about you and Lynda, and all I can say is it's about time."

"Pam," Troy mumbled, "I'm not sure that's honest news." He looked at Clyde, and his eyes held a question.

"Probably not," Clyde admitted.

As the song ended and they sat down, Clyde realized Lynda had been right after all. The Parker sisters had been on a rampage, and it hadn't even been twelve hours.

Dodd mounted the stage, traipsing back and forth behind the podium and pulling Clyde's attention back to where it belonged. The preacher had mellowed in the two years he'd been at the Trapp church. His accent had softened into a drawl, and his homespun Bible training had given way to a broader version of the gospel. Not that Ruthie's husband would ever be a pushover, but he could no longer be called naive.

"God doesn't want us to sit back and wait for Him." Dodd's eyebrows bounced. "He wants us to run into His arms, to get busy and work, to show others His love."

Clyde didn't see how his own mundane routine would please or displease God either way. He kept to himself, stayed out of other people's business, and worked hard to pay his bills. He tithed regularly and was kind to others ... whenever they got close enough. *What would he change about his life ... if he wanted to?*

Dodd's mother coughed into a tissue, and Clyde's gaze slid from her to Ruthie, then down the pew to Fawn, JohnScott, and Susan. His insides tightened.

He had made a mess for Susan years ago, and maybe God expected him to clean it up now, but the woman didn't need anything. She had Fawn and Nathan. She had a huge ranch house and a fancy car. She had friends here at the church. She had a million civic responsibilities that kept her busy. And she had Neil.

Dodd wrapped up his sermon with a final challenge. "Get out there and use the gifts God blessed you with."

Clyde stood for the last song, but this time he didn't even hum. He was too busy pondering Dodd's statement. There was only one thing Clyde could think that he truly wanted to do with his life. And that was to make Lynda Turner smile.

CHAPTER ELEVEN

"Lynda, I'm about to melt into a puddle right here in the middle of the Trapp City Park." Velma fanned herself with a wrapped Golden book while I poured a bit of water on the nape of my neck.

"You're not the only one." I leaned back in my camp chair, happy to be at Nathan's first birthday party but silently wishing the Blaylocks weren't there.

Fawn claimed she chose the park because it was Nathan's favorite place, but more than likely, she feared the roof would blow off her double-wide if the families got too close to each other—like paint fumes to a pilot light. Not only did the outdoor venue provide better ventilation for the heated personalities, but it also included convenient escape routes.

Velma and I had come appropriately dressed in shorts, and Ansel, sitting catty-corner in a lawn chair, wore a pair of thin coveralls. Our grown children had changed out of their church clothes and were buzzing around us. JohnScott and Fawn hung balloons on the playground equipment while Dodd and Ruthie filled Styrofoam cups with ice.

Opposite us, at the park's lone picnic table, hovered Neil and Susan—the Blaylock faction. Susan arrived straight from church services in her ridiculous dress and heels, and even though Neil hadn't attended worship in more than a year, he seemed to have gone out of his way to dress the part—Western slacks, starched shirt, drawstring tie, and, of course, his trademark cowboy hat.

Susan shot a fake smile toward us, but Neil didn't even glance our way. He paced in front of the picnic table, and I recalled Clyde's adjective. *Antsy.*

Nathan, joyfully oblivious, toddled around the table, using the bench for balance. When he got to Susan's knees, he paused before continuing his circuit.

"Come to Pops, son." Neil picked him up under the armpits, and the baby kicked his feet, clearly wanting back down again, but Neil merely walked around the table and handed the child a Cheeto.

"Daddy, he'll get you all orange," Fawn called. "Proceed with caution."

"Noted."

JohnScott stood with one hand resting on the metal slide. "Fawn, should we open gifts first? That way we can hold lunch until everyone gets here."

She gazed up the street. "I suppose it's time."

"It'll take Nathan twenty minutes to open each gift anyway," Dodd said.

Fawn nodded but didn't smile. I figured she wanted to wait for Clyde, but no one dared make the request.

An enormous, ornately wrapped box sat on the edge of the cement slab near the table, and Neil squatted next to it, resting Nathan on his bent knee. "You ready for your surprise, boy?"

Nathan squealed and slapped his palms against the side of the box.

I noticed Clyde walking toward us from down the street, but not until then did I remember his car was broken down. He lifted his chin in greeting to JohnScott and Dodd, then positioned himself away from the commotion. Leaning against the slanted metal pole of the swing set, he glanced around casually, and then his gaze bounced to me.

My lungs felt as though a hundred dragonflies had taken flight during a windstorm, and I bit my bottom lip. Clyde couldn't even get to his grandson's birthday party on time, so there was no good reason for me to be feeling all fluttery inside. It was ridiculous.

He ducked his head as he watched Nathan, and I peered at him a moment longer, wondering if I should offer to trim his hair. His blond ponytail was the exact same color as Fawn's, only shorter. It was surprising more people hadn't figured out she was his daughter long before that news flash made the gossip circuit. In fact, nobody had figured it out. A swell of injustice crowded the dragonflies out of my lungs.

My gaze wandered to Clyde's hands, one shoved in the pocket of his jeans, the other absentmindedly gripping the chain of a swing, and suddenly it seemed like a million years ago that I had felt the urge to hold his hand on the side of the road. Everything had happened too fast yesterday, and I had foolishly let Ansel's prognosis and Velma's despair drive me to Clyde for comfort. *And I let him hug me.*

Stupid.

I forced my mind and my eyes back to the party, only to find Susan watching me.

Her mouth twisted into a tight knot, but when she looked back toward Nathan, her smile spread.

The toddler had managed to expose only a corner of the box by ripping the paper piece by piece. He threw the strips over his shoulder, but Fawn was there to intercept them.

"Here we go, son." Neil slid his hand under the edge of the wrapping and tore off a large chunk, exposing the label for a battery-powered, ride-on car. "Look there, Nathan. Look what Pops got for you."

"And Mimi." Susan's plastic smile slipped momentarily. "I'm responsible for that snazzy wrapping job."

"Let's see what's in here." Neil's eyes widened along with Nathan's as he tore away the box to reveal a miniature replica of a Range Rover.

Child-sized, yet far too large for a one-year-old.

"Well, would you look at that." Neil smiled at Nathan, but the boy pointed at a bird.

Susan bounced around the two of them, taking pictures with her phone, but Fawn glanced doubtfully at JohnScott before picking up more pieces of torn paper.

The car had doors like a real automobile, and Neil opened the driver's side to nestle Nathan behind the wheel. "Ready, little guy?"

The toddler leaned forward and backward in the seat as though he could make it roll just with momentum, and Susan cackled.

"Hang on, and Pops will get you going." Neil flipped a switch, and as the car began to roll, he walked alongside, steering to keep the child safely on the sidewalk.

Susan squawked that Neil should be careful, and Fawn and Ruthie waved and cooed and tried to get Nathan to look at their cameras.

Even though I despised the flamboyance of the gift, I smiled in spite of myself. I didn't know which of them was acting the most juvenile. When I looked at Clyde, he winked at me, but I pretended not to see. That sort of thing would never do. I chided myself for agreeing to hike with him to Picnic Hollow after the party, but at least that would give me plenty of time to let him know how I felt.

Nathan spied Clyde by the swing. "Cyde?" The child held his arms through the open roof, flexing his wrists back and forth.

"Let's try this little hill over there, son." Neil steered the car away from the playground and toward a raised place in the sidewalk, but Nathan turned around in the seat and stood up.

"Cyde?"

As the distance between the Range Rover and Clyde lengthened, Nathan's face screwed into a ball of emotion, and Fawn shuffled after them, retrieving her child from the plastic prison and laughing softly.

Tension settled over the playground as though we had all been sprayed by a crop duster. Neil's behavior was odd, even for him. Something was definitely up with him, and I decided right then and there that *antsy* was too light a term to describe it.

CHAPTER TWELVE

"You think we're on the right track?" Two hours later, Clyde pulled back a mesquite branch so I could pass without getting scratched. After twenty-some-odd years, we were having a dickens of a time locating any landmarks to help us find our way to Picnic Hollow.

"Maybe." We had gained access through a Corps of Engineers service site, driven through a bumpy pasture as far as we could, then took off hiking. I shielded my eyes from the late-afternoon sun. "Who owns this land?"

"Way back when, it belonged to Hector Chavez's grandpa. I reckon it's still in the family."

Obscured below a rocky bluff on our left side lay the lake, but even though we couldn't yet see it, the fishy scent of the water wafted on the breeze, filtering through the crags and crannies as we searched for the declivity that would lead us down to the hollow.

"Here we go." Clyde ran-walked up a boulder, then jumped from the back side. He turned to wait for me. "Remember that time Hector used this rock as a stage? We're almost there."

I laughed, partly from remembering our old escapades and partly from relief that we weren't going to be hiking much longer. "I never would have thought he'd turn out to be the sheriff."

"Sure enough." Clyde looked behind us as though we were being followed. "I bet he's been busy out here this week."

"Not this far east," I said. "Those bones were found closer to Rock Creek."

I scooted past him and hurried the last few yards, my steps quickening because of the sloped curve of the solid rock beneath my feet. I figured the lake to be less than twenty yards away, but because we were sheltered in a tiny canyon of sorts, we still couldn't see it. Waves lapped against the sandstone at the water's edge, sending wet echoes bouncing off the walls to tease us with the sound of its coolness.

"Take it slow, Lyn."

But I couldn't. I hurried around the bend, curving to the right, where I stopped in the broad hollow created years ago by wind or water or time itself. I turned around and gazed at the sheer cliff behind us. A sandy wall rounded down from fifteen feet above our heads, creating a slanted ceiling of rock and sheltering us from the late-afternoon sun. I smiled.

"Ain't that something?" Clyde's fingertips brushed along the surface as he studied the names carved in stone. "There's my grand-pappy right there. And Ma."

"And my parents." I pointed to their names, carved deeper than some, one above the other, with a heart in between. "How old do you suppose they were?"

"If I had to guess, I'd say teenagers." He chuckled. "Don't seem like a grown man would carve that heart." Unexpectedly Clyde slid one arm around me and firmly gripped both my elbows.

I stiffened. *What on earth?* I hadn't yet had time to set him straight about my feelings toward him, but I'd done nothing to give him the impression I wanted him to *touch me.* But when he tilted his head toward the ground where the wall sloped at a sharp angle, I realized he was only trying to keep me from screaming. A diamondback rattlesnake lay coiled in the shade of all those names.

Clyde dropped his arms to his sides, leaving me feeling unprotected. "He won't bother us, if we don't bother him."

I knew that to be true, but I took three steps backward anyway. My attention was divided then between the carvings and the reptile, but I forced myself to drink in the sights and the memories, knowing I might not be out there again soon. Slipping my phone from my back pocket, I spent the next ten minutes zooming and focusing and clicking, but then I stopped to examine a picture once cut deeply into the stone but now weathered away. One of the oldest markings, a wagon train, toiled endlessly from east to west, complete with oxen pulling the covered Conestogas and a set of initials below each of the wooden wheels.

I imagined settlers, stuck in the area for days because of sickness. Maybe a couple of them found this little spot, pulled out a pocket knife they brought from back home, and started whittling to pass the time. Maybe they even settled in the area. I searched the wall, deciding they probably hadn't. The next identifiable time frame was a bold *1927* far above my head. "How do you reckon?"

Clyde looked where I pointed. "Probably sitting on horseback."

My gaze bounced to the rocks at my feet, then to the jagged ravine above and below us, then to the snake still pretending to sleep. "Life was so hard back then."

"Hard now, too." Clyde wore a canteen over his shoulder, and pulling its strap over his head, he offered me a drink and then let the water pour into his own mouth. "Funny you can't see the lake from here, and we're so close." He held the jug above his head, just long enough for a splash to wet his hair, and then he blinked as droplets clung to his eyelashes.

"A lot of things aren't what they seem."

"But a lot of things are." He sat on a rock and crossed his arms, and I knew he was looking at me.

"Is your name up there?" I asked.

"I reckon."

My gaze skittered across the rock methodically, left to right, up and down, searching for any rendition of the name *Clyde Felton*.

And then I found it. *C.F. + S.S.*

"You and Susan. That day." My voice sounded as hollow as the nook where the rattlesnake rested, and I instantly regretted calling attention to the double date that echoed so gracelessly through my memory. Even though the evening had been innocent enough—two young couples hiking together—the weeks following it were so filled with pain that I wished it had never happened.

"Long time ago," Clyde said.

"Yeah, it was." Without wanting to, I let my eyes wander to the bottom left corner where the wall slanted parallel to a boulder. Neil and I had been in our early twenties then, and we had sat there together. I had lain back on the rock, sunbathing, while he carved

L.B. Nobody but the two of us knew it stood for *ladybug*, and I wasn't about to share that tidbit with Clyde. I squinted at the letters, realizing Neil hadn't carved his own initials.

"I bet your name's up there a time or two," Clyde said.

I studied his profile, wondering what he meant, what he knew. Two years after I sunbathed on that rock, I had come to this place with Hoby. We were married then and brought our baby daughter way out there for old times' sake. Hoby insisted on carving our names—probably to prove to himself and the world that we were really together—but he barely got started before Ruthie needed a diaper or a bottle or had some other urgent baby crisis. Half an *H* would forever mock me from the middle of the cliff, two shallow scratches among the solid indentations of all the others.

"Lyn—"

Clyde's words were interrupted by a loud noise—an explosion—from down near the lake. We turned in time to see a geyser of water shoot above the rock line, bringing with it the foul scent of rot from deep in the lake and showering us with fine mist. Just as quickly as the spout appeared, it fell back to the water level, but my heart didn't stop racing from the surprise.

"*Holy cow.*" Clyde watched as the snake slithered slowly away from us to disappear into a crevice between two rocks.

"What was that?" I asked.

"Must be the Tarrons dynamite fishing again. The game warden was talking about it at the DQ last week, and I reckon if those boys get caught, they can kiss the military good-bye."

Rowdy shouts and whoops bounced up the crevices.

"Where do they get the dynamite?" I asked.

"Don't know. Might not be dynamite, seeing as how it's hard to come by these days. Could be C-4 or even hand grenades for all I know." Clyde put his fists on his hips and stared at the carvings, but I could tell this time he wasn't seeing them. He was frustrated about something, and it wasn't the Tarron boys' fishing methods. "Lyn?" He cleared his throat, and for some reason, the sound sent a tremor of apprehension through my mind like the rumble of distant thunder. "I've been wanting to ask you out, but every time I start, something always comes up."

My gaze landed on his hand, where it rested near his belt, and I mentally slapped myself for hugging him at the Dairy Queen. For giving him the wrong impression. For making him think anything could ever happen between us. I frowned at the letters near the boulder, wanting to tell him no but unable to flat out reject him. "We're here, aren't we?" I shrugged. "And we went to the windmills the other day."

"The side of Highway 84 don't count, and this"—he glanced to the crack where the rattlesnake had disappeared—"this is closer, but it still ain't right."

Irritation spread through my core like an angry infection, but close to the surface, a calming balm covered my pain, and I yearned for his baritone voice and strong hands. Squeezing my eyes shut, I blocked out the names that all seemed to be whispering advice, and I tried to focus on the sound of the breeze through the ravine, the waves slapping against rock, the call of a scissortail flying overhead. Real sounds.

Without meaning to, I sighed. A frustrated release of breath, not a dreamy one, and I spoke quickly to cover my error. "Well, what did you have in mind?" My eyes snapped open.

"Dinner maybe? I heard about a new steak house in Lubbock. Supposed to be pretty good."

The whispering voices fell into silence, leaving me with no answer. No rebuttal. No excuse. I felt helpless, with no real reason to refuse him. My mind told me to say yes, but the ghosts in my past insisted against it. I crossed my arms, shook my head, and started counting the names. One, two, three …

I heard him take a step, and he paused a few seconds before moving in front of me, turning his back on the crowd of names to look me in the eye. When he spoke, his voice was deep and rough. "Will you go out with me, Lyn?" His eyes were sad and determined at the same time, and it hurt to look into them. Instead, I peered past his bicep to the wagon train and the lightly scratched *H*.

He stood motionless, towering over me, and I sensed his sadness changing to fear.

Our eyes locked for a few seconds before mine wandered to a few hairs hanging down the side of his cheek, having pulled loose from the tie at the base of his neck. The wind nudged them an inch toward his ear, then an inch back, and my gaze followed his jawline down to his chin, covered with stubble. Clyde almost always had stubble. I wondered what it would be like to touch his chin and feel the roughness of his face. What it would feel like to be the one buying him shaving cream at the United. What would happen if I rubbed my lips against his cheek.

Almost without thinking, I stepped toward him and slipped my hand into his, wrapping my fingers safely around one of his.

For a second it seemed as though he leaned away from me, an automatic reaction to approaching danger, but then his eyebrows lifted slightly and he grinned.

I shook my head, already regretting my actions, but Clyde's laughter bounced off the walls and echoed through my heart, and I realized I hadn't heard him laugh like that since before he went to prison. His voice boomed as if his happiness came from deep inside, and the sound startled me so much, I took a step back and stared.

Wanting to hear more.

CHAPTER
THIRTEEN

I could have kicked myself for holding Clyde's hand. *Good grief.* He and I were not hand holders. We didn't touch each other. Or hug. Truth be told, nowadays I never touched anyone except for bumping elbows with Ruthie when we sat too close at football games.

But Clyde's hand felt different than Ruthie's elbows.

I had lain awake thinking what his skin felt like against mine. The moistness of his palm. How my fingers smelled like him afterward, an unrecognizable scent that teased me until late into the night. Was it cologne? Deodorant? Some kind of cleaner from the Dairy Queen?

By lunch on Monday, it had long since washed away, but I ran the back of my forefinger beneath my nostrils, pretending to rub my nose. All I smelled was hand sanitizer.

I stood in front of Velma's living-room window watching the skies darken over her back pasture. Drops of rain plopped quarter-sized circles on the top of the old picnic table, and a metal lawn chair rocked back and forth in the grass, threatening to tumble. Through the thin panes, I could feel the temperature dropping, but

Velma—always the older sister—was too busy interrogating me to pay any attention to the weather.

"What time do you go in today?" She sat at the computer desk in the corner of the room, her head tilted back as she looked through her bifocals. *Paying the bills was typically Ansel's job.*

"One thirty."

"You worked much overtime lately?"

"Not really."

"What you been doing with your free time then?"

Even for Velma, she was extra-inquisitive, but I began to understand. I let my head drop to one side as I crooned, "What have you heard about me?"

Her lips puckered. "Clyde Felton."

It hadn't been twenty-four hours since I held Clyde's hand at Picnic Hollow—not to mention we had been alone—so she must have heard from the Parker sisters about the stroll down Highway 84. "We were just walking down the road."

She stopped clicking her mouse but didn't look at me. "They were saying you held his hand out at the lake."

"But nobody was even—" In my voice I heard the whine of my fourteen-year-old self, insisting to my older sister that I would be good if only she gave me permission to go to the skating rink in Lubbock. *But I wasn't asking permission for anything.*

"Aw, it don't matter, Lynda. You and Clyde were bound to end up together." She leaned back in the oak desk chair. "Does Ruthie know?"

"It's not like we have anything to tell." I frowned at the box monitor. "We're just talking, that's all."

She reached for a Kleenex and wiped the computer screen, scrubbing firmly on a few fingerprints, and I wondered if Ansel had been eating popcorn while he played solitaire. "It's clear Clyde's crazy about you. Has been for a while now." She let her palms fall to her thighs. "But I bet he has a thing or two he'd like to say to Hoby."

Naturally she would cut straight to the crux of my worries. Even though I no longer had feelings for my husband, I did still have … a husband.

"A lot of us have a thing or two we'd like to say to Hoby." I leaned my forehead against the cool surface of the sliding-glass door. Outside, dirt and gravel swirled across the porch, and in the distance, lightning shot starkly through the blackened sky. The pasture was alive with frenzied movement, and a dull grumble sounded every now and again, but in contrast, things lay still in the house. Only the faint scent of dust gave any indication that the storm brewing outside might ever reach us in our cozy nest. If I dated Clyde, I might be creating my own storm.

"I can't go the rest of my life waiting for Hoby," I said.

"Clearly he ain't coming back."

Her words cut like a knife across my pride, but I said nothing.

My sister was silent for a moment, and without looking I figured she had that stop-feeling-sorry-for-yourself expression on her face. She exhaled softly. "I reckon I'm borrowing trouble, but if you ever try to legally separate yourself from Hoby, he could mess with your mind again."

My body wilted like a day-old carnation, and I slumped against the doorframe. It had been quite a while since I considered the notion that my husband might come back to Trapp. Right after he drove away in that bright-red wrecker of his, I had hoped and prayed he would come back, but after a while, I stopped praying.

The bedroom door down the hallway creaked open, and Ansel hobbled into the living room. "You girls solved all the world's problems?" He chuckled at his own joke.

"Not just yet, but we're working on it," Velma said.

I smiled at the gray coveralls my brother-in-law wore. Velma had purchased the gently worn garment at Harold Porterfield's yard sale, but when she sat down with her seam ripper to remove Harold's embroidered name from the front pocket, she had stopped short halfway through the task and decided there was no need to continue. Over the years the coveralls had become Ansel's favorite work-around-the-house uniform, partly because they were comfortable and partly because his wife had teasingly labeled him *old*.

Ansel sat in his recliner and raised the footrest, and I imagined his joints rusted like an old tractor. Within a few minutes, he was snoring softly.

"How's he doing?" I asked.

"Same."

I glanced at the churning clouds and noticed Ansel's cattle making their way to the barn. A calf jumped and kicked, adding to the maelstrom in the sky.

Velma, a little rusty herself, stood and took four slow steps to the adjacent kitchen. She glanced back at the recliner, and her eyes turned into empty pudding bowls, scraped clean of their usual rich, chocolaty goodness.

"I'm not going to change," I said.

"I know you're not." She smiled gently while she used a hand-cranked can opener on a can of pork and beans. "But I sure don't know what I'd do without you, Lynda."

It wasn't like Velma to talk that way. Her strength and independence defined her motherly take-charge attitude in all she did, and she never needed anyone. Certainly not me. I stepped to the kitchen and pulled a pitcher from the cabinet just as a gust of wind pelted sand against the house like mosquitoes on a screen door. "Do you think we should take shelter in the bathroom?"

Velma waved the can opener toward the computer desk, her determination renewed now that I needed advice. "The weather radio will let us know if it gets that bad, but lawdy, I hope I don't have to wake Ansel."

I tore open a packet of lemonade mix and spilled the yellow powder into the pitcher, inhaling the lemony cloud it produced. As I let the faucet water run, I coughed to clear the bitterness from my lungs, wishing it were so easy to cleanse the bitterness from my heart.

"You'll make it all right when Ansel's gone," I said softly, unsure of this new role I was taking on as the encouraging sister. It felt like a lie. It *was* a lie. "You won't be alone."

She reached into the refrigerator for a package of wieners, and her silence echoed as though the tiny kitchen were a vast underground cavern.

I didn't know what else to say. My feeble words couldn't prevent Velma's pain any more than they could save Ansel's life.

"I'll be fine," she said.

I stirred the lemonade with a wooden spoon, watching specks of powder spin on the water's surface, unable—or unwilling—to dissolve. "Maybe I won't talk to Clyde again. We sure don't need any more drama around here."

Velma wielded a paring knife to cut small pieces of wiener into the saucepan with the beans. She said nothing, so I tossed the spoon into the sink.

"No." A sigh slid from her lungs with that one little word, and it sounded as if the rest of her strength went with it. "You need Clyde."

I stared unseeingly at the calendar above the sink, wanting to be a source of encouragement to her, yet unable to pull my selfish thoughts away from my own problems. "I'm scared, Velma. What if he's like Hoby?" A sob made its way up from my stomach, but I quickly stifled it. "What if I just get hurt again?"

Her spoon gently scraped the bottom of the saucepan. "Aw, Lynda. Clyde Felton's not going to hurt you."

"He could have changed."

"Nobody changes that much."

I wanted to believe her. I wanted to embrace her words and hold them close until they seeped through my chest and nestled in my heart. But I couldn't. Somewhere in the back of my mind, a silent demon still whispered.

"He even goes to church now." Velma calmly removed a blue serving bowl from the cabinet. "Now that I think about it … if you and me went to church, you'd see Clyde more often. And I'd see JohnScott more, too."

What on earth? She jerked me from my thoughts and tossed me under a speeding locomotive. "What are you saying?"

"The folks down there are different now, right?"

I bit the inside of my cheek, not hard, just enough to worry the skin. Velma and Ansel weren't churchgoing types, and she knew better than to suggest I was. "From what I hear, a lot of them have changed, but I'm sure a few are still holding out for Christ to come back."

She lifted the saucepan with one hand and spooned beanie-weanies into the bowl with the other. "I don't mean to beat a dead horse, but I'd kinda like to see JohnScott somewhere other than the sideline of a football game. Don't you think it'd be worth it to see Ruthie more often? And hear her husband preaching the words?"

I didn't need to attend worship service to hear Dodd Cunningham preach at me. Clearly I was his number-one target recruit, and he pelted me with subtle encouragement nonstop. But as Velma rinsed her Revere Ware under the faucet, I realized she wasn't talking about me. Or Clyde. Or even JohnScott. After all I had been through with that stinking church, she would never shove me toward that white-frame building unless she had a darn good reason. And that reason was snoring in the recliner.

"Ruth Ann knows where to find me." I mumbled the excuse, not wanting to think about the true source of our discussion.

Velma smacked her lips as though her tongue were covered in taffy. "What's that mean?"

"She's married, going to college, wanting a baby." I shrugged. "She's got a full life."

"You want a cart of cheese to go with that whine?"

"I'm not whining. Just stating facts, and she don't need me."

Ouch. I hadn't meant to say that last part.

A spray of angry raindrops pelleted against the window as the clouds finally dumped their water on the ground below, beating the dry grass as the wind moaned against the roof. Velma and I both froze for a few seconds, awed by the power of the storm, and then she carried our gourmet lunch to the table and plopped the bowl down on the vinyl tablecloth. "Hmmph."

I sat next to her and peeled a paper plate from the stack in the middle of the table. "I hate it when you make that sound."

"I know."

Of course she knew. The woman had raised me since I was fourteen, and we'd been through hell and high water together. She knew what irritated me, what worried me, what made me happy. And she knew, without my telling her, that I'd like to see Ruthie more often. That I wanted to see Dodd, too. That I even wanted to hear him preaching the words. But she also knew my frazzled emotions had more than they could deal with just thinking about Ansel.

And she knew I couldn't … wouldn't … go back to the church. Not yet.

"I know," she repeated.

CHAPTER FOURTEEN

Clyde dropped by Lynda's house after work, hoping he could get things straightened up in her yard before it got too dark. Her place had wind damage from the storm, but the house would fall down around her before she'd ask for help—from anyone other than Ansel. Clyde figured he was doing them both a favor.

Two clay flowerpots had blown off the porch and now lay broken on the ground, their long-dead plants spilling out like unearthed corpses. Clyde picked up the pieces and dumped them in the trash barrel under the carport, then took an ax to the fallen limbs of the mesquite tree. From the looks of it, the largest one had missed Lynda's front window by only a few inches.

He worked quickly, and when she pulled up, he was piling the last of the brush at the side of the house.

"I could have done that myself." She slammed the door of her little hatchback so hard, Clyde thought it might have dented. He laughed to himself. Ansel had kept that car running for years. Wouldn't it be funny if she ruined it with a tantrum?

"No need to get riled up." He reached for his ax. "I'll be on my way."

"You'd best come in and get a drink of water first."

Clyde smiled. She'd have to do more than slam the car door if she wanted him to believe she was angry. "You hear about that tornado?" he asked.

"A hundred times. Every single detail." She rolled her eyes. "It touched down in Slaton. Minimal damage. Metal roof ripped off the feed store. Forty-five years since the F5 hit Lubbock." She paused as she unlocked the front door. "Though it seems like yesterday to Old Man Guthrie, as told to Sophie Snodgrass and the ladies' quilting club that met at the diner for their after-piecin' piece of pie. Lemon meringue."

"Long day?"

"Not too bad." Her eyebrows quivered. "I shouldn't complain though, should I?"

He hadn't meant the comment as an accusation, so he didn't answer. He followed her into the kitchen, where he folded himself into a maple dining chair and watched her fetch him a glass of ice water.

"You hungry?" she asked.

"Sure. Pork chops and carrots?"

"Frozen pizza and ranch dressing."

He chuckled. "I like you better at Dixie's."

"Everyone does." She opened the freezer and removed a Tombstone pizza, then flipped on the oven. "I hate cooking."

Clyde fought to keep his laughter buried in his chest. Lynda had hated cooking ever since her ninth-grade homemaking class when she burned her German chocolate cake. "Why do you cook for Dixie?"

"It pays more than waitressing." She ripped away the plastic shrink-wrap, tossed the pizza on the oven rack, and twisted the timer. "It's different at the diner, though. I don't have to think about it, or care. The customer orders a pork chop, and all I have to do is throw it on the grill, then slap it on a plate. There's no planning or shopping or recipe hunting. It's mindless."

"It's a job." He hated that for her, though he had suspected as much.

"It's a job," she said softly.

Clyde's gaze fell to the table, where he noticed a few folded papers. He reached for them and opened the first. It was a letter, and he immediately felt sick to his stomach. "Why is Neil Blaylock sending you—"

She crossed the room and snatched the papers away from him. "It's nothing. Just something I found cleaning out a closet." She tossed them in the plastic trash can near the sink and rested her hands on the counter. "How tall are you?"

So she didn't want to talk about her old mail. His eyes briefly skimmed the ceiling. "Why?"

"I was just thinking you're enormous, and I wondered how enormous you actually are."

He rubbed the back of his thumb along the seam of his jeans. "Maybe six and a half."

"Six feet, six inches?"

"Last time they measured."

She opened the fridge and snatched the ranch dressing from the door, then thunked it on the table in front of him, glaring as though he had said a curse word. "I don't like the way you talk. *They* measured you. *They* weighed you. *They* cut your hair." Her shoulders shivered. "It's like they owned you or something."

He looked through the back-door window and noticed the neighbor's hound in the glow of their porch light, loping from one end of the chain-link barrier to the other. "That's because they did." He lowered his head. For a fact, the State of Texas had owned him, but he was doing everything in his power to be different now. Lynda didn't get it.

She had her back to him as she washed her breakfast dishes at the sink, one knee bent. He studied her. She didn't have to do the dishes while the pizza cooked. She could've sat down and talked to him for ten minutes, but there seemed to be a shadow of doubt over her actions—slamming the car door, misunderstanding his comments, washing dishes when she normally would've let them pile up—as if the two of them had become strangers at Picnic Hollow. As if she was sorry it had happened.

A surge of panic swelled through him, and he stood almost without thinking, driven by the overwhelming urge to make sure she knew him. To tell her he was different now, and that in the months and years ahead of them, he would be even more different. He walked up behind her, and when she turned, her brow wrinkled.

"What?"

"*They* don't tell me what to do anymore," he said quietly, afraid that if he spoke louder, she would startle like a deer and run away. "I do what I want."

Her eyes widened but then slowly narrowed. "And just what is it you want?"

"You." He shrugged.

"Me?"

Her eyes begged for something—maybe reassurance—but he didn't know the words to explain the whirlwind of thoughts thrashing through his mind. He answered by bending down and gently pressing his mouth against hers, trapping her between his arms as he reached behind her to grip the edge of the sink. He didn't move, couldn't move. He felt frozen in fear of what he might lose and what he might never have.

Hesitantly she moved her mouth against his and laid her palms on his chest. Clyde focused on the sensation. Few people ever touched him, and the pressure of her lips and hands sent his thoughts racing. He pulled back, looking into her eyes before he took a step away.

Her lips were parted as though he had interrupted her mid-sentence, but then the oven timer buzzed. "Go back over there, you." She busied herself with their dinner and with not looking at him. After a few minutes, she slipped into a chair and put pizza slices on two paper plates. He could tell she was thinking about that kiss, and Clyde got the feeling she hadn't been all that pleased.

He bowed his head to pray and laid his hand palm up on the table, hoping she would hold it, but after three empty seconds, he began without her. He intended to say a short prayer for the food, but somehow he drifted over to Ansel's health and then to Velma's grief. And he tacked on a bit about Dodd and Ruthie wanting a baby. He was almost to the *amen* when she slipped her tiny hand in his, and then he considered praying for an hour, just so he could feel her skin. Instead, he gave her fingers a squeeze and reached for a napkin.

She nibbled a slice of pizza but wouldn't look at him, and he realized that if he wanted to know what she was thinking, he was going to have to pull it out of her. "Lyn? Is it all right that I kissed you?"

"I ... I think so."

"But?"

She set her pizza on her plate, then watched it as though it might fly away. "Maybe not just yet," she whispered. "I don't know about it all."

She didn't know about it all. She didn't know about him. "I understand." He grabbed the ranch dressing, removed the cap, and squirted a blob of dressing on his plate. "No need to rush things."

"Can we try it again later?"

Her last six words erased the doom created by the others, and he released a shallow breath. "Sorry, but this is all sort of new to me."

She took a bite, but then her chewing slowed, and after she swallowed, her eyes bored into his. "You ... haven't kissed many women."

His face warmed as though the sun hung from the ceiling directly above the table, and under his shirt, a drop of sweat trickled from his armpit down to his waist. "Just the one."

"Susan." She sounded as if she might pull every hair from Susan's big blonde hairdo, if given the chance.

Clyde didn't understand why they had to talk about it. He could see Lynda was gradually figuring things out in her head, picking up the bread crumbs he had left for her to follow, finding her way to the truth of his past. She had a question in her eyes, *the question*, but instead of asking it, she dropped her gaze to somewhere near his heart.

He answered her anyway. "It was only the one time with me and her." He cleared his throat. "And it was ... quick."

Clyde ran the tip of his pizza through the dressing, then shoved it into his mouth, tearing off a portion large enough to occupy his tongue with something other than talk. There had already been enough conversation to last him for weeks, and it had done nothing but put them both on edge.

When he sneaked another glance at her, he knew she was just as scared as he was. Afraid of having old memories dredged up from the bottom of a deep well. Afraid of not being able to forget the past. Afraid of not being able to move forward.

He almost wished he hadn't kissed her.

But not quite.

CHAPTER FIFTEEN

"Lynda, hush. I can't hear." Dixie leaned through the pass-through window, pretending to count open tables, but I knew the truth. She was eavesdropping on a group of boys—strangers to Trapp—who had shoved three tables together and pulled up extra chairs.

I raised my eyebrows questioningly.

"Boy Scout troop from Lubbock," Dixie whispered. "They're helping the Rangers out at the lake."

"Those bones?"

"Yep. I heard the kids talking about it. They form a line, walking four feet apart, and search every square inch of land."

We studied the teenagers as we worked the grill, both of us trying to pick out tidbits of information, but their talk had shifted from work to dirty jokes.

I moved away from the window and dropped an order of fried zucchini into hot oil. "Lake Alan Henry is eleven miles long. Finding more bones out there would be like finding a needle in the Grand Canyon."

Dixie's eyes twinkled. "Girl, go take your break and find out what they're saying."

"That sounds like work to me, and you don't pay me for breaks."

"I'll pay you for this one."

"Deal."

She nodded toward the dining room, but as I walked away, she seemed to have second thoughts. "Just ten minutes, Lynda!"

Three male Rangers sat at a table near the Scouts, and one of them made eye contact and motioned me over. "Lynda, is it?"

"That's right. What can I do for you?"

"I was wondering if you happened to know the closest liquor store."

I pointed north. "You passed CJ's on your way into town, back about half a mile."

"Seems I remember that, now that you mention it." His skin was tanned except around his eyes, where he had two pale circles from wearing sunglasses.

He leered at me, but I ignored him. "You boys working out at the lake?"

"All day long with nothing to show for it," a red-haired man, who looked younger than JohnScott, whined from across the table. "I'd rather be working with a real crew than these little kids."

"Will they likely run tests on those bones," I asked, "to figure out who it is?"

"Can't." The young man shrugged. "Not enough DNA left. They're too old."

"So what are you doing out there now?"

The first man sat up straighter. "At this point, searching for a shallow grave, a few displaced bones, or anything out of the ordinary like—"

Red-Haired Boy interrupted him. "I don't see why they extended the search site and called in all these Boy Scouts, though." He squinted at the third, silent man before lifting his chin. "In spite of the teeth marks on them bones, no animal would drag a carcass more than twenty yards or so. I've got experience with this sort of thing."

"It's not that simple." Sunglass Tan shook his head. "If a mother coyote is hunting for her pups, she might haul their dinner as far as a mile away."

My stomach turned. "So you'll be around here for a while, I guess." My last question had less to do with the bones and more to do with when the diner would be back to normal.

"Could be weeks." Sunglass Tan leaned back in his chair, letting his eyelids close partway. "And we'll be back in here often between now and then."

Good grief. "Can I get you boys anything else? Maybe some apple pie?"

"Pie isn't what I had in mind." He let his gaze slide to my hips. "What time do you get off?"

"Not anytime soon." I didn't smile. "I'll have the waitress bring your check."

"Come on, babe, I can wait around."

"Jim." The quiet man must have been a foreman. "She said she doesn't get off anytime soon."

"I might get off, though."

Jim's comment received a snicker from the redhead. "Bring a friend for me, why don't you."

"Lynda." A firm hand gripped my elbow, and I turned to see Hector Chavez with his bushy, black mustache. "Tea?" He waved his glass in front of my face. "Today?"

"Coming right up, Sheriff." Not only was Hector the sheriff, but he was also a friend of mine from way back in grade school. I knew he hadn't interrupted the conversation simply because he wanted a drink refill. Apparently the Rangers realized that, too.

"You her bodyguard?" The redhead scowled.

"Now, Cory," Hector said patiently, "I've been working just as much as you, and I need me a refill of sweet tea before we head back out in the heat."

The two obnoxious Rangers grumbled, but the quiet one gave Hector an apologetic shrug as the sheriff followed me to the counter.

I grabbed the pitcher and sloshed tea into his glass. "I had things under control."

The Rangers noisily made their way to the cash register, where they paid the waitress, but I forced my gaze to stay on Hector.

"I reckon you did," he said.

"I'm not a helpless damsel in distress."

"Nope. For sure, you're not that." He chuckled.

I squirted the counter with vinegar water from a spray bottle, then wiped it with a cup towel. "Neil used to do and say that sort of thing," I said. "I guess I got used to it."

Hector gingerly set his glass down and looked away from me. "Neil Blaylock's a friend of mine, Lynda."

My spine stiffened.

The sheriff glanced toward the street, where the Boy Scouts congregated on the sidewalk, throwing Skittles into the air and catching them in their mouths. "Yet still ..."—Hector pulled a twenty-dollar bill from his pocket and dropped it on the counter next to the register—"sometimes I think that man needs a thrashing."

CHAPTER SIXTEEN

"Momma, Ansel doesn't belong here."

Tuesday afternoon, Ruthie and I stood on the front lawn of Trapp's beige brick nursing home. We had promised Velma we would check out the facility, but now that we were here, we couldn't bring ourselves to walk the last few steps and through the door. Even from our perch twenty yards from the entrance, I could smell the telltale scents of disinfectant and body odor. On the front porch, a shriveled woman sat in a wheelchair, listing heavily to one side. The welcoming committee.

"No, he doesn't," I said as I shoved my hands into the front pockets of my jeans. I didn't want to lose Ansel, but almost worse than losing him would be visiting him in a place like this while he slowly withered. "We should check on home care."

Diverting my gaze from the woman on the porch, I thought how nice it would feel to pound my fists against the nearest car bumper. I pushed the thought away as a ray of sunlight bounced off the shiny grill, causing me to squint at the brightness. The sun seemed out of place in such a dismal setting, but when I stopped to examine the parking lot, I noticed the neatly trimmed hedges, the hanging flowerpots, the tree-lined sidewalks. Clyde would say there's always good among the bad. Clyde said a lot of things—without ever speaking much at all.

We wandered to a wooden bench beneath a pine tree. The bench had been recently whitewashed, yet *Go Panthers!* had already been scratched into the clumpy paint. Ruthie and I sat side by side, and I spoke quickly, not wanting to think about Ansel anymore. "You probably heard the rumors about Clyde and me."

Her right eyebrow curled into a question mark, pulling the corner of her mouth along with it. "Yep." She gazed at her fingernails, flipping her palm over to inspect the cuticles. "But what about Daddy?"

I held my breath.

"I mean I'm glad you're with Clyde and all, but—"

"I'm not *with* him."

"Whatever." She smiled as though she knew better. "But ... I mean ... there's no way Daddy's coming back, right?" Her smile faltered.

Until that moment I hadn't realized she was still hanging on to the notion. When Ruthie was small, she would ask me every few days when her daddy was coming home, and generally I would answer her impatiently, wishing she would stop asking, stop waiting, stop hoping. *Stop reminding me.*

"He almost came back once, Ruth Ann." Instantly I regretted having started the conversation, because the thought of sharing one of my secrets, even with Ruthie, made me feel as if I were peeling away the plates of protection I had placed around my heart. And without them, I might be exposed to the elements, like a brand-new butterfly crawling out of its cocoon, only to be swept away by a dust storm.

Her eyes grew wide. "When?"

"I got a letter from him several weeks after he left. I still have the silly thing." I studied my Converse sneakers, tapping them against each other, wanting to keep the details buried where they belonged. I carefully selected a few tidbits of information to help Ruthie make peace with it all. "He apologized for believing Neil's word over mine and said that once he had calmed down, he realized I would never be unfaithful." My lungs weren't getting enough air, and I consciously took a deep breath before continuing. "He said he was coming back, and we could talk. Go from there."

Ruthie stared at me as though my words made a difference.

"I thought he meant it, Ruth Ann." I laughed nervously. "He said he had been a fool to believe Neil's lies, and that he was ready to give up the bottle, but he needed me to help him."

Her eyebrows quivered. "I don't remember him coming back. Ever."

"He didn't show." My words were knives, and I regretted the wounds they left on my daughter. "I never heard from him again."

Ruthie froze for ten seconds before she laughed unconvincingly. "It's just as well. I mean … it's been so long, and you … you probably don't love him like that anymore."

My heart broke. Right there on the bench in front of the nursing home, it shattered because Ruthie clearly still clung to a childlike dream that Hoby and I would get back together. All those years I had been locked away, drowning myself in bitterness, my daughter had been waiting for her daddy to come home.

I looked into her eyes. "No, Ruth Ann."

In the lull that followed, a pickup drove past us on the street, its gears racing loudly as the driver shifted out of sync, trying to force something that should have come easily.

Ruthie smiled too widely. "I guess I always imagined him coming back and making everything better. Just driving into town in his red wrecker, but that's ridiculous. That truck would be really old now." She shook her head as though to clear the memories away like cobwebs. "And I really do like Clyde. You two are perfect for each other. Everybody says so."

A steady rhythm beat in my ears, filling my mind, my heart, my soul, because I had no idea what would happen between Clyde and me. Multiple scenarios played out in my mind, but none of them had a happily-ever-after ending. I squinted at her. "Everybody?"

"Yes." She laughed through the word, and it became a light shush that floated on the breeze and bounced around my shoulders. Then her gaze jerked toward the street. "Now I've seen everything."

My mood took a few seconds to shift, but I followed her gaze and saw Clyde walking down the sidewalk pushing a stroller. "Oh my."

Ruthie suppressed a laugh but then giggled, and I couldn't help but join in. Clyde was so tall, he had to bend slightly to reach the stroller, and plastic grocery bags hung from the handles. A half gallon of orange juice lay across Nathan's lap.

The baby gripped a long packaged stick of beef jerky, waving it in the air, but when he hit himself in the face, he started crying.

"We better help," Ruthie said.

"We'd better hurry."

We jogged past the hatchback and Ruthie's El Camino, hurrying away from the shadows of the nursing home and into the sunshine of babies and strollers. And Clyde.

"What on earth?" Ruthie called to him.

He had stopped and was bent over to tend to Nathan, but when he heard us, he seemed to cringe before looking our direction. "We're just on our way home from the United."

"Why are you on foot?" I asked.

"Well, now … my car's still on the blink."

He lifted Nathan from the stroller, but the child still fussed, pulling at his diaper. "Boo-boo," Nathan whimpered.

Clyde ducked his head and motioned to the bags. "I think I got too much stuff. The kid kept pointing at things."

"I'll take you home," I said.

"Aw, Lyn. We'll be all right once he settles."

Ruthie sniffed. "Smells like he needs attention."

Clyde's mouth hung open momentarily, but then he held Nathan higher and sniffed while the child squirmed and arched his spine.

Ruthie raised her voice to be heard. "He did that once when I was with Fawn. Something in his poop was burning his backside. He wouldn't stop until she cleaned him up and soaked him in the tub."

"Boo-boo, Cyde," Nathan moaned, giving his pants another tug.

Clyde's eyebrows wrinkled as though he just realized he held an alien from Mars.

I grabbed three grocery bags and headed to my car while Ruthie folded the stroller.

"Where'd you get this old thing?" she asked over Nathan's wails. "It's not Fawn's, is it?"

"Naw, I found it at a garage sale in Roscoe. Comes in right handy when we decide to take ourselves a walk."

Ruthie laid it in the back of the hatchback next to the groceries. "Hate to run off at a time like this, but I'm due at work."

I waved to her as she headed to her own car, and then I turned to Clyde, still standing motionless on the sidewalk. "I'll have you home in thirty seconds."

"But I don't have a car seat for the little guy. Fawn wouldn't like it."

Nathan's face was turning red and blotchy, and he drew in ragged breaths between his cries. "This is an emergency," I said. "Come on."

We buckled ourselves into the car, and as I drove, I watched Clyde out of the corner of my eye, surprised by the way he held the baby firmly against his shoulder, trying to comfort him with soothing tones.

As we turned onto Main Street, Clyde cursed under his breath, and anger burst into my head from its convenient resting place between my shoulder blades. I glared at him. He never spoke that way in front of Nathan, and Fawn would have a conniption if she heard him do so.

But when I saw what Clyde was looking at, I almost cursed, too.

Neil Blaylock stood on the sidewalk in front of city hall talking to Lee Roy Goodnight, and as we passed, he craned his neck to watch us.

My nerves rattled, not because we'd been caught with Nathan out of his car seat or because Neil would surely tell Fawn all about it, but because Neil should have looked furious. He should have been concerned for the safety of his grandson, but instead of anger, his expression was calculating, as though he were putting together pieces of a 3-D puzzle, and he had just found one that fit perfectly.

CHAPTER
SEVENTEEN

In the past two years, I'd never had reason to go inside Clyde's trailer, but now I stood in the middle of the living room, snooping a little while he tended to Nathan. The furniture looked worn, and the carpet radiated the faint scent of pets, but other than a few newspapers on an end table, the place was neat. Next to the front door, there was a hole in the wall, but when I looked closer, I noticed the thin paneling and figured it could have been an accident. Maybe.

When I heard bathwater running, I trailed my fingertip across the splintery edge of the hole, then went to help Clyde.

An hour later we had Nathan cleaned up and powdered, and by the time JohnScott and Fawn arrived, Clyde had cooked four steaks on the grill and convinced me to stay for dinner. As we sat down at the small table in the kitchen, I realized I was uncharacteristically nervous in front of my nephew and Clyde's daughter.

"Aunt Lynda, can you reach that stuffed giraffe?" JohnScott motioned to the counter behind me, and I stretched for the toy, then handed it to Nathan who sat in an outdated high chair that I assumed was another of Clyde's garage-sale finds.

"Hopefully that will keep him quiet long enough for us to pray." JohnScott held his hands palms up on the table.

Even though I no longer got caught with food in my mouth during the prayer, I still felt awkward participating in the ritual. My right hand met JohnScott's solidly, but my left barely slid into Clyde's. I bowed my head, keeping my eyes focused on Clyde's fingers that wrapped completely around my palm and covered the back of my hand.

"Dear Lord," Clyde began, "thank You for this food and for these friends."

My gaze traveled from Clyde's wrist to his bicep, where his tattoo teased from the edge of his shirtsleeve. It looked like the number *nine*, but I had never seen the whole tattoo.

Nathan squealed in the high chair and clapped his hands, spurring Clyde to finish quickly. "And thank You for the little guy, who keeps us all on our toes. Amen."

Clyde rubbed the back of my hand with his thumb, then let his fingers trail away. His soft touch made the skin around my wrist itch, and I pressed my hand against the edge of my chair until it stopped.

"He's not so little anymore," JohnScott said.

Clyde smiled at Nathan. "Still seems pretty small to me."

The two of them, side by side, made quite a contrast, and I found myself wondering if Nathan would look more like Clyde the older he got.

"Little fella," Clyde said, "you be good for your momma and JohnScott."

The baby giggled as if the idea was absurd, and then he squealed again. "Daddy!"

Clyde rubbed his chin with the back of his hand. "Does he call you *Daddy*?"

"Yep, Fawn's been encouraging it lately." JohnScott looked at his wife, then back to Clyde. "We figured he could call his biological father *Dad*. It may sound awkward for a few years, but when he's older, it'll suit better. And he can call me *Daddy* till I'm old and gray, and it won't bother me."

I grunted. "I can't imagine Tyler Cruz being called *Daddy*. Now or ever."

"No, it don't really fit," Clyde agreed. "He doing all right?"

"Good," Fawn said. "He's working on his ranch again. And his mental health is stable."

"Glad to hear it."

Fawn dug into her baked potato, then scooped a spoonful onto the high-chair tray. "Thanks for grilling out, Clyde. I haven't had a steak in a while."

"Me, neither," he said. "Everything down at the Queen is cooked in oil." He glanced at me. "And Dixie only serves chicken-fried and salisbury steak. It's about time for an honest-to-goodness T-bone." He forked a steak from the platter in the middle of the table, but then his eyebrows quivered.

JohnScott laughed out loud. "Those steaks are bleeding all over the plate."

"Eww ..." Fawn pressed a hand to her stomach. "I like mine well done."

Clyde rubbed the back of his hand across his mouth. "I can't always tell when meat's done. When I grill the hamburgers at work, I watch the clock, but I guess steaks are different." He smiled sheepishly. "They're the same color either way."

JohnScott snickered. "If I'd remembered you were color-blind, I never would've risked eating here."

Clyde swooped up the platter and stomped to the back door, calling over his shoulder, "Five more minutes ought to do it."

"Maybe more," JohnScott crooned.

Nathan stared at the back door as it clicked shut. "Cyde?" He slammed his hand on the high-chair tray, sending chunks of potato bouncing to the floor.

Fawn reached for his hands. "He'll be back once the steaks stop mooing."

Silence fell over us until JohnScott started telling Fawn about a pistol one of the other coaches had bought. Bless my nephew for filling the silence.

He leaned his elbows on the table. "Makes me want to get my concealed-handgun license."

"Seriously?" Fawn asked. "If you are, I am too. That way I can pack heat in the diaper bag."

"You two are nuts," I said. "I've never wanted a gun."

"I can't picture you shooting a gun, Aunt Lynda," JohnScott said.

My nerves calmed as a happy memory came to mind. "I shot your BB gun that year at Christmas."

"I don't remember you shooting it. I remember you spilling the ammo in the grass."

Fawn picked three chunks of tomato out of her salad and tossed them on the high-chair tray. "My dad let me shoot his pistol once when I was a little girl, but I don't think I've shot a gun since then."

JohnScott formed Nathan's hand into a finger gun while Fawn insisted he "stop that right now."

My thoughts scattered.

I remembered that pistol of Neil's. He had brought it back from TCU his freshman year, bragging that it had belonged to Buddy Holly and had even been in the singer's overnight bag when his plane crashed. He expected his parents to buy a glass display case, but Gerald Blaylock had the gun appraised and discovered his son had been duped. After that, Neil kept it stashed in the glove box of his pickup, and he and his friends—Clyde and Hoby included—used the thing for target practice on the side of every barn in Garza County.

JohnScott sighed as his laughter faded. Then he looked at me. "So ... you and Clyde?"

I took a sip of tea and shrugged a little. "I don't know. Maybe."

Fawn's gaze bounced between the two of us, and she tried to hide a smile. "We don't mean to pry. We just want you both to be happy."

But they didn't know what would make me happy. I didn't even know.

The door opened, and Clyde held the tray above his head before setting it on the table. "Let's try this again."

JohnScott boldly cut into his meat and shoved a forkful into his mouth. "Now that's a steak, Clyde. That's a steak."

Fawn laughed. "In spite of that, I'm wondering if you should look for a job that doesn't involve cooking."

"Aren't too many options around here." Clyde glanced at me. "Troy Sanders has been pestering me about working on the wind farms, but I'm not sure what I think about that."

I had just taken a bite of potato, but I now found it difficult to swallow. Was Clyde actually considering working on the turbines?

Fawn tore off part of a roll and gave it to Nathan. "That's a big step considering your PICS."

"Aw, now …" Clyde salted his salad with a vengeance.

"PICS?" I asked.

Fawn looked from my eyes to the saltshaker in Clyde's fist. "Sorry. I didn't know it was a secret. It's just something I studied in a class last semester."

After a long pause where no one seemed to breathe, I snapped, "Well, I don't need to hear anyone's secrets, that's for sure."

"It ain't a secret," Clyde spoke quickly. "It's post-incarceration syndrome, that's all." He chopped his fork into his baked potato, mixing in butter and grated cheese. "When I first got out, I had some trouble, but things are better now." He stirred his potato long after it was mixed, not meeting my gaze.

JohnScott leaned forward and cleared his throat. "The birthday party was a success, don't you think?"

"Bir-day!" Nathan lifted both hands above his head as though he were calling a touchdown, and then he rubbed butter deep into his dark curls.

"All things considered," Fawn said, "it went all right."

The party had been strange, and Fawn knew it. Neil and Susan spent an hour traipsing after Nathan with their flashy gifts while the

Pickett side of the family chatted in our lawn chairs, trying not to make fun of them.

Clyde's movements stilled, and he looked at his daughter. "Maybe I shouldn't have come. I could've given the boy my gift anytime."

"No way." JohnScott shook his head. "Neil will not dictate the guest list for our son's birthday parties. I'm glad you were there."

He didn't say as much, but I had the feeling it was easier for JohnScott to stand up to his father-in-law when Clyde was around.

"Your parents doing all right?" Clyde asked Fawn.

"I guess." She looked doubtful.

Clyde set down his fork and slowly finished chewing. "We saw your dad in town earlier, and he didn't look any too happy with us." He lowered his head. "I already told you I had the boy out of his car seat."

"I would have done the same thing," Fawn said. "In my book, a screaming baby trumps a traffic law any day." She glanced at JohnScott, who gave a subtle nod. "I'm not sure I should say anything, but I've been worried about my dad."

My gaze met Clyde's for a brief moment. Maybe this was the *antsy* behavior.

"I'm not sure there's really a problem," JohnScott said. "He seems stressed to me, but that's all."

"He's different now, though. Mom, too."

With my finger I wiped a line of condensation from my glass. "How?"

"He's been talking crazy lately, and Mom's freaking out. He says he might sell his livestock and the ranch and move away."

So that was it. My mind instantly cluttered with questions. The thought of the Blaylocks moving away from Trapp seemed as far-fetched as the pope moving in. Still, the idea nudged my heart with hope … and apprehension.

Fawn glanced at Nathan, then lowered her voice. "I think Mom's a little scared."

A sick feeling filled my stomach, not quite nausea but close. I'd seen that scared look on Susan's face before—scared of Neil, scared of her circumstances, scared of life—but in the past few months, she had seemed better. More confident.

Nathan held his cup over the side of the high-chair tray, then dropped it. Immediately he peeked over the edge and giggled at the cup where it lay under the table.

JohnScott bent to retrieve it. "We're worried there might be abuse there again, but Susan denies it."

"She always did," I snapped.

Fawn squinted at me, but then her eyes softened. "You're right, but this seems different somehow."

JohnScott pulled out his cell phone and checked the time. "We better get Nathan home."

"I'm sorry to bother you guys," Fawn said. "I just don't know what to think."

She started unbuckling Nathan from the high chair, but Clyde laid a hand on her arm. "We should pray."

Fawn looked startled for only a second before she lifted her hands.

This time when we bowed our heads, I slipped my hand firmly into Clyde's and let my fingers wrap around his pinky. Two prayers in one night was a record for me, and praying for Neil felt downright backward. But as I listened to Clyde pray for the man who had done so much damage to my life—to all our lives—an unfamiliar emotion settled around my shoulders like a mink stole.

I was concerned for Neil Blaylock.

CHAPTER
EIGHTEEN

The feedlot on the edge of town had been in business all Clyde's life, yet he had never had reason to set foot on the place. Until Wednesday morning. Riding shotgun in JohnScott's old pickup with Ansel nestled between them, Clyde scanned row after row of fenced holding yards, all jammed with livestock. "This place is big." It was a nonsense thing to say, but Clyde felt the urge to fill the cab with something other than sadness and stench.

Ansel sat with his hands casually resting one on top of the other, but his right thumb rubbed against the knuckles on his left hand until Clyde thought he might wear a hole in the skin. "That it is," Ansel said.

JohnScott had been encouraging his dad to sell some of his herd, and after the latest prognosis, the old man finally agreed. His rusted stock trailer bumped along behind the truck, full of cattle, and occasionally Clyde could feel the weight yanking the pickup just like the sale of the herd was bound to yank Ansel's pride.

"Pull up right here, Son." Ansel pointed at a louvered metal building labeled *office*. "Sam will be in there."

"Want us to come in with you?" JohnScott slid the truck into neutral and put on the brake.

"I reckon I can manage on my own."

Clyde and JohnScott climbed out of the truck, and Ansel followed, scooting across the seat to the passenger side. He leaned heavily on his cane as he made his way across the gravel parking lot, and the three steps leading up to the door prompted him to cling to the pipe rail.

"You sure he don't need help?" Clyde asked softly.

"He won't have any trouble negotiating a price with Sam, but I'm a little concerned about him running into my father-in-law." He motioned toward the shiny, black-and-gray double-cab parked at the far end of the lot. "I'm sure Dad noticed it, though, so he's on his own."

"I never knew Ansel to be crossways with anybody."

"It was a long time ago, but Neil cheated him in a cattle deal. Sold him some sick heifers, and we lost five or six of them within a month."

Clyde ran his fingers through his hair, then held the mess out of his eyes as he gripped the back of his neck. He didn't need another reason to be disgusted with Neil.

"Dad keeps it to himself," JohnScott said.

"When did it happen?"

The coach took off his cap to scratch his head. "About five years ago, I guess."

"Huh." Clyde rested his forearms on the rim of the truck bed, and across from him, JohnScott did the same. "So they've been uncomfortable around each other for that long?"

"Why do you think we didn't invite our parents to our wedding?"

"I thought it was just Neil and me."

"Yeah, well …" He chuckled. "Mostly."

Clyde sighed, thinking back to his time in the pen, the regularity of it, the boredom. So much had happened in his little hometown while he was away. So much had changed.

To their left stood a large metal barn, painted blue, and Neil sauntered out of its gaping door. At first he didn't see them because of the angle of the sun, and as he stepped around a portable cattle chute, he removed his cowboy hat and rubbed his eyes. He stopped walking, seemed to take a deep breath, then put his hat back on.

Only then did he see JohnScott and Clyde. He stood up straighter and pulled his hat down more firmly, then hesitated for a split second before striding toward them.

"Coach," he said loudly. "That grandson of mine giving you any trouble?"

"Every day."

Clyde was glad Fawn's husband had a relationship with Neil, even if it was shaky.

"He's a feisty Blaylock." Neil cut his eyes toward Clyde, but Clyde didn't take the bait. Not only was he tired of fighting, but he didn't give a hoot whom Nathan took after. The child may have shared Neil's last name, but he didn't share his blood.

JohnScott's gaze bounced between the two of them. "Yep. Fawn says she probably deserves anything he dishes out, seeing as how she was a handful herself."

"She certainly was." Neil grinned as broadly as a shady politician. "Kept her momma and me busy." He looked at Clyde again, and his smile faded.

Clyde thought JohnScott's shoulders wilted, but just then, the office door opened.

Ansel paused when he saw the three of them, but he called, "Son?" He motioned for JohnScott to come inside, and then he disappeared again.

JohnScott shook Neil's hand. "You and Susan still planning on dinner at our place Saturday?"

"You know it."

As JohnScott walked toward the office, Neil took two steps as though he were headed to his truck, but when the door closed behind his son-in-law, Neil paused at the tailgate. He patted Ansel's trailer. "So, the old man's selling a few head?"

"I reckon. Can't say I blame him, though. Getting up in years." Clyde gestured to Neil's truck and trailer. "You selling, too?"

"Maybe. Why do you ask?"

Neil lifted his chin and stared at Clyde, but Clyde only shrugged. There was nothing that needed saying. For a while Clyde looked back, but when it became an obvious attempt on Neil's part to intimidate him, Clyde felt foolish. He and the other boys used to have stare-downs back in sixth grade. Surely Neil wasn't still doing it.

As soon as Clyde broke eye contact, Neil laughed once. "So, I hear you and Lynda are together now."

"Not necessarily."

"That's not what Fawn says." Neil's chin lowered, and he peered at Clyde like a detective drawing out a confession. "From what I hear, the four of you had a double date just last night."

Clyde's patience stretched. "I'm not sure I'd call it that." He wasn't sure Lynda would call it that either. He wasn't sure Lynda wanted to be with him at all.

"You ever thought about taking her away from here?" Neil rested a boot on the trailer hitch. "If I was you, I'd head off to somewhere nobody knows you."

Clyde rubbed his chin, not trusting what he was hearing. "Don't know if that'd be such a good idea. We've both got family here."

"It's none of my business, really. Just offering a suggestion, but your family will be tended to whether you're here or not." He smiled. "You're not all that good for the boy anyway."

"Fawn would disagree."

The rancher shook his head. "You don't take good care of him. I saw you yesterday."

Suddenly Neil was a spoiled child pitching a fit worse than Nathan ever had. "Yesterday was a bit of an emergency," Clyde said.

Neil scanned JohnScott's truck, then looked back toward the barn, and he had a strange expression on his face that Clyde couldn't quite make out. "I'm just saying that if you leave town with Lynda, it might be the best thing for everyone involved."

Clyde's fingers tightened into a fist. "Nathan is my grandson, Neil. And his momma—*my daughter*—wants him to know me."

Neil grinned. "Watch that anger of yours."

The office door opened, and JohnScott held it while Ansel shuffled out.

Neil lifted his hat in greeting. "Ansel, you get a good deal for your stock?"

Ansel didn't answer at first, only limped to the truck looking worn and tired. "Not bad."

JohnScott's eyes met Clyde's across the bed of the truck, and in a split second, Clyde knew the old man was broken. Selling his herd was akin to digging his grave, and even though he still had a few head left on the ranch, this day marked the beginning of the end.

Neil chuckled as he shook JohnScott's hand, either not seeing or not acknowledging Ansel's discomfort. "We'll be at your place Saturday night." His eyes cut once more to Clyde. "Wouldn't miss it for the world."

CHAPTER
NINETEEN

"Lyn, Hector told me about those Rangers giving you grief yesterday."

"No big deal." I didn't see why the sheriff thought he needed to share that tidbit of information, but I didn't say as much to Clyde. He sat on his usual stool at Dixie's counter, eating his usual lunch, and I saw no reason to discuss Hector or the Rangers. I reached for a stack of menus so I could update them with tomorrow's special.

"And he told me what you said about Neil."

I gritted my teeth. "I didn't realize you and the sheriff spoke much."

"Some."

I slapped a menu against the counter, then calmed myself as I removed today's card, slid in tomorrow's, and flipped the menu to the bottom of the pile. I stopped for a second, deciding if I really wanted to talk about what I was thinking, and then I huffed and went on to the next menu. "It was a long time ago."

"What did Neil do to you exactly?"

I shrugged. "Crude humor and innuendo when he saw me in town. Sometimes touching me when no one was looking. But he was good enough, nobody ever caught on."

Clyde's cheeks reddened. "Sometimes I want to beat that man senseless."

"You'd get arrested."

"I don't know. The cops might be on my side."

I shook my head. "Neil has those two wrapped around his pinky finger. I'm not sure about the sheriff."

"Well ... he shouldn't have treated you like that."

"He doesn't do it anymore. Not since everybody found out about all of it and he left the church. Now people are watching him. Curious." I snickered softly. "He's a different person—sort of—and it seems he's trying harder since Nathan came along."

"Why are you defending him?"

"Give me a break. I can't stand the man." I focused on my work but thought about what he had asked.

Every time I pulled out those blasted letters, something tugged at my heart and wouldn't let go, but it wasn't Neil. It was more of a lost promise. When he cast me aside, my life never seemed to catch up to the dream. Not even when I married Hoby.

But just because Clyde had kissed me in the kitchen didn't mean I was ready to shine a light on all my secrets. "So, tell me about this post-incarceration thing Fawn mentioned."

He studied me for a second, and I knew he didn't appreciate my changing the subject from my sore spot to his. "It's nothing," he said.

I nodded, knowing he would have already told me about it if it was *nothing*.

"It's like this," he said. "While I was in prison, all my decisions were made for me. When I got out, it took a while for me to remember how to do stuff on my own."

I clucked my tongue. "Like haircuts."

"I'm still working on some things, but at least I've figured out how to treat people."

"That explains your house."

He looked up. "What's wrong with the trailer?"

"It's old and kinda ratty."

He walked around the counter in slow motion, then helped himself to a piece of pie from the case and fetched a clean fork. Finally he returned to his stool. "Okay."

Frustration niggled at the muscles in my jaw, but I wasn't sure if it had anything to do with PICS. "I could have gotten that for you."

"You're busy." He forked a bite into his mouth that was equivalent to a third of the piece of pie, then looked up quickly as if he had just remembered something he wanted to ask me. He swallowed and took a swig of tea. "Can I pick you up for the game Friday?"

I didn't reply, unsure whether or not he was asking me to sit alone with him on the far side of the scoreboard.

"The view's not as bad as you'd think."

So he meant for me to sit with him. My teeth ran across my bottom lip, pinching slightly. *Everyone in the stands would see us.*

"Or you could come to worship with me tonight." He shoved another bite into his mouth, but I thought he smiled.

I chortled so loudly, two people at a table near us turned to look. "I'm not going to church with you. Tonight or ever."

He put his fingertip on the edge of his empty plate and pushed it an inch. "We don't have to go to the Trapp congregation. We could go to Slaton. Or Snyder."

"No need." I slapped another menu on the counter.

Clyde pressed both palms against the counter and pushed himself to a standing position. "Friday then?"

He was bribing me, and we both knew it. "People will talk."

"Yep. Hester Prynne and Magwitch."

"Who?"

"Hester Prynne, the adulteress in *The Scarlet Letter*, and Magwitch, the escaped convict in *Great Expectations*."

I rolled my eyes. "Books."

He bent at the waist until his face was even with mine, and I found myself wishing Dixie didn't insist we wear brown polyester uniforms.

"What?" I snapped.

His eyes wrinkled as if he were laughing out loud, but he didn't make a sound. He only stared at me until I looked into his eyes, but then his gaze dropped to my lips.

Warmth spread up my neck as though my clothes had been set on fire, and even though my brain screamed at me to take a step back, my body involuntarily leaned toward him.

He chuckled. "Lyn? I may suffer from PICS, but there are two decisions I'm not struggling with anymore."

"Oh?"

"First of all, I need God. He's the only thing that gets me through the hard times, and He's going to be part of my life no matter what."

I lifted my chin in defiance, not so much against Clyde but in defense of a million other conversations I'd had about God. "And the second?"

"You." He took a step back, and suddenly we were in the middle of the diner again. He tapped his knuckles on the counter twice. "I want you in my life."

When he walked out on the street without looking back, I felt as if a high-powered vacuum was pulling me toward the door, and I had the urge to sprint after him. My heart longed to tell him that I wanted him, too, and I was ready to give in and give up. But my doubt still held me firmly behind the counter, where Dixie's laminated menus busied my hands with a concrete task that I clung to as a means of avoiding the obvious.

I was falling for Clyde Felton.

And I was falling hard.

CHAPTER TWENTY

Clyde pulled into the church parking lot on Wednesday evening, wishing Lynda had agreed to come with him. Maybe he had been foolish to push, but he wanted her to enjoy all the things in life that he enjoyed. He had waited twenty years to live, but truth be told, so had she.

He backed his sedan into a parking space, glad he had finally managed to get it repaired, and then he stared across the church lawn with his hand suspended above the gearshift. He froze.

Neil Blaylock was walking toward the front door, coming from the other side of the parking lot with Susan by his side.

She patted his arm and leaned to speak in his ear, but in spite of her prodding, Neil seemed to drag his feet. He almost didn't look like himself because his behavior was so drastically different from usual. His face was red, and he looked like he might be sick at any moment.

Clyde knew that feeling. He had walked up that same sidewalk two years ago, anxious about coming to the little church in his hometown—where he was known for only one thing. It hadn't taken him long to realize he'd be better off at the congregation in Slaton.

He had attended there for a while, but in the end he couldn't stay away from Fawn. And the baby. Even JohnScott had become like a son to him.

Clyde cut the ignition and rested his fist on top of the steering wheel, opting to wait a few minutes before going in.

JohnScott's truck pulled past the sedan, and soon he and Fawn were hurrying up the sidewalk. Neither of them noticed Clyde. JohnScott was carrying Nathan, and Fawn was scurrying ahead of them, wielding a purse, a diaper bag, and a stack of construction paper. They surrounded Neil in front of the door, forming a huddle of encouragement.

Fawn tilted her head to the side, and JohnScott slapped Neil on the back. Susan took him by the hand, almost pulling.

Clyde's hand tightened around the gearshift as envy tightened around his heart. He should have been glad Neil was returning to the church. Clyde had begged the Lord's forgiveness for years of bitterness against the man, and he had finally gotten to the point he could let it go. Now here he was feeling the sting of resentment again.

He didn't want Neil to be back at the church. He didn't want him sitting on the pew down at the front. Didn't want Nathan to crawl in his lap during services. Didn't want Fawn to smile at him. He didn't even want him there for Susan.

But when Clyde examined his heart, took a close look, and came away with a verdict, he realized it wasn't that he didn't want those things for Neil. He did. He wanted the best for him, but he also wanted Neil to be the best he could be. The best father, husband, and grandfather that his family needed. No, it wasn't that Clyde didn't want it for Neil.

It was that he didn't believe it.

As he slid down in the seat so as not to be noticed, his memory swept back to his senior year of high school. He and Hoby had been first-team all-district offensive linemen guarding Neil all season, protecting him. Clyde was used to watching Neil. He had watched him back then, he had watched him in his memory for twenty years in prison, and he watched him now on the sidewalk in front of the church. And Clyde knew.

Neil was faking left.

Three running steps, a mock pitch to the left, then straight on to the end zone. Neil only used the trick play once in the entire season, though the Panthers had practiced it all year. The coach—and Neil—wanted to save it till it counted. The state championship. If they had revealed it anytime before that, the play would have been worthless. In the end it ran without a hitch. No team expected Trapp to run a sneak, because Blaylock was a passing quarterback, and when he completed that perfect play in Austin, it landed him first-team all-state, first-team all-American, and a full ride to Texas Christian University.

On the sidewalk in front of the Trapp congregation, Neil's family finally coaxed him through the doors, and Clyde stared at the spot where they had stood moments before. A few latecomers scurried into the building, but Clyde stayed put. Thinking.

Neil had seemed nervous going in, but was it anxiety from returning to the church after eighteen months, or was it fear of something else? Clyde didn't buy the penitent-sinner routine, but he couldn't imagine why Neil would go back to the little congregation if he didn't mean to repent of his ways.

Clyde peered out the side window of the sedan. Charlie Mendoza was on his tractor behind the church building—uncharacteristic for a Wednesday night—and Clyde figured the old guy was dutifully reciting his midweek prayers as he circled the field. Maybe Clyde should worship on his own, just him and God. He could go up to his property on the Caprock, because up there he was always three hundred feet closer to heaven.

His eyelids dropped as though they were weighted with lead. *No.* That wasn't how God wanted it, and that wasn't how Clyde had planned it. Even if the baptized believers were a tangled mess of problems, God wanted Clyde in the middle of them—worshiping, forgiving, tolerating. If he expected them to overlook his faults, he needed to overlook theirs, too. Especially Neil's.

But Clyde wasn't sure he was up to it today.

He opened his eyes just as the glass door swung open and Neil stepped out of the building.

He held the door, speaking to someone just inside, then raised one finger and mouthed the words "Be right back." Letting the door close behind him, he stepped around the hedges and out of sight of the front windows. He took a deep breath, looked at the sky, and then rubbed the back of his neck as if it were tight.

Then he noticed Clyde. Neil squared his shoulders and crossed his arms, but he only hesitated a moment before he … *laughed.* Instantly all traces of his nervous jitters evaporated, and Neil once again became an arrogant rancher.

Clyde got the impression Neil was making fun of him for hiding in his car, slumped down in the seat, but Clyde didn't change his position. He continued to watch Neil, wondering at the speed the man's temperament had changed, wondering at the cause behind it. Wondering if the man had ever been what he seemed.

Neil put his hands on his hips, shook his head as though he had just heard a good joke, then walked confidently back into the building.

Coldness crept up Clyde's spine, not because he was afraid of what Neil might be up to, but because he was afraid for Neil himself.

CHAPTER
TWENTY-ONE

"Thank God you're here, Lyn."

Clyde pulled me through his front door on Thursday afternoon, holding Nathan awkwardly in one arm. The child had stopped crying long enough to see who was at the door, but now he resumed his wails and viciously rubbed his wet nose against Clyde's shoulder, leaving a moist trail on his T-shirt.

"Why are you babysitting again?" I had intended to rake him over the coals, but when I saw his disheveled state, I changed my mind. It looked as if Nathan had run him through a gauntlet already, even though Clyde had said the boy had only been there forty-five minutes.

"Never mind the why. Fawn said he's teething. What does that even mean? You'd think the kid was dying."

"He's just getting new teeth is all. It hurts when they're breaking through the gums."

"She said she'd only be gone a few hours, but ..." The skin wrinkled around his eyes. "Can you take him for a while?"

I looked at Nathan. "What would I do?" I'd never been very maternal, even when Ruthie was a baby.

"I don't care." Clyde shoved him toward me, but Nathan began to howl as though I were a stranger.

As I stumbled into the living room, Clyde shut the front door, but not until he had peered up and down the street as if harboring a crying baby was a crime. While he ran his hands through his hair and took several deep breaths, I bounced Nathan on my hip and tried my hand at baby talk. Ruthie's childhood had passed so quickly, I didn't have time to figure out the difference between diaper rash and diaper cream, and Velma had done most of the mechanics of it anyway.

I patted Nathan's back. Under different circumstances, Clyde would have called my sister to help instead of me, but under different circumstances, Nathan would have been with Velma—his grandmother for all practical purposes—in the first place, not here with the two of us.

"Does he have any of that tooth gel in his bag?"

Clyde's head jerked at the possibility of deliverance. "What's that?" He grabbed the bag and turned it upside down, emptying its contents onto the couch.

Nathan held out his hand and stretched for something, but when I leaned toward the pile of goods so he could show me what he wanted, he only screamed louder and threw his head back.

"There." I pointed at the small tube. "Squirt some on my finger."

Clyde's oversize hands gripped the tube, completely covering the end of my finger with reddish gel, but I didn't mind the quantity. I shoved my finger in Nathan's mouth and rubbed all around his gums.

"Is it helping?" Clyde asked. "Why is he still crying?"

"It takes a second."

Nathan's eyes had gone big when he began to feel the numbing effect of the gel, and he licked his lips, looking slightly confused. He whimpered, but not loudly, then rubbed his forehead against my shoulder.

"Here, let me walk him around a spell." Clyde gently took the baby, and I noticed his nerves seemed to have calmed right along with Nathan's—just as quickly as mine had deteriorated.

He pressed the baby's chest against his own and stalked from one end of the small trailer to the other, and then he turned and repeated it, over and over, until I thought I might get seasick. With each rotation, Nathan's eyes drooped a little lower—probably unable to keep up with the room spinning around him—and then finally he laid his head against Clyde's collarbone, and his eyes didn't open again.

"He out?" Clyde asked.

"Just. Better give him a few more laps around the bases."

"Gotcha."

I leaned back against the couch cushions. "So what's the deal with Fawn bringing him over here again?" I asked quietly. "I understand her not wanting to bother Ansel and Velma, but what's wrong with Neil and Susan?"

"You want the kid to spend more time over there?"

"Not really." I picked through the diaper-bag items, tossing them into a pile. "But I don't want you to get strapped with the job either."

"I don't usually mind it."

"Still, it seems like Susan could take him. Or hire someone to do it for her."

Clyde sat down in an upholstered chair and rubbed the baby's back. "Aw, Lyn, I like having the little guy around."

I studied Clyde then. He had left his hair down today, and his blond locks blended with Nathan's black ones, creating a tangled mix of swirling tiger stripes. I laughed softly. Clyde wasn't the same person I knew in high school. He wasn't even the same person I'd known last week. He was different, unusual, interesting. He rocked babies to sleep and enjoyed being a grandpappy. My skin warmed as I watched him.

"What?" he asked.

"You don't look like a grandfather."

He glanced down at himself, shirtsleeves stretched tight by muscles, with part of his *nine* tattoo showing from under the cotton fabric.

"Guess I don't, do I?" he said.

His gaze slid cautiously from his body to mine, and I spoke quickly. "Why did you punch a hole in the wall over there by the door?"

He peered at the window even though the dusty blinds were shut, and his lips twisted. "Lyn ..." He exhaled, and his eyes said everything he couldn't verbalize.

I wished I hadn't asked. "But it's better now?"

He nodded once. "It was bad right after I came back, but I've worked through the worst of it. Now I only get riled if something really, really irks me."

"Like a crying baby?"

Clyde grunted. "Naw, things like that don't set me off. It's more like when a bully kicks a puppy. That sort of thing." He curled a lock of Nathan's hair around his finger. "Last week a teenager cut in front of Algerita Parker at the red light. Her reactions are a little slow, you know. And she had to slam on her brakes so she wouldn't hit him." Clyde's eyebrows pulled together as he remembered the incident. "I've never seen her scared before, but I reckon she was shook up pretty bad, because she pulled over to the curb for a while."

"And you got mad about that?"

"Not mad enough to punch a hole in a wall, but sure, I got a little ticked at the kid."

I looked back at the hole. *Who was the puppy that got kicked that day?* Clyde was already avoiding my gaze, so I didn't ask.

"Fawn and JohnScott seem happy." It wasn't the type of thing I would say, and Clyde knew it. His eyes met mine, and he laughed without laughing.

"Before you go changing the subject, let me get this out." He crossed an ankle over his knee. "You told me the other day that Neil used to pick on you when nobody else could see or hear."

"So?"

"Two years ago when I found out what he'd been putting you through …"—he stared at me intently—"let's just say that really, really irked me."

Without thinking I glanced at the hole, then away quickly. Clyde found out about Neil a few months after he came back to Trapp. A lot of people found out then. When Neil left the church, the story spread all over town faster than a stout case of chicken pox.

"He's making you sweat." I motioned to Nathan. "Why don't you lay him on the couch?"

"How? Won't he wake up?"

"It's worth a try."

Clyde slowly got to his feet, crept to the couch, and bent down, hovering a foot above the plaid tweed. When he shifted Nathan, it took both of us to lay him gently on the cushions, but he didn't wake up.

Easing off the couch, I followed Clyde into the kitchen. It was open to the living room, and we were both afraid of waking the baby. We ended up sitting on the floor and leaning against the cabinets so a few layers of imitation wood would block the sound of our voices.

We sat in silence for a few minutes, and I let my gaze fall on his tattoo. The number *nine*, like the tail end of a Nazi prison brand. Surely they didn't still do that. "What's your tattoo?" I pointed, snapping the words quickly before I lost the nerve.

"What, this?" He pulled his sleeve to expose the rest of the ink—*Joshua 1:9*—stenciled in script across the curving bulge of his arm.

I looked away. "A Bible verse?"

"What'd you think it was?" He laughed softly.

"Did you get that in prison?"

"Yep." I felt him looking at me then. "Gave us something to do, you know?"

"Oh?"

"I stopped with five," he said, "but some guys were covered by the time they got out."

I tried to inspect his body without turning my head. Clyde always wore jeans and a T-shirt … but now I wondered.

"Fawn says I shouldn't get any more, and I reckon she's right …" His voice trailed off, but then he mumbled, "You think Fawn needs anything?" He bent one leg and picked at the seam of his jeans. "I want to help her somehow."

"What could she possibly need? They've got a comfortable living, and as long as JohnScott keeps winning games, his job security is good."

Clyde's shoulders sagged.

I thought back over the past months and years. Clyde had helped Fawn before she married JohnScott by letting her stay in his run-down house on the Caprock. I was never sure that was a blessing to the girl, since the house was in such bad shape, but he had been able to help her then because Neil wouldn't.

My heart hurt for him. Didn't he know there were other ways to show he cared? Like babysitting her teething toddler?

I poked his shoulder with the tip of my finger. "You know you can never outgive him."

He raised his eyebrows and for a moment attempted to feign ignorance, but he knew good and well what I meant. Neil was the richest man in Garza County, and Clyde was one of the poorest.

"That girl doesn't need stuff," I said. "She just needs you. You've got tons more to give her than he ever will."

Clyde tilted his head back and peered at the overhead light far above our heads. "Neil came back to church last night."

"Holy cow," I whispered. "What happened?"

"I don't know. I didn't go in."

"Why not?" *Clyde wasn't a coward.*

"I thought it would make it harder for him, if I was there. He needed the worship service more than I did."

"So he didn't see you?"

Clyde straightened both legs and crossed his ankles. "He did. In the parking lot."

"He talk to you?"

"Didn't have to."

I shivered as if the air conditioner had kicked up a notch. "And to think you wanted me to go with you."

"It wouldn't have been so bad, would it?" His eyebrows lifted in the middle until they almost touched each other.

"Neil Blaylock and Lynda Turner showing up at worship on the same night?" I snickered, and it sounded evil to my ears. "I'd say that would have been pretty bad."

The way Clyde's jaw clenched and unclenched told me he wasn't happy with what I'd said, and I realized I didn't want him to be upset with me. He was staring at the space between the refrigerator and the cabinet when I slid my hand over his and squeezed his thumb—a silent apology.

He looked down at our intertwined hands, seeming to study them for an endless time. Then his lips curled into a smile, and he pulled me gently toward him.

When my head nestled against his shoulder, I felt as though I had just lain down to rest after running a mile. As though Clyde could ease my worries and help me be a better person. As though I was home.

CHAPTER
TWENTY-TWO

The football game on Friday night was the first public appearance Clyde and I made together. I say it was a public appearance, but that might have been stretching the truth. I wasn't sure it counted as an appearance if nobody could communicate with us.

"You want to stay in the car awhile longer?" He touched the volume knob on the radio with the tip of his index finger, rolled it clockwise, then counterclockwise. If it had been turned on, the music would have blared across the pasture and fought the squawking of the Panther band.

"No, I'm good." We would be more visible to the home stands once we were out of the car, but it was past halftime, and the news had certainly already circulated that Clyde and I were together. No reason to hide.

When he opened his door, the breeze swept through the car, in one door and out the other, blowing away my tension. He sat on the hood, and I leaned against it, glancing at the back of the scoreboard. "What's the score?"

"Twenty-eight to six."

I felt more uncomfortable talking to him now that we were out of the car, but that was ridiculous, of course, and I forced myself to keep up the conversation. "Nathan still teething?"

At the mention of the child's name, Clyde's face brightened. "Fawn says he's better today. Probably over there with her and Ruthie right now, crawling up and down the bleachers."

"Sometimes the cheerleaders get ahold of him and carry him around."

"I know it." Clyde's laugh came from deep in his chest. "I've seen him running on the track in his tiny football jersey. Wonder where they got that."

"Susan had it custom made." I shouldn't have said it. I shouldn't have squelched his joy, but it tumbled out of my mouth.

I ran my teeth across my bottom lip, tempted to bite down as I listened to the announcer's voice and the band's muted tones rolling across the field like tumbleweeds.

The people looked small.

"It's nice over here," I said.

"Yeah."

"It feels like they can't see us, but I know that's not true."

His head turned. "You having regrets?"

Maybe. "No." I shifted to lean against my other hip. "After all, Blue and Gray already spread the news."

"This is different."

I crossed my arms. Uncrossed them. Scratched my elbow. "Maybe we should have waited."

"For what?"

For things to be different. Easier. "Hester Prynne, right?" I said.

His shoulders sagged. "You don't have a scarlet letter, Lyn."

"Might as well. After everything this town has thought about me, talked about me, it's like I'm finally living up to their expectations. *Great Expectations.* Isn't that the one with the convict? What was his name? *Your* name."

"I never should've said that."

"Tell me his name."

He bent his knee so his boot rested on the bumper. "Magwitch."

"Magwitch." I let the name float over my lips. "Magwitch and Hester."

"Hush up, Lyn."

Clyde's elbow rested on his knee, and his shoulder and upper arm created a barrier between us—or at least I felt like they did—but I wasn't sure I wanted a barrier anymore. I wondered if I would ever know what it would be like to be happy with Clyde. Without thinking, I touched two fingertips to the skin just below the sleeve of his T-shirt, where the Bible verse teased me again. He was warm, and the muscle was hard, but when his gaze met mine, I pulled my hand away. "Sorry."

His eyes held mine for five seconds, and then he blinked and smiled. "Are you?"

"No."

He didn't look back at the field, even when the announcer declared another touchdown for Trapp, and the band played another stanza of the fight song. Even when the final buzzer sounded, he only looked at me, into me, and it felt as if he could read my mind, my heart. Then his gaze dropped, and I felt my face flush as he looked at my body.

"I want to kiss you again," he said.

"Might not be the best time for it."

"We could really give them something to talk about."

I cocked my head for fun, but when he leaned toward me, I stood up abruptly and took three steps away from the car. Gazing at the field, I calmed my heart, which was beating faster—and probably louder—than the bass drum at the top of the bleachers. I shoved my hands in the back pockets of my jeans and didn't dare turn around.

I watched as townspeople filtered onto the football field like marbles rolling across a kitchen floor. They were happy. Proud. Free.

"Why do you care what they think?" Clyde's voice was gentle.

"Because I've been Hester Prynne for years."

"No, you haven't. Neil just wanted them to believe that."

"They would have thought that even without his—"

"Stop defending him." The gentleness was gone from his tone, and the bitterness in its place ignited a slow burn of defensiveness between my shoulder blades.

I turned to confront him face-to-face. "I'm not defending him. I'm just stating a fact. The people in this town would have looked down their pointed noses no matter what Neil said."

Clyde crossed his arms and glared. "What is it with you and him?"

My neck involuntarily turned my face away from his. "Nothing," I mumbled. "I can't stand him, you know that."

"That's what confuses me, Lyn. I know good and well you can't stand him, but I feel like I'm fighting him for you." He gritted his teeth. "I'm already fighting Hoby."

My mind grew foggy from the shock of his statements, and I felt like a crystal vase left outside during a hailstorm. Even though I knew the answer to his complicated question, I wasn't sure I wanted to admit the truth. Not to Clyde. It would make me sound crazy, simpleminded, *pitiful.*

My cell phone rang, and after a few startled moments, I pulled it from my pocket. I didn't recognize the number, but I answered it anyway.

"Yeah?"

"Did you enjoy the game?"

I blinked and looked at Clyde. "What do you want, Neil?"

Clyde's eyebrows went up questioningly, but I turned away, scanning the empty stands.

"I wanted to talk to Clyde, but I don't have his cell. Does the man even have a phone?" Neil's voice drawled lazily. "Do you happen to have his home number?"

Of course I had his number, but I wasn't about to give it to Neil. "I can't get to it right now." Only a half lie.

"Would you mind just putting me on speaker then?" Neil's tone mocked me. "It's important I talk to him tonight."

I spun on my heel as Clyde muttered, "What does he want?"

"You." I pushed the button for speaker and set the phone on the hood of the car, then backed away as though it were a serpent.

Clyde's chin jutted forward as he scanned the stadium and parking lot, searching.

"Clyde ..." The voice on the phone seemed too loud for the evening air. "Glad you made it to the game tonight, but it's too bad you couldn't sit over in the stands with Fawn and the boy. And me."

Clyde scrutinized a dark truck parked on a side street. He crossed his arms.

"I know that looks like my truck, but it's not. You remember, mine has a toolbox on the back. That's probably Cliff Worlow. Over from Slaton? From what I hear, he's courting Maria Fuentes. There's a lot of that going on."

Clyde jerked his head toward the phone, his eyes shining red in the shadows of the stadium lights. "Why did you call?"

There was a pause on the other end of the line, and I wondered if Neil was also fighting to control himself. When he spoke, his words were clipped. "Like I said the other day, I want what's best for my grandson."

Clyde sighed, but it wasn't a humble, tired sigh this time. It was an angry huff of hot air. "Fawn is my family, too, Neil, and I'm not staying away just to suit you."

"That might not be such a good idea. You see, I know about your anger problem."

Clyde clenched his fists and turned to search the town again.

"See? There it is now," Neil crooned. "You really should watch that temper of yours. The State of Texas looks down on men who can't control themselves."

Anger slashed across my mind. "What do you want?"

"Lynda, sweetie. You were always one to cut right to the heart of the matter, weren't you?" He snickered, but then his voice turned to steel. "Clyde, it's like this. Seeing as how you're an ex-convict, you're not fit to be around my grandson. Not *safe*."

"What are you talking about?" Clyde said. "I haven't done anything."

"Not yet, you haven't, but I'm not willing to risk it. Come Monday morning, my lawyer will serve you a restraining order forbidding you to come anywhere near Nathan."

The flame of irritation that had been crackling silently at the base of my neck grew into a raging brush fire, and I lashed out, catching myself before I hurled the phone across the pasture. "Clyde isn't going to hurt Nathan, and you know it."

"Lynda, you of all people should know it doesn't matter if he does anything or not, and just to be on the safe side, you might want to stay away from him. I know he's been coming on to you, but you've got to keep in mind that the good citizens of Trapp know Clyde to be a convicted rapist. He can't be trusted, and he's making you look bad."

As Neil was speaking, Clyde's eyes met mine, his brows forming a hostile point.

We stared at each other, and Clyde's head shifted a centimeter to the left, then the right, denying Neil's accusations. I returned the gesture, and at Neil's final threat *making you look bad*, Clyde took two steps and yanked my body toward his, shoving his mouth against mine.

My palms floundered at his waist, but I didn't push him away. I kissed back, allowing my anger to release through my actions and willing Neil Blaylock to read in my rage the simple message that he would not control my world any longer.

The phone still hummed on speaker, and without pulling away from Clyde, I reached over and disconnected the call.

Clyde growled deep in his throat and settled roughly on the hood, drawing me onto his lap with my knees on each side of his hips. Years of anger surfaced and resurfaced, billowing like clouds of smoke and obscuring our logic, our inhibitions, our willpower. Even our common decency.

When the stadium lights went off, we were swallowed up by blackness, and our kisses slowed, then waned into nothing, and I slipped from his legs with an exhausted sigh and stumbled back a few paces, breathing hard and afraid to speak. Afraid of what we had just started and what it might mean down the road.

And afraid of Neil.

CHAPTER
TWENTY-THREE

I stood three feet away from Clyde. Embarrassed. Surprised. Regretful. Back when Neil and I had dated, his influence impressed me so much, I was blinded to his character, but now I knew better. The power Neil wielded in our little town demanded respect. And caution.

And Clyde and I had just smeared his nose in cow manure.

"Guess we've done it now," Clyde said.

I couldn't see him to know if his left eyebrow curved upward in a challenge, but I imagined it did. He usually had that expression on his face whenever Neil was around. I tugged nervously at a lock of my hair. "I don't defend him."

Clyde shifted on the hood, but he didn't say anything.

"I don't," I repeated. "I hate him."

"You shouldn't hate him, Lyn."

"Don't you?"

He paused. "Not anymore."

"But he sent you to prison."

"Actually, Susan's daddy did that. But I can't say I didn't feel more than a little satisfaction when I heard that man had passed on."

"Neil married Susan when she was pregnant with your child. Isn't that enough to warrant a little hatred?"

"Aw, Lyn …" He was quiet for a while, but the silence rang as he decided what to say to me. "When I was in prison, it took some time before I could even believe what he did. But sure, for a while there I was ate up with hate."

The breeze whipped past the scoreboard, causing the metal to creak and moan. The sound made me lonely and I shivered, wishing I had controlled my anger.

Anger.

I squinted at Clyde's shadow. "You really do have an anger problem, don't you?"

"You're one to talk."

"You shouldn't have kissed me like that."

He spoke his next words slowly, and I wondered if he were fighting his anger right then. "Lynda, I wasn't the only one angry, and I sure as heck wasn't the only one kissing."

His tone was like a warden explaining broken rules to a delinquent, and my fists tightened in rebellion. "You started it."

He laughed then, loudly, and I suddenly worried that Neil was still in the area, listening. But no. The wind would cover our voices. Thank God for the wind.

Clyde's laughter faded. "Lyn, you're such a toddler."

"Shut up." It was a hard phrase, and I usually delivered it with a kick, effectively masking any emotions I wanted to avoid, but this time a sob rose halfway up my lungs before I stuffed it back where it belonged.

"Hey, now," Clyde whispered. When I didn't respond, he groped for my hand in the darkness, then slid his index finger into my palm. The action comforted me like mashed potatoes with gravy, and when I tightened my grip around his finger, he pulled me slowly into his embrace.

He was still sitting on the hood of the sedan, and as I stood between his knees, I relaxed into the soft spot between his shoulder and neck. "We shouldn't be doing this." I rubbed my nose against his skin, inhaling his sweaty, soapy scent.

"Why not?"

"Well … technically, I'm still married."

"Most people wouldn't think so."

"The church would."

We both fell silent as we held each other. Him running his free hand through my hair. Me clinging to his waist as if I were drowning. Maybe I was. Drowning in years of bitterness toward the two men who had hurt me, toward the church, toward a lifetime of hard luck.

Clyde combed his fingers through my hair, from my scalp all the way to the ends, causing a tingling sensation as though he'd poured bubbling champagne on me and let it trickle down my body. Then he hooked his thumbs though the belt loops of my jeans and let his palms spread across my hips. His breath warmed my forehead. "Are you saying you don't want this?"

His question scared me because I knew it was time I gave him an answer—a real answer—but no matter what I said, my life would never be a fairy tale. There would still be problems to deal with and pain to overcome, not to mention the judgment of a community of people who thought they knew us. I loosened my grip on his waist and pulled away from his embrace.

I waited, thinking, wishing the decision were easier.

He sighed—a defeated sound that communicated more emotion than a hundred sentences could have—and suddenly I found it difficult to breathe.

I heard him stand, take a few steps away, then turn back. "We're not kids anymore," he said. "We've known each other more than half our lives, and there's no reason for us to dillydally around. I want to make you happy, and I want to start doing it now. I'm going to ask you one more time, and after that, I'll never bring it up again. I'll take Neil's advice and move on, leave you alone." He seemed to hold his breath for a count of three before inhaling. "Do you want to be with me or not?"

Good Lord. In forty-three years of living, I'd only ever loved three men. One of them dumped me for a woman he didn't love. One of them left me alone with a child. And one of them—whom I'd always loved like a brother—was standing in front of me giving me an ultimatum.

A thunderhead stormed through my mind, shadowing my mood until I thought I might lose myself in its whirlwind of doubt, but surprisingly when the worst of it passed, only a bank of gray puffs remained, and a sliver of moonlight pierced through the thickness. As I felt its warm promise of hope, I realized three things. First, Clyde didn't just want to date me. He wanted me forever and always. Second, deep down in my soul, in the place I never allowed myself to visit, I probably wanted him, too. And last, but at the forefront of my thoughts, I desperately needed to free myself from the bars that imprisoned me in memories.

It had been only eight days since Dixie had set off that tangle of thoughts in my head when she mentioned Clyde, but it seemed as though a year had passed. A year of confusion and disbelief. But I could no longer deny the feelings I had for this man. No matter what baggage lay in our past or what difficulties lay in our future, Clyde Felton—with all the problems that came along with him—was my present.

I stumbled forward, and when I placed a palm on his chest, he bent down and his body melted around me. His arms roughly encircled my shoulders, and his core trembled as if he were fighting back emotion.

"Yes," I whispered. I couldn't say aloud everything I wanted to say. I couldn't tell him I lay awake at night and wondered what it would feel like to have him next to me. I couldn't verbalize that he was the only person who made me feel alive. I couldn't say I wanted him just as desperately as he wanted me. My voice and mind and lips froze into a solid mass of anxiety. "Yes," I repeated.

It was all I could say, but it was enough.

Clyde buried his face in my neck and wept.

CHAPTER
TWENTY-FOUR

Saturday afternoon, Clyde stood in front of the deep fryer at the Dairy Queen, knowing he was using his work as a means of ignoring the worry in his mind. He had already talked to Hector Chavez and discovered that Neil was blowing hot air. Child Protective Services wouldn't even get involved unless Clyde had custody of Nathan—but Clyde was still anxious. Neil had made a threat, and even if his accusations wouldn't hold up in court, he clearly wanted to make trouble for Clyde, and he had plenty of power to do it.

"Hey."

Clyde hadn't seen Lynda come in, and her soft greeting surprised him.

Her gaze met his, but she looked away quickly. "You get off soon, right?"

"Few minutes."

She glanced at the time clock, then the parking lot, then the bubbling oil. "I'm sorry about last night."

Clyde lifted a basket of chicken strips and hooked it on a rack to drain. "I'm not."

Her hand fiddled with the neck band of her shirt. "I don't mean I'm sorry about everything. I'm just sorry … it took me so long."

She was sorry.

Clyde separated two cardboard trays and scooped fries into them. Lynda just apologized for being so strung out on memories, she couldn't function in the present. He couldn't figure how to answer her. He looked past the ice-cream machine, through the plate-glass windows, and into the parking lot. "If you keep showing up right when I get off work, I'm going to get the wrong idea."

She finally exhaled. "You're not the only one."

He noticed an old Honda pulling into the lot. "There's my replacement."

"Ellery Leach can cook?"

"It's just the Dairy Queen, Lyn. Anybody can do it."

"Evidently."

The teenager swerved into a parking space, loped across the asphalt, and shoved the glass door so hard it slammed against an adjacent table. When he came around the counter and into the kitchen, Clyde felt the instinct to brace himself as though a high wind were about to smash through the restaurant.

"Have you heard?" Ellery's face was pinker than usual. "It's all over town."

Clyde rested an elbow on top of the slush machine. "Guess not."

Ellery paused with his apron halfway over his head and stared at them. "Everyone's been talking about it up at the school." He methodically wrapped the apron strings around his waist, then tied them in slow motion. "You know the Tarron boys have been drop-ping grenades out there in the lake?"

"Grenades?" Lynda picked at a hangnail.

Ellery rushed his words. "Yeah, and yesterday they blew up a spot down by the cliffs, and a rearview mirror blasted out of the water. Landed on shore twenty feet from where they were standing."

"A mirror, huh?" Clyde walked to the time clock.

"Turns out the Tarrons found a car down there. It was too deep for them to see it much, but the Lubbock police are checking into it." He smiled so widely, his braces looked like train tracks, and then he swiped his hand beneath his nose.

Clyde held the soap dispenser toward the kid and gestured to the sink.

Ellery peered from the soap to the sink, then shrugged and began washing his hands. "It's probably been out there awhile, so you can only imagine the shape the driver's in by now. Slimy, I bet."

Lynda gave a disgusted grunt and walked away, and Clyde fol-lowed her.

"What?" Ellery called after them, but Clyde only shook his head and lifted his hand in a wave.

Lynda led him out the door, but her steps slowed until she stopped between two red outdoor tables.

"Want to go for a drive?" Clyde no longer felt an urgency to take her out on a real date. He would still do it eventually—court her like she ought to be courted, like she was something special—but after Neil's unexpected behavior last night, all Clyde wanted to do was be with her, hold her, pretend they were somewhere else.

"I don't know why I came by." In answer to his question, she walked slowly to his car. "If you've got something else to do, I can head home."

Clyde slid into the driver's seat and tried not to smile. In spite of all their problems, he thought it was cute, her showing up when he got off work, yet unable to admit she wanted to see him. "I've got nothing else," he said.

"We could just drive around town."

Clyde studied her. Crossed arms, tightened lips, furrowed brow. He started the car but then paused with his hand on the gearshift. "I told you CPS won't get involved. Neil's way out of line this time."

She peered out the passenger window, looking away from him, and Clyde felt they were separated by a million miles.

"What about the car-seat thing?" she asked.

"Hector said it could only result in a Class C ticket. Nothing as dramatic as a restraining order."

She released a heavy breath, then looked at him. "It'll be all right?"

"It will."

When he backed out of the parking space and stopped at the street, JohnScott and Fawn pulled in. They were in JohnScott's truck, with Nathan strapped in his car seat between them.

With both vehicles blocking the entrance, Clyde rolled down his window and greeted his son-in-law. He would never get used to having a son-in-law, or a grandson, or a daughter. He would never get used to having a life at all.

"You already off?" JohnScott grinned at Clyde, then ducked so he could see his aunt Lynda.

"Just now."

Nathan clapped his hands and squealed. "Cyde!" The baby leaned forward in his seat, slammed his head back, and then he did it again, laughing.

"What are y'all up to?" Clyde asked.

"Neil and Susan are coming over for dinner. We're just picking up a bag of crushed ice."

"That right?" Clyde studied JohnScott, wondering why he looked older.

"The Blaylocks are pushing for Nathan to spend more time with Tyler." JohnScott draped his wrist over the steering wheel. "I know it's the right thing, since he's Nathan's dad and all, but it still feels wrong."

Fawn opened her truck door and walked around to stand by the passenger side of the sedan, and Clyde heard Lynda huff as she rolled down the window.

Apparently Fawn didn't want to discuss her problems, and Clyde couldn't blame her. He blocked out the women's small talk and lowered his voice. "JohnScott, do you ever feel like Nathan's got one too many dads?"

"Sometimes, yeah. I love the kid, and I'd give anything to be his kin." His mouth curved downward. "Besides, it would be a lot easier without Tyler in the picture, babysitting problems or not."

"Yep," Clyde agreed. "Sometimes it's that way with Fawn, only I don't feel like I'm the one who's kin." He cleared his throat, wanting to tell JohnScott about Neil's threat but not wanting to burden him. "I don't wish Neil away, but things would be simpler if she only had one of us in her life."

Nathan kicked his feet and clapped, and JohnScott laid his palm on the baby's head, running his fingers through his curls.

He looked at Fawn and Lynda, then pulled his chin in. "Fawn says her mom's been moody lately. Crying a lot. So there may be something going on between them that's made Neil crankier than usual."

Fawn interrupted. "Hey, have you guys heard about the fuss out at the lake?"

"Sure enough." Clyde knew Lynda would be ready to hit the trail, but he figured he ought to follow through with the conversation before suggesting they leave. He'd learned it was the polite thing to do, especially with friends and family. "Can't believe there's been a car on the bottom of the lake, and nobody noticed it."

"They say it's in one of the deepest spots, but the lake is a little low"—Fawn laughed lightly—"and with the explosives those crazy boys have been using out there, things are getting stirred up."

"Are they just going to leave it down there?" Lynda asked.

JohnScott's arm hung outside the truck, and he tapped his fingers against the door. "One of the coaches heard they're bringing a crane to pull it out."

"When's that happening?" Clyde glanced around the DQ parking lot, almost expecting to see townspeople scurrying to the lake.

"Sometime this afternoon. They're rushing it on account of those bones." JohnScott pooched out his bottom lip. "We can't go watch because Neil and Susan are coming over."

"We could go." Clyde turned to Lynda.

She shrugged. "Free entertainment, I suppose. What kind of vehicle is it?"

"A pickup truck," JohnScott said. "I wonder if it'll turn out to be an oil-rig worker. Or a wind tech."

"I bet not," Fawn said. "If it was a company truck, it would have been reported missing."

"Maybe it was," he answered. "It'd be hidden on the bottom of the lake either way."

Clyde's mind conjured up a wacky scenario that he wanted to share with JohnScott, but just then another car stopped on the street, waiting for access to the Dairy Queen entrance.

Fawn bounced around the two cars and back into her seat, and JohnScott lifted his ball cap, then replaced it on his head. "See y'all later."

Clyde eased away from the parking lot, turning the steering wheel to head out of town. He didn't care if they ended up at the lake, or at the windmills, or a hundred miles away where nobody knew them. "This could be our first official date if you wanted it to be."

"No candlelight dinner? No romantic movie? No flowers?"

"Nope. Just me. And a crane pulling a car out of the lake. It don't get any better than that."

Lynda sighed dramatically, looked behind them as if checking for witnesses, then unhooked her seat belt and slid next to him. "Sounds like my kind of date." She reclicked the middle seat belt, tightening it around her waist and anchoring herself solidly next to Clyde.

Suddenly he felt as if one of the Tarrons' grenades had exploded inside him, sending a spray of anticipation and peace through the interior of his old sedan. He chuckled, put his arm around Lynda, and pulled her snugly against his side. Right where she belonged.

CHAPTER TWENTY-FIVE

Clyde and I were sitting so close together, our bodies touched all the way from our shoulders to our knees, and I thought my pulse might cause a blood vessel to burst behind my ear drums. I hadn't been on a date since Hoby left—hadn't really even wanted to talk to a man—but now, suddenly, I felt more attracted to Clyde Felton than I had ever felt to any other man before. And for the first time in years, I thought my cup might be half full.

"So …" I let the word hang, unable to verbalize my thoughts. Since I had plastered myself by his side and allowed him to pull me into his armpit, anyone who passed us on the highway would get an eyeful. The entire town would know, but I had come to the point that being with Clyde was more important than invisibility.

"So." Clyde said the word with finality, with confidence and purpose. He squeezed my shoulders. "You all right?"

"Feeling a little unsure at the moment."

"Unsure? Or exposed?"

And just like that, he hit the nail on the head, driving a shard of clear crystal into my doubts and allowing a ray of sunshine to penetrate the darkness. We were speeding down the highway, just below the Caprock where the turbines flailed their arms like happy children waving streamers in the wind. Streamers that swept away my concerns.

"You ever dreamed you forgot to get dressed, and you walked into a party stark naked?" I asked.

"That's pretty exposed I guess."

"Hester Prynne probably felt that way."

"You been reading *The Scarlet Letter*?"

"I watched the movie. Got it from the Video Barn."

"Hmm. I reckon Hester felt exposed when she was in the stocks in front of the whole village, but Lyn ... you're not her."

"Maybe not, but thanks to Neil Blaylock, I was in stocks in front of the entire town for a while."

He fell silent for a few moments before asking, "Why do you reckon he told the church you were unfaithful to Hoby?"

"He said it was because he never stopped caring for me, but I figure it was simple meanness and jealousy."

"Sure don't sound like love."

I peered at him then, studying the side of his face. His ear, his jaw, the ever-present scruff on his chin. Clyde had changed since we were young. Now he spoke less and said more. "How do you know the right things to say?"

He blinked. "I don't."

"You don't think you do, but you do."

He stared down the highway, frowning slightly. "When I read books in prison, it was sort of like I traveled all over and saw lots of different things, good and bad and beautiful and ugly." His mouth twisted. "But I really didn't see anything but a cell, so I'm nobody to say the right things."

I hadn't meant to send him back to those memories, and already I wanted the smiling Clyde back by my side. "I can't picture you reading."

"Not much else to do." He turned on the main lake road, tugging my gaze away from the merry children. "Any idea how to get to that spot they were talking about?"

"Not a clue."

"I'll follow that guy." He pointed to a white passenger van in front of us.

"Good Lord. Channel Eleven?"

"This is breaking news, Lyn."

We passed cacti and pastures and curved around trailer parks and bait shops, following the van on a maze of turns. We ended up on a narrow, rocky road, a trail really, that seemed to be leading away from the lake. There were crags and small canyons and bluffs, and then we climbed up one last incline and suddenly I could see the lake snaking thirty feet below us.

The news van rolled to a stop, and Clyde pulled past it.

He reached through the steering wheel and shut off the ignition with his left hand, then pulled me closer with his right. "This isn't a typical first date, is it?" he asked.

"We're not a typical couple." It felt strange to refer to us as a couple, but I supposed that's what we were.

The news man opened the back of his van and hurriedly removed a camera and tripod, but we stayed in the car watching him. He ran-walked to the edge of the bluff and popped the tripod open in one swift movement, and within a matter of seconds, he had the camera trained on the ground far below at the bottom of the cliff.

From the front seat of the sedan, we were too far from the bluff to see what was happening below us, and curiosity whispered to me, but it paled in comparison to the bullhorn blare created from being so near Clyde with the security of his arm around me.

He focused his gaze on my face, seemingly unconcerned with whatever was happening in the water. "We may never be a typical couple." He brushed his lips across my forehead.

The tip of his nose traced a path from my temple, across my cheek, and then he paused with his lips millimeters from mine. I tasted the cinnamon of his breath just before I lost myself in the weightlessness of his kiss. At that moment I didn't care if the whole town knew about Clyde and me. I didn't care about anything at all except being with him, in the safety of his arms, knowing he wanted me, too.

When we pulled apart, the cameraman was looking at us. His shoulders shook gently with laughter before he went back to work, and my soul felt light. That stranger had acted as though we were any other normal couple. So maybe we were.

"We don't have to stay here," Clyde said. "We could just go back and watch the windmills."

"The side of the highway isn't any more private than this."

"We could go on up the Cap. Maybe find an access road to get to the wind fields. Maybe even up to the base of a turbine."

I felt as if a burst of wind energy swept through the car, leaving me exhilarated. The possibility of being that close to one of the huge windmills charged me with excitement, but even more than that was the thought of being there with Clyde, who knew me well enough to figure I would enjoy it.

"Surely you don't want to go parking on our first date," I teased.

A surprised laugh puffed from his lungs. "I wouldn't mind parking on every date, Lyn."

My neck and chest warmed.

"I love it when you blush," he said.

"I don't blush."

"Yes. Yes, you do. When you're nervous or embarrassed. It's beautiful." His thumb rubbed a small circle on my cheekbone. "Because you're so pure."

In a snap, my confidence vanished, and I pulled back just enough to distance myself from the discomfort of his words. I looked away from him, out the window, watching the news guy shifting from foot to foot as he waited for something to film. "How long do you suppose that truck's been down there?"

I felt Clyde's sigh as much as I heard it, almost condescending, as though I were an unruly child he couldn't control. "Years, I reckon, but they built the lake a few years after I left town, right? So it couldn't be longer than that."

The truck didn't interest me, and I couldn't have cared less how long it had been at the bottom of the lake, or how long the lake had been there. The only real thought in my mind was whether or not Clyde's love was real. Or if it was even love at all.

"I'm afraid you'll leave me," I said, wishing I could manage a first date without bringing up my past lovers.

"I know you are."

"So how do I get over that?"

"Maybe just let me prove it to you."

I scooted to my side of the seat, feigning interest in the lake. "That could take a long time."

His gaze fell to my hand gripping the door handle. "We've got the rest of our lives, Lyn, and I'm in no rush."

"But you said we're not kids anymore. You said you don't want to dillydally around."

"I don't mean to dillydally, but I'm not going to rush you either." His smile sent another wave of heat across my skin. "Not much at least."

The intensity of his meaning compelled me to flee, and I yanked the handle. "Let's go see what's going on down there."

Clyde followed me to the front bumper of the sedan. "Do you know this place?"

I studied the terrain, the jagged cliff edge, the way the road curved past two pump jacks, the rocky bluff on the opposite side of the chasm. Yes, I knew this place. "Neil used to bring me here. Before you went to prison." I blinked away the stupidity of that last statement. Neil and I had roasted marshmallows and sat on the edge of the cliff tossing pebbles over the side and watching them fall to the rocks below. That was way before the lake was here.

I grunted, disgusted with myself. "You think we'll ever be able to have a conversation without mentioning Hoby or Neil?"

"That might take a while, too." Clyde slipped a finger into my palm and pulled me toward the edge.

I followed him willingly, stepping over devil's-head cacti as the knee-high grass itched my shins, but I wasn't prepared for what lay below us. The lake came right up to the bluff beneath, but an arc of dry ground formed where once there had been water. Police cars and news vehicles scattered near the waterline, and a crane lay to our left, its highest pulley almost even with our feet. People were everywhere: officials in uniforms, Boy Scouts, townspeople. Several cameras were already rolling, and reporters jabbered in front of them.

I glanced at the man just down from us. "Isn't he the clever one?"

"We got lucky with him as our guide."

Two scuba divers surfaced in the middle of the lake, swimming to the shore, and I noticed a metal cable traveling from the crane into the water, where it disappeared into the depths. The smell of the lake, stronger than usual, wafted toward us as the sun shone across the surface. Everything seemed to be happening in a flurry of activity, but from our perch above it all, I felt like a spectator watching a movie, uninvolved and distant. I squeezed Clyde's finger. "What did you read?"

"Read?"

"In prison."

"Oh." He shifted his feet. "Everything. Anything."

"We're on a date. You should answer my questions."

He chuckled. *The Firm ... Anna Karenina ... Mein Kampf ... 1001 Ways to Stuff a Turkey ... Harry Potter.*"

A man below yelled orders, and the engine of the crane revved and began to move. The line grew taut, but I turned to Clyde, more interested in him than all the turmoil below us. "That all?"

"Not hardly."

"Clyde Felton, you just rolled your eyes."

He smiled down at me. "You're a bad influence, I guess." Slipping his arms around my waist, he leaned over and kissed me right there in front of half the town. His bravery sent a jolt of rebellion across my heart as I realized that any of those people would see us … if only they looked up.

He pulled away, chuckling, and his breath brushed against my cheek.

"So those are your favorite books?" I asked.

"I wouldn't say that, no." He left one arm around me.

"So what's your favorite?" The crane jerked and strained when it began supporting the weight of the vehicle, and the commotion on the shoreline calmed, but the activity happening below us seemed insignificant compared to the scene playing out next to me. Clyde was talking about himself, sharing secrets, and enjoying it.

"Favorite book?" He pulled me a little closer. "That would have to be the Bible, I suppose." The corner of his mouth lifted, and I could see a hint of his teeth, but then his gaze slipped toward the waterline, and he frowned.

I followed his gaze to see a muddy automobile bumper just breaking the surface of the water. Gooey, brown sludge cascaded from the vehicle, leaving a silty circle in the lake as it revealed two rear tires and a red towing mechanism. "The Bible?" I whispered.

The wind that had been nudging me now vanished, leaving me stifled in the heat of the late-afternoon sun. Water and mud poured from the windows of the truck as the crane pulled it farther out of the water. It wasn't a pickup. It wasn't the truck of an oil-field worker or a wind tech. I knew without a doubt it was the truck of a mechanic.

It was Hoby's wrecker.

Emptiness welled up from deep inside me, gently expanding like a hot-air balloon to suffocate me with its nothingness. "I should have known," I said.

The water around the truck swirled, and the shoreline slid away, and the people became foggy and blurred. When the ground beneath me began to spin out of control, I felt Clyde's arms around my back and under my legs. He swooped me up and held me tightly against his chest just before the world went black.

CHAPTER
TWENTY-SIX

When my husband left me fifteen years ago, I thought I would never recover from the heartache, but now that he was dead, I felt nothing at all. Hoby had given in to the pull of the bottle one last time and had driven off a cliff before he could make it home where I could help him.

After all those years of bitterness, waiting and angry, I found my life becoming a void of emptiness that swallowed me up more thoroughly than Lake Alan Henry had consumed that wrecker.

I sat on the side of my bed staring at the wall—at that oval-shaped chip in the semigloss—but all I saw was that muddy wrecker being pulled from the water and Hoby's mud-covered skull right there on the driver's side. I whimpered, then toyed with the idea of ripping the Sheetrock from the studs. Getting rid of the old, deteriorating facade in lieu of something fresh and clean. *Wouldn't help, though.* The house would still be old. Things would never change.

A water glass sat on the floor next to the bed, and I bent to pick it up, wrapped my fingers around it, and squeezed, hoping the pressure would shatter the glass so its shards would cut me. When it didn't budge, I reared my arm back and slammed the tumbler against the wall, hoping to trigger my habitual angry feelings. The silly thing only broke into three pieces, though, and for some reason I laughed. I had expected a satisfying crunch, and the pitiful thunk didn't come close to quenching my thirst for emotion.

I searched the room, my gaze landing on a porcelain lamp resting on my bedside table—pink roses against green lace—not my taste at all. My style would forever be wood and iron and denim. Hard, sturdy, usable surfaces that could survive the trials of life. I stood, gripped the lamp with two hands, and jerked the cord from the outlet. When I hurled it against the wall, the lamp merely fell to the floor and lay at an angle, its socket and bulb dangling and its shade askew and bent.

I sobbed once and fell to my knees. The lamp had sat on an end table in my living room when I was a child, and I remembered my mother cleaning it with a feather duster. I picked it up and returned it gingerly to the nightstand, shoving the shade back down like a winter hat on a runny-nosed preschooler. The porcelain hadn't even chipped.

Maybe roses and lace were more durable than they seemed.

The drawer of the nightstand was open, and the letters peeked out at me, teasing, taunting, but I let them be and sat down on the edge of the bed. They would only make things worse. Make me crazier. I slid to the rug and sat with my knees bent, heels shoved against my thighs.

My parents never should have died in that wreck. It didn't take a psychiatrist to figure out that I wouldn't have been so needy had they survived. I would have had a normal childhood and grown into an emotionally healthy adult, and I never would have thrown my mother's lamp against the wall.

A guilty voice inside my head sang a sad song of relief, crooning that I was free from Hoby's memory, but the vise-grip pressure on my chest left me no peace. Before my husband left, I wanted him to trust me and be happy, and after he left, I wanted him to come back. Both times he let me down, and over the years, I grew more and more angry. At life. At myself. At Hoby. I wanted him to pay. I wanted revenge.

But I never wanted him dead.

Dead was final. Dead was hopeless. Dead was incomprehensible abandonment. Dead was my parents.

Slowly I leaned over with one elbow on the hardwood floor. Then I lay down on my side and pulled my knees to my chest, wrapping the lamp cord around the fingers of my empty hand and drawing the other hand to my chest, crushing its contents.

My thumb rubbed across the paper, and I grunted in disgust. Somehow the letters had found their way into my hand, and I lay gripping them against my heart like a numbing anesthetic. An anesthetic called bitterness.

CHAPTER
TWENTY-SEVEN

Sunday after work, Clyde pulled out of the Dairy Queen parking lot and decided he had left Lynda on her own long enough. When he dropped by her house to check on her, he was surprised to find reporters in the yard hovering around the property line like vultures around a wounded animal. A few of them approached his sedan, but when he pulled himself from his car, he towered above them with a scowl, and they backed away. In spite of that, he figured they would find out who he was, and his name and his past would be splattered on the news stations right along with Lynda's and Hoby's.

No wonder Lynda hadn't shown up at work.

At lunchtime, Dixie told him Lynda had called in sick, but neither of them believed that to be true, so Clyde had promised to check on her. He tapped on the door and waited, imagining how she would lock herself away. He couldn't leave her there no matter what was going on in the front yard. He knocked louder but still got no answer.

Clyde thought for a second about going by the United and asking Ruthie for a key, but that would only upset the girl. She and Lynda had enough issues without him reminding her.

He pulled his wallet from his back pocket, slipped out his driver's license, and used his body to shield his actions from the onlookers with their cameras. He had the door open in less than three seconds. Lynda might be angry with him, but he was used to that.

"Lyn?" He stepped into the living room, closed the door behind him with a soft click, and then he listened for a few seconds. *Empty silence.* The lights were off in the kitchen, so he knocked on the bedroom door. "Lynda, it's me. You in there?"

He knew she was in there. Where else would she be? In the best of situations, she might have gone to stay with her sister, but Velma couldn't handle anything else, and Lynda was still healthy enough to admit it.

He knocked again, this time louder.

"What do you want?" Her voice sounded clear, not as though she had been crying. Clyde realized Lynda rarely cried.

The knob turned easily. *Thank goodness.* Breaking in through her front door was one thing, but her bedroom was something entirely different. "Figured you needed checking on."

"I don't."

Clyde paused in the doorway and waited for his eyes to adjust to the dim light. She was lying across the bed wearing an old T-shirt and what looked like oversize men's pajama pants. "Mind if I turn on the light?"

"Why did you come here?"

Clyde ran his fingers through his hair, looked back up the hallway to the living room, and then sighed. Sometimes Lynda could be testy, and she didn't always know what was good for her. He flipped the light switch.

Lynda pulled the pillow over her head and rolled to her side. When she drew her knees up to her chest, her T-shirt crept up, exposing four inches of her spine.

Clyde looked at the floor as he walked to the side of the bed and poked her knee with his finger. "You can't stay in here forever."

She didn't move, so he pulled the curtains back to let in sunlight.

"Stop it." Her voice was muffled beneath the pillow.

He sat on the side of the bed. Waited. Looked at her. The way she was lying on her side made her hips curve away from her waistline. He noticed a throw blanket on the end of the bed and pulled it over her, but she kicked at him, sending the blanket cascading to the floor.

"I'm not cold."

He jerked the pillow from her head, and when she flipped the other one to cover herself, he was faster and caught it in midshift, leaving her pillowless and as irritated as a diamondback on hot sand.

She jerked to a sitting position and scooted herself back. "What?"

"You can't stay in here, Lyn."

"Give me a break. It hasn't even been twenty-four hours." Her face wrinkled into a fierce glower, but her hair jumbled on top of her head, and her anger didn't make it all the way to Clyde, who was trying not to smile.

"Twenty-five."

Her eyes bounced to the clock radio, and then she slumped against the headboard.

A maple dining chair stood in the corner, and Clyde pulled it to the side of the bed and sat. She would talk when she was ready, and Clyde would stay until it happened.

He watched her for a while, but when she didn't move, he took another look around the room. Bare walls. A dresser with a junior-high-aged picture of Ruthie in a frame, and next to it, a pink baby Bible. The bedside table held a fancy antique lamp with a whopper-jawed shade. A pile of clothes had been dumped in the corner—mostly brown diner uniforms—and her Converse tennis shoes were next to it. And near the baseboard, what looked like a broken glass.

So she had thrown a tantrum.

Her head lolled back, and she bumped it softly on the headboard. "Life is just so hard. Will it never ease up?"

He figured she didn't want an answer, so he didn't give her one, but she was right. Life was insanely difficult. So hard it took his breath away at times. So hard he often thought about locking himself in his own house, just as she was doing.

She sighed. "I hate when I whine, but I can't seem to stop."

"Least you hear yourself doing it."

"Does that give me extra credit or something?"

"Yep."

She crossed her arms and stared out the window.

Not wanting to rush her, he lowered his gaze to the floor, but when he did, he noticed crumpled pieces of paper between the bed and the nightstand. One of them stuck out farther, just catching the light from the lamp. They were the letters from Neil that he had seen in the kitchen last week. The letters she had thrown away.

He poked at a few items in her open bedside drawer, pretending to be curious, and then he leaned over and dropped his hand smoothly to the floor. Sliding his palm across the letters, he folded them with one hand and slipped them into his pocket. He looked back at her, expecting her to snap at him for being nosy, but she was still looking out the window, not seeing. "You hungry?" he asked.

"No."

She needed to eat. She needed to keep up her strength so she could fight off the desperation. She needed to tell him the truth about whatever he had in his pocket.

"I'll make you a sandwich." He stalked away, but as soon as he got to the kitchen, he flipped on the light and pulled out the letters.

The first was nothing more than a scrawled note.

Since you won't talk to me, I've resorted to the postal service. Lynda, he would want you to let go of the past. You know he would. Let me help.

Clyde stared at the paper in his fist, wondering—no, fearing— when Neil had written it. The paper didn't seem fresh, but it was nowhere near as worn as the longer one. He turned the stationery over to read the words of the letter, and his heart catapulted from the top of a guard tower, landing on an electrified, razor-wire fence.

Lynda, my ladybug.

The phrase jolted Clyde back to a night years ago, when he'd been sitting at a card table in the bay of Hoby's mechanic shop. Neil had leaned over and made Lynda giggle with his absurd words. "Lynda, my unlikely little ladybug, I love you and like you and lust you, and I long for later when a license makes us lawful."

Clyde could almost hear the dominoes clink against each other as Hoby shuffled them. He and Hoby had moaned while Neil and Lynda laughed. That was before Susan. Before everything. The four of them had been such good friends.

And Hoby had loved Lynda as long as Clyde had.

They even talked about it once their senior year. The two of them were on the offensive line, protecting the quarterback, and they joked about how easy it would have been for Neil to get hurt. But letting Neil get injured wouldn't have solved anything. They both knew neither of them stood a chance against Trapp's golden boy. Besides, Neil was their friend.

Lynda coughed in the other room, and Clyde snapped back to the present. He yanked food items out of the cabinet while he skimmed the rest of the letter.

... still love you ... can't live like this ... miss you so much I could die ... Susan will never know ... wasn't what I wanted ... had no choice ... please forgive ...

A deep burn ignited beneath the soles of Clyde's feet, and it gradually grew stronger, engulfing him in flames until he thought he might explode into a hundred fireballs. He looked at the top corner of the paper to the date scrawled in Neil's handwriting. The letter had been written during Clyde's trial, just a few weeks after Neil married Susan.

There was another letter with different handwriting and an old church bulletin, but Clyde shoved them into a pile. The hate he felt for Neil Blaylock was so intense, it pressed on his shoulders, and he carried it back to the bedroom, supporting its weight as if he were carrying an invisible iron yoke.

Lynda had insisted she had no feelings for Neil, and Clyde believed it. She couldn't fake that kind of hatred. So why did she hang on to these letters after so many years?

When he entered the bedroom with a paper plate of peanut-butter sandwiches, she was running her fingers through her hair, releasing the tangles. Well, that was an improvement. His burden shifted slightly but didn't ease.

He held the sandwiches toward her.

"Not hungry."

He stood like a statue, the plate extended. He wouldn't leave until he saw her eat at least half a sandwich, and if Lynda thought about it, she would know as much.

"Fine," she snapped.

He set the plate on the foot of the bed and raised a sandwich to his lips, and they ate in silence. Staring. Chewing. Thinking. And then he slipped into the kitchen and brought back two cups of ice water, having avoided the pitcher of cloudy tea on the counter.

Lynda had sneaked another sandwich while he was gone.

Clyde reached for another and took a large bite, then settled back in his chair. He swallowed. "Might serve you well to get out of the house."

She lowered her arm, letting her sandwich rest on her thigh.

He took a swig of water and wiped his mouth on the back of his hand. "Not all at once, but a little farther every day."

"A little farther?"

He motioned to the hallway. "Take on that door first."

She glared at the door as if it were a demon in need of a thrashing. "I guess Hector will come by."

"I asked him to give you a couple days. He said he had information for you, but he didn't say what."

"Hmm."

Clyde leaned forward and dropped the letters back on the floor. "You talked to Ruthie?"

"A few minutes last night."

"She needs you."

Lynda pulled her knees up to her chest and curled her toes into the quilt. "I know she does, but what do I have that she would want?"

"Just you."

Clyde anticipated how the conversation would play out. He had read enough novels to know this was where she was supposed to break down into tears, but Lynda wasn't a typical woman, and right at that moment, she gritted her teeth in a calm fury.

"Ruth Ann hasn't needed me in a year or more, if she ever did."

"The girl clearly needs you. Especially now."

"But she left me, just like the rest of them." Her eyes opened wide, searching his, as though she might find a solution to a problem there.

"No … now. She didn't." He shook his head.

"Yes, she did." She clawed her fingers through her hair until she held handfuls tightly in her grip.

Clyde shifted on the chair, realizing she had a point. Even if it hadn't been Ruthie's intention to abandon her momma, she had—sort of—left Lynda alone when she married Dodd.

Just like Lynda's parents. Just like Neil. Just like Hoby.

And now Hoby had left her all over again.

No wonder Lyn was a mess.

He moved to sit next to her on the bed and worked her fingers out of her hair. When her arms dropped limply to her side, he held the glass of ice water toward her and waited until she took it and drank.

Clyde knew she was in a deep, dark place, but he also knew she could dig her way out. "That door, Lyn. Start with that door."

Her eyes followed his arm until she was gazing blankly toward the hall, and then she looked back at him, her eyes childlike and wide. "If you say so."

He slid his palm into hers, but this time, her hand wrapped so loosely around his finger, he could hardly feel it. As though she were barely there.

CHAPTER
TWENTY-EIGHT

"Lynda?" Hector Chavez knocked on my front door bright and early Monday morning, and when I peeked out the diamond-shaped window, I saw that the sheriff had been followed by more news reporters and cameras. The desperation I'd worked so hard to repel now crept silently across the hardwood floors of my living room and crouched behind me.

As if finding my husband's vehicle at the bottom of the lake wasn't enough, now I had to discuss it with an old friend while being hounded by a crowd of strangers. *Why bother?* Hector would only explain that they had found Hoby's wrecker, that he was dead, that he had been dead a long time.

I opened the door but shielded my face with a Kleenex box when I saw cameras pointed at me from the street.

Before either of us spoke, Hector entered, clearly wanting to avoid the media as much as I did. He pushed the door closed behind him, then leaned against it. His eyes quickly swept my tangled hair and worn pajama pants before he cut his gaze to the front window. "I won't stay long, Lynda." Without moving from the door, he reached over and pulled the curtain cord, closing out any unwanted attention I might receive from the spectators.

"Thanks." I crossed my arms and waited for him to decide if I was thanking him for closing my curtains or for not staying long.

"When I leave, I'll try to get them to give you a break for a while." He closed his eyes for a second and seemed to take a deep breath to prepare. "I guess you've heard about the Lubbock Police Department finding Hoby's wrecker out in the lake."

"I thought it was the Texas Rangers."

"No, the LPD has jurisdiction over the actual lake."

I nodded, not trusting my voice.

"This is hard for me, Lynda. Hoby was a good friend." He held his cowboy hat in his hands, rotating it endlessly. "And Neil."

"Neil?"

"I keep thinking about one summer. The three of us did target practice on the side of his dad's barn." He chuckled. "That was before I was in law enforcement, of course. Years later I ran a report when Neil's pistol was stolen."

"I never knew it was stolen."

"Right out of his truck in downtown Trapp." Hector shook his head. "During the Christmas parade for the volunteer fire department. Don't that beat all?"

Silence invaded my living room as we both lost ourselves in memories, but then Hector shrugged, ever so slightly, as though to plunge on through his dirty deed. "They didn't find a body, Lynda."

A body.

Suddenly I was in a crime scene television show, with my husband playing the part of this week's victim. I stumbled to the couch and plopped down heavily. "But I saw—" *What had I seen?* When the wrecker came up out of the water, it had been filled with silt from the bottom of the lake, but as the mud sifted back into the water, I could have sworn I saw a skull through the back window.

"I know what you think you saw." Hector followed me and sat on the very edge of the recliner. "Most all the spectators saw the same thing, and at this point, we're letting them believe it was a body, but it was actually Hoby's old hard hat hanging from the gun rack."

"A hard hat?" I had forgotten Hoby even had a hard hat. He used to wear it as a batting helmet when he played softball. My teeth bit gently on my bottom lip, and I looked away from Hector toward the empty kitchen, through the window, to the backyard and freedom. "So he's not dead?" With my worn emotions, I didn't know what to think, and it crossed my mind that I probably wasn't behaving the way a widow should behave. *Was this some kind of test?*

"The boys from Lubbock are speculating, but everyone in town assumes it was either an accident or suicide." His face scrunched. "That's probably what you're thinking, too." He leaned forward. "Hoby had been diagnosed with depression, right?"

"Yes." My head seemed full and empty at the same time, and when I tried to talk, my tongue tingled. "What should I be thinking, Hector?"

"I'm sorry to be so blunt," he said. "I'm not really involved in the investigation of the vehicle, but I have a little to do with those bones that were found."

I bent one knee to tuck my icy toes beneath the opposite thigh, not seeing the connection.

"At this point," he continued, "the Rangers are considering the possibility that those bones belonged to Hoby."

"Wh-what?" My thoughts spun in wild arcs, and I struggled to make sense of them. "Why?"

Hector shrugged. "Because there was no evidence of a body in the truck."

"But everyone's saying the Tarrons' grenades could've moved things around." A feeling of dull nausea settled in my stomach. "If his body wasn't in the wrecker, then it's still on the bottom of the lake."

"Actually …"—Hector shifted, and his holster pressed against the arm of the recliner—"the CSI team from Lubbock had a lot to say about what would happen to a body under those conditions, especially with the windows open on the truck."

I didn't want to know what would happen, but surely I was supposed to ask. A good wife would ask. "What would happen?"

Hector studied the cuticle of his left thumb before returning his gaze to me. "Let's just say that if Hoby had been in the cab when the truck entered the water, his body probably would have surfaced in a day or two."

Even though I hadn't eaten anything for breakfast, my stomach churned in protest, and the mild nausea from a few minutes ago flared into a serious threat. My dead husband's bloated body had risen to the surface of the lake, only to be ripped apart by animals and left to rot.

"I'm sorry this is happening, Lynda. Hoby was a good friend." Hector continued talking, unaware that my brain was only catching half of what he said. "Also, the Rangers sent those bones to an anthropology expert down in Austin. The preliminary report showed there wasn't enough DNA to make an identification."

Bones … DNA … identification … Hoby. I couldn't take any more of Hector's verbiage or assumptions or speculations. My husband was dead one minute, alive the next, then dead again. Or maybe it wasn't him at all. "I think I've got it now, Hector." But really I didn't. It didn't make sense at all.

He rose, walked stiffly to the door, and then stopped. He turned back to me, and his eyes were sad. "Lynda, I don't think you fully understand what I'm saying."

I pressed my forearms against my stomach in an attempt to settle it. "Okay."

"You see ... at this point, the Rangers don't know if the bones belonged to Hoby, or if the body was in the truck when it went into the water. They don't know if the bones were ever in the water at all. They'll know a lot more once they get the rest of the results from Austin."

"What are you saying?" If he told me anything else, I might not be able to handle it, but I had to ask. I was supposed to ask.

He held his palms in front of me as though he would catch me if I fell. He spoke slowly and softly. "I'm saying they think there may have been suspicious circumstances." He pressed his lips together and dropped his gaze, seemingly unable to look me in the eye. "I can't tell you everything right now, but I can tell you that things aren't adding up."

"I don't understand."

"I know, but you're going to have to wait a few days. Wait until we have more evidence." He reached for the doorknob. "But I need you to keep this between the two of us until I talk to you again."

"Why?"

"Because I'm not sure who I can trust."

CHAPTER
TWENTY-NINE

"Momma?" Ruthie knocked on the front door twice.

"It's open, Ruth Ann." I rubbed my eyes, pulling myself up to a seated position.

It had been four hours since Hector left, and I had sat on the couch the entire time, but at least I hadn't gone back to my bedroom. I kept telling myself I would take a drive later today. Maybe not all the way to the windmills, but surely I could handle a trip to the Dairy Queen drive-through. After all, Clyde would expect me to get out.

Ruthie came in the house, then stood just inside the door, arms crossed, peering at me. The look on her face was the same as when she was five years old and had to drink the thick, pink medicine— stubborn and willful. "Dodd said I had to come over here and talk to you, or he was going to go nuts. He's not picking me up for an hour."

From where I sat on the couch, I could see the El Camino pulling away from the house. Apparently the reporters had given up. "He's a good man."

Ruthie sat down next to me even though there were two other chairs in the room. "Yeah … he is."

Shooting the breeze wouldn't help either of us, but it was the best I could do. "What's his sermon topic this week?" I had a warped habit of asking. "Tell me it's not forgiveness again."

"No, I think he's gotten all the mileage out of that one. This Sunday he's preaching on repentance."

"Ah, he's talking to Neil."

"Momma, Dodd wouldn't preach to one person in the audience. That's not cool."

"I don't see how he has a choice."

"What do you mean? Nobody tells him what to preach."

"I'm just saying Neil's been on his mind lately, so he's bound to be influenced. It's just where Dodd is right now."

She laughed lightly. "But Neil has been on his mind ever since he started preaching here two years ago."

"No wonder he's preached on forgiveness until he's blue in the face."

Ruthie pursed her lips as if she wanted to say something else, but she only looked away and shook her head.

Ruthie was hurting.

She was hurting, and I didn't know how to help her. I had never known, and my own pain had always overshadowed hers until I barely knew my own daughter.

Her eyes clouded. "Why do I miss Daddy?"

I froze, unable to think of anything other than Hector's insistence that I not talk to anyone.

"He's been gone over fifteen years," Ruthie said. "I stopped missing him years ago—or at least I stopped dreaming he'd come home, but now I miss him again. It's stupid."

"That's not stupid."

"Explain it, then."

I couldn't explain it. "I just know I feel the same way, and we can't both be stupid."

She peered at me for a few minutes, then bumped my shoulder with hers. "But you've missed him all along."

"Sure, I've missed him, but I also wanted to slap him. I wanted to get him back for leaving the two of us. I wanted to make him pay."

Ruthie's gaze bounced around the room, looking for a place to land.

I cringed. "But I never wanted him … dead."

She inhaled a shallow breath, and I could hear a stifled sob around its edges. "I know, Momma."

A gust swelled outside, and dust pelted the window. We both turned our heads that direction, stared without seeing, then turned back. Like so many other times, I noticed our similarities and marveled at how much we were alike. Was there any trace of Hoby in my daughter? Was there anything left of him?

While she picked at her fingernails, I studied her. As a child, Ruthie had a gap between her front teeth, just like Hoby, but braces had changed that. She still had Hoby's eyes, of course. Right after he left, those eyes of hers had almost driven me insane, but somewhere over the years, I had all but forgotten their constant reminder, and Ruthie's eyes had become her own, not Hoby's.

She sighed. "Dodd says I miss him now because I know he's never coming back, but it's more than that." She spoke louder and faster as though she would feel better—*cleansed*—once she had tossed the notion out into the room where we could look at it, examine it, poke it with a stick. "Now we know where he was all that time." Her eyes widened. "He wasn't deliberately staying away."

The same thoughts had somersaulted through my head, but after the sheriff's visit, I didn't know what to think. "It makes sense, Ruth Ann. I could always reason out why he left me, but it was wildly out of character for him to leave you." Then I realized the truth of my words. No matter what Hector had been trying to tell me, Hoby being dead was the only thing that made sense.

A tear trickled down her cheek. "I've spent so many years believing he didn't want me." She slumped back, seeming to let the cushions soak up her tension. "Momma, what do you think Daddy would say if he were here?"

"Why do you ask?"

"Oh, I don't know." She shook her head. "I've just been thinking. What would he have done if he had been at my wedding? What would he think about Dodd? Would he be happy that I'm in college? I mean, I suppose I know the answer to those questions … but still … I wish he could be part of my life."

I was beginning to understand. "What else have you been asking yourself?"

"I ask myself what might have happened if things had been different. What if he hadn't gotten drunk? What if he had just slammed into a telephone pole or something? Yes, he would have still died, but we would have known about it. What would our lives be like now?"

I shivered. "Things would definitely be different, but there's no way to know if they'd be better or worse."

"Seems like they'd have been better."

My finger rubbed at a rough spot on the couch cushion. "Yeah, it does." *Sort of.* My thoughts had just undergone a shift, and in my mind, Hoby was so dead, I couldn't imagine him alive. "Let's go get a dip cone."

"You just want to see Clyde."

"He's not working today."

She lifted her head and smiled. "Okay. A dip cone."

As we walked down the front steps, the outdoor air felt foreign to me, and I could hear it whispering that I should go back in the house, stay home, stay safe, but in defiance I lifted my face and let the sunshine warm my cheeks. *I can do this.*

Ruthie paused, squinting into the sun. "I wish I had more memories of him."

So do I. The most vivid memories were always the bad ones.

"The two of you used to swing a jump rope for me," she said. "Daddy sang a chant while I jumped. I don't remember it, though."

I took one step to the car, then stopped. "Cinderella dressed in yellow went upstairs to kiss a fellow."

Ruthie finished the rhyme. "Made a mistake and kissed a snake. How many doctors did it take?"

My mind wandered back to that time. Not long before Hoby left, he had been working a lot, but he had always made time for our daughter. "He was the first one to give you a nickname," I said. "And I used to call you Ruthie just like he did. Do you remember that?"

She didn't answer right away, and I knew it wasn't easy to think back that far. "Maybe. Why?"

"I haven't thought about that in so long. He only called you Ruth Ann if he was sad. When he left, I was mad at him, and I started calling you Ruth Ann all the time. I told everyone it was because I wanted to emphasize the names of your grandmothers, but really I was just angry with him for leaving."

The two of us stood in the middle of the yard, halfway between the house and the hatchback, but in the past thirty minutes, we had covered so much emotional ground, we were miles closer than we had been in years.

She smiled. "Thank you for telling me that, Momma."

CHAPTER THIRTY

Clyde felt a wave of heaviness pressing on his chest. After he saw Hoby's wrecker being pulled from the lake, he had expected to be sad—even angry—but the chained-down feeling surprised him, as if he was a vicious dog tethered to a post in a weedy front yard. His friend had died, and Clyde hadn't been around to do anything about it. A match struck deep inside Clyde's gut, starting a slow burn of helplessness that quickly flared into fury.

He walked to the back door and peered at the old shed in the corner of his yard. It would feel so good to take an ax to the rotted two-by-fours, to relieve his stress in blow after blow on the dry wood, to vent his anger and frustration.

But that would never do.

Chain-link fences separated his yard from five others, giving his neighbors a front-row seat from their kitchen windows. A front-row seat to witness his rage that, even though justified, would not necessarily appear so to others.

There were just too many things to deal with. If it were only he who was hurting, it wouldn't be so bad. Clyde gripped the door handle with his fist, unable to hold back his fear. Fear of how Lynda would deal with everything happening in her life.

Would she lock herself away again? *Would she hold herself accountable?* Clyde could only hope she'd work through the pain more quickly this time, but Lynda wasn't good at that. She was fragile. She needed someone to help her through all of life's battles, because she had been through too much strife on her own.

And there was so little Clyde could do for her.

He wrenched the door open, shoving aside his concern about the neighbors. That shed was coming down.

✳✳✳

Three hours later, he once again held the door for Lynda at the bookshop, hoping an outing would do her good.

"I always thought the old post office was a strange place for a store." Lynda's negative comment put a smile on Clyde's face. Sunday her eyes had shown little or no emotion, but two days later, a hint of irritation had returned.

As they entered the shop, Clyde noticed Pamela Sanders on the other side of a display of greeting cards, just before she stuck her head around the corner.

"Hey, Clyde. You back again?" She smiled as she wiped her forehead with the back of her pudgy wrist, but when she saw Lynda, she scooted into the open. "Oh … Lynda … I heard about what happened out at the lake, and I'm so sorry." Her face mirrored Lynda's pout, and she emphasized the last word as though she felt the pain herself.

"Thanks, Pam."

Lynda's eyes settled, and Clyde was surprised at the soothing effect Pamela had on her.

"It's not as big a deal as you would think," Lynda half lied. "It happened so long ago."

"Death is always a big deal, sweetie." She grasped Lynda's hand briefly, long enough to solicit a slow blink from Lynda but not long enough for her to pull her hand away.

"Had many customers?" Clyde asked.

"Hardly any so far, but I'm still having the time of my life." Pamela beamed. "I never realized how bored I'd gotten since Emily went off to school. This shop is just what I needed, and I absolutely *love* the setup in the back. Even if the reading room doesn't take off, it gives me a place to rest my feet." Her eyebrows lifted comically. "You should show Lynda how we changed things around. Since she's here and all."

"I guess we'll just sit back there a spell," Clyde drawled, "if that's all right with you."

Pamela's palm went into the air as if she were swearing an oath. "Take all the time you want."

Lynda rolled her eyes softly, but she followed Clyde to the back room, where a leather couch and chair had replaced a few of the bookshelves. "Clearly you and Pamela are working a plan."

"Yep."

She put her hands on her hips and inspected the layout of the room, but even while she turned and frowned and sighed, Clyde got the impression she didn't hate the space. "It's bright in here now." Her eyes swept the ceiling, taking in the skylight, then the fresh coat of paint on the walls. "Light yellow. I like that."

"Troy and Pam have worked hard on this place," he said.

"I get the impression you have, too. Oh goodness." She pointed at Ellen Mendoza's old VHS collection, displayed in a couple of stacked milk crates.

"Aw, now … once Pam gets the coffeepot working, it'll practically be a Barnes and Noble."

"Coffee would definitely help."

Clyde sat on one end of the couch. "The smell of old books reminds me of memories. Or imagination." He shrugged, embarrassed he had said it. "Or something like that."

She perched on the opposite end of the couch and rubbed the toe of her tennis shoe across dried paint splatters on the cement floor. Her gaze wandered to the shelves of books, the scented candles on a table in the corner, the buzzing fluorescent light high above their heads. "This is better than my bedroom," she said.

"Yep."

Her eyes opened slightly wider than normal. "This was nice of Pam, wasn't it? She's been kind to me. Through all of it." She shook her head. "For years."

"She always thought Hoby was a *peach*."

Lynda smiled big enough to show her teeth. "Exactly how Pam always described him." Her eyes darted to the lighted exit sign above the back door, and her smile vanished. "How did you know what to say to me Sunday? When I was stuck in bed?"

He shrugged. "I was locked up awhile."

"But that was against your will. I locked myself up all on my own."

He wished she would let him hold her again. "Sometimes being locked up is safer than being out in the world."

A cricket inched its way across a rug near a squat metal shelf packed with children's books, and Lynda watched it intently. When the insect disappeared beneath the books, she looked back at Clyde, and her eyebrows asked for more explanation.

"For a while … in prison … it was good to be distant from the pain of what had been done to me. Against me. But once I had forgiven them and accepted my fate, then I just felt locked up, and the real imprisonment started."

"Are you saying I should forgive Hoby for being a drunk?"

"Maybe."

She gritted her teeth. "I'm just so mad at him, you know?" She trembled. "He was so selfish."

Clyde wanted to tell her it would be all right, ask her to let go of the pain and get on with life. "You should read."

She seemed to grope for the lighter topic like a lifeline. "I'm not going to read a psych book, if that's what you mean."

"I hadn't thought about that, but it's not a bad idea."

When he pretended to search the nearest shelf, she kicked him. "Here's one. How to deal with crazy women."

The second time she kicked, he caught her foot and held it across his lap. At first she pulled against him, but when he rubbed his hand up and down her shin, she settled. Clyde kept his gaze focused on her shoelaces for a few minutes, worried she would be glaring when he looked up, but when he lifted his eyes, he was surprised to find her with her head resting against the couch cushion and her eyes closed.

"Do I really need a psych book?" The edges of her mouth teased upward.

"Aw, Lyn. I don't know what you need. Everybody grieves different."

"How would you know?" She spoke with impatience in her tone, but she immediately shook her head. "Forget I said that. You have more in your life to grieve than just about anybody I know."

"Depends on how you look at it."

She opened her eyes. "How did you know to tell me to tackle the bedroom door?"

"I've heard things over the years. From prison ministers. Or books. And now that I'm home, your son-in-law tells me stuff. He's got me talking to one of his therapist friends over in Snyder."

"You're in therapy? But it's been two years."

Suddenly his personal life lay exposed on the couch between them. "Can you believe there's a therapist in Snyder of all places?" He knew it wasn't fair to avoid her questions when he was the one who had started the pushing, but Lynda had enough problems without worrying about PICS.

She looked at him out of the corner of her eye, then blinked and rolled them, letting the shift in topic pass without argument. "Okay," she said with finality. "No, I didn't know there was a therapist in Snyder. Is he in the old post office?"

Her sense of humor tickled him around his Adam's apple. "In an old house, actually."

"How cozy."

"You should try it sometime."

"An old house?"

"A therapist."

"But I only just now made it to the Trapp Door."

He shut his mouth and looked her in the eye, but her gaze darted away as though she had looked directly into the sun.

"Are you going to make me read a book?" Her chin lifted.

"Might as well. How about that brown one?"

"Brown one?" She pulled her foot off his lap and stretched to the shelf behind her. "This brown one?"

He sighed. She could be cute, but she could also be snooty. "It's not brown, is it?"

"As green as grass."

"Whatever."

She leaned forward with her elbows on her knees. "Remember when we used to play Chicken Foot with those multicolored dominoes, and you couldn't tell the colors apart?" She smiled but didn't quite smile. Her memories seemed to keep spiraling back to Hoby, no matter what she tried.

"Aw, now …"

She chuckled for real then, and the sound soothed Clyde's worried nerves like the salve his grandmother used to put on his sunburn.

"We better be going. I've got work in a few." He lifted his eyebrows, silently asking her about her job, but it was her turn to ignore a question. He stood up.

"Aren't you going to get a book?" she asked.

"I guess not."

"Why?"

He hesitated. "I've read them."

"All of them?" She looked down at the book in her hand. "Even *Anne of Green Gables?*"

"Okay, I ain't read that one, but I've read most of them." He didn't feel like adding that he had donated a good portion of them. Books he'd found at garage sales in the past two years, read, and then passed on to Pamela.

"Why did you bring me here if you weren't planning on buying a book?"

He held his breath for a count of three, then jumped off the high dive. "I'm comfortable here, and I thought you might be, too."

She gazed around the room. "You know ... I sort of am."

A vibrating rumble eased through Clyde's chest. He could tell Lynda wasn't completely recovered from discovering her husband might be dead—who would be?—but she could see beyond the pain. And someday, when she came further out of the shadows, she might once again notice him in the sunshine.

CHAPTER
THIRTY-ONE

"Ansel, how you doing today?"

Wednesday morning, not only did I get out of the house, but I did it all by myself. Clyde would have been proud had he known, but I didn't call him. I called Velma.

"Aw, Lynda, I've been worse," Ansel said.

My brother-in-law's chair of choice was his recliner, and that's where he was today. Only instead of his usual position, sitting with the foot support lifted, he had the chair laid all the way back. His head rested to the side, and his hands lay limply on the armrests. I wondered if he even had the strength to change the channel on the television.

"I'm better now the TV reporters have left us be." His eyes met mine, and without words, he conveyed compassion for my loss. I was startled to realize I had briefly forgotten about Hoby. Losing my husband, whom I hadn't seen in nearly seventeen years, paled in comparison to Velma'losing her husband, whom she had seen every day for over thirty.

Velma motioned toward the sliding-glass door. "They've been out in the pasture with their zoom lenses."

"Blasted photographers." Ansel seemed to have rallied his strength to make the outburst, and then his head sank back down on the headrest.

"JohnScott posted signs." Velma pursed her lips. "That did the trick."

Ansel grunted. "Thank God."

"The old man's been talking a lot about the Lord lately," Velma said. "Seems to think he needs to get right."

"Now, Velma," he said slowly. "I've got plenty of time to set things straight with the Big Guy. I'm in no rush."

"No … no rush." I tried to sound carefree, but in the back of my heart, hidden where nobody could see, lay an urgent secret. Now that I was looking at Ansel's approaching death, I couldn't bear the thought of him not knowing God. An involuntary chuckle slipped from my throat. "The people down at the church wouldn't know what to think if Ansel Pickett walked in."

"Good Lord," he rasped, and then a laugh turned into a coughing fit. When he had quieted and wiped his lips with a cloth handkerchief, he insisted, "I'm not thinking of going to a worship service. God's here at the house, too, ain't He?"

Velma clicked off the television. "Ansel heard that Neil Blaylock went back to the church a week ago."

"I heard that."

My brother-in-law reached for a toothpick on the end table, then placed it between his teeth and talked around it. "Reckon they'll make him an elder again?"

"Surely not," Velma said.

He shrugged his shoulders weakly. "Wouldn't put it past 'em."

My insides turned to Jell-O. "So you won't be headed to Sunday services anytime soon?"

"Naw, not me," Ansel said. "Velma might get a hankering to go, though."

"Not without you, I won't." My sister pulled a crocheted throw pillow into her lap and fluffed it. "I only go there for weddings and funerals and such."

Her face went white.

"Mom and Dad's funeral was the first time I'd ever been in the church building," I said.

"You don't say." Ansel joined me in making the best of Velma's accidental funeral reference.

"That was a strange time," Velma said.

"I barely remember it." Except for the parts I did remember. Like the women who patted my shoulder with their squishy, warm hands. The emptiness in my lungs, as though I couldn't draw in a good breath. The caskets at the front of the room, shut tight because the accident had been so gruesome.

"You were in shock, I reckon," Velma said softly as she picked at the yarn on the pillow.

We sat in silence until Ansel drifted to sleep, his toothpick falling from his lips and down into the inner parts of his recliner.

Velma put the pillow in the crook of the couch and gave it a good thump on the top edge. "Nowadays we've got all these talk shows telling us what we should've done back then so we wouldn't be in the shape we're in now."

"We're a mess, aren't we?"

"Ansel's a mess." The lines around her eyes deepened when she looked at him. "He was talking about visiting the church before Neil started stirring things up down there. Now, he'll be dead before he gets around to it."

I looked at my brother-in-law, his worn hands folded over his chest as if he were already lying in rest at the funeral home. But I reminded myself what Ansel had said. God was at the house, too. I clasped my hands together, locking my fingers tightly, and squeezed with all my might, hoping Ansel was right.

CHAPTER
THIRTY-TWO

The kitchen in Clyde's trailer house was nothing more than two short counters with a gas stove and a tiny refrigerator, but the scents that swirled as I watched him chopping vegetables smelled like a five-star restaurant. "What are you making?" I asked.

"Salsa. To go with the enchiladas. They're in the oven."

He had four tomatoes, two of them bright red and juicy, two of them still green, and he was slicing them quickly with a butcher knife.

I leaned my hip against the counter as I watched his movements. "How do you not chop your fingers?"

"I read a book once—"

"Of course you did."

He paused, blinked, seemed to suppress a sigh. "Some famous chef explained it. See?" He shifted so I would have a better view of his paper-plate cutting board. "You let your knuckles guide the side of the blade, so your fingers don't get under the knife."

His hands made the butcher knife appear small, and I recalled his demonstration the first time he took me to Pamela's shop. "Don't you mean a *shiv*? What other words are different in prison?"

He shook his head. "Again with the prison questions."

"Never mind, then."

He continued chopping. "Okay. Deodorant was *foo-foo*, and weights were the *iron pile*."

"Do you ever slip and accidentally use a prison term?"

"Only once. One day at the Dairy Queen, I called Bernie Guthrie's cigarette a *fug*. He almost swallowed the silly thing when I told him they weren't allowed in the restaurant." Clyde's head fell two inches, and his face warmed to a pale burgundy. "He thought I said something else."

I bit my lip, picturing Old Man Guthrie's reaction. "By the way, I brought this." I nudged a plastic container sitting on the counter next to two jalapeño peppers and a clove of garlic.

"Bean dip?" He chuckled. "You could have just brought it in the can. Didn't have to get all fancy with the Tupperware."

After turning the dish upside down, I inspected its contents. "It's guacamole."

"No kidding?"

"It's green with bright-red chunks of tomato." I looked around the counter for a cookbook. "Don't you use a recipe?"

"Not for salsa. I just do it." He reached for an onion, but before he started chopping, he pulled a small box of matches out of his pocket and clamped one between his teeth.

"Does that work?" I asked. "Does it keep the onion from burning your eyes?"

"Sort of." He spoke around the match, then smiled as his eyes watered anyway.

"Dixie and me just chew spearmint gum."

He spit the match on the counter. "Does it work?"

"Sort of."

He put the matchbox back in his pocket, then tossed his vegetables in a large bowl and added a few leaves of parsley. When the oven timer buzzed, he removed the enchiladas and positioned my guacamole next to them on the stove. Finally he opened a bag of tortilla chips. "I've been thinking about you saying I need another place to live."

"Praise the Lord."

He leaned with both palms on the counter, looked me in the eye, and laughed. Loud. Then he pushed away and handed me a plate. "Help yourself."

"Why did you just laugh like that?" Using a metal spatula, I placed a cheesy enchilada on my plate and added a scoop of guacamole and a small portion of his homemade salsa.

"I figured you might help me pick out a place."

I pretended I didn't hear him, then lifted my plate and sniffed. "Have you ever thought about opening your own restaurant?"

"No. Why?"

"You cook good enough." I sat down at the table. "And you obviously enjoy it, because you even cook on your days off."

"I cook because I got to eat."

"No. I have to eat, and I never cook."

"You made guacamole."

"Ruthie made it."

He paused, then smiled slowly. "Sounds like you're the one who needs a new job."

I forked a bite of enchilada and blew on it to cool it. "I guess I liked waitressing better than cooking. Talking to the customers, tending to their needs." I shrugged.

Clyde scooped a dollop of salsa onto a chip and put the whole thing in his mouth, but then his chewing slowed, and he got a quizzical expression on his face. He swallowed, set his fork down, took a drink of his tea. "I make salsa all the time. Why would it turn out wrong the one time it matters?"

I smiled, partly because he cared what I thought about his cooking but also because he had given me the opportunity to razz him again. "Could it have been the green tomatoes?"

He stared at the salsa on his plate, poking it with a chip. "Seriously? They were green?"

"Only half of them."

His huge shoulders slumped, and he looked as if he might cry.

"But the enchiladas are great," I said, "and my bean dip ain't too shabby either."

✳✳✳

Thirty minutes later, we were still sitting at Clyde's kitchen table, and our paper plates had been pushed back to make room for sliced peaches. Clyde called the fruit a *light dessert*, but I called them *breakfast*. When he brought out a can of whipped cream and let me spray it over both our bowls, I decided the peaches might be dessert after all.

"This is good," I said as I licked my spoon.

We ate in silence for a few minutes before I poked him for information.

"So," I said, "it's Wednesday night."

"It is."

"You're not at church."

He crouched over his bowl, pushing peaches from one side to the other, silently screaming for me to stop asking.

But I couldn't. "You don't want to face Neil."

His eyes met mine.

"Does Fawn know he threatened you with a restraining order?"

He shrugged.

"You haven't talked to her."

"No need." He finished his last bite, then leaned back in his chair, watching me. "Want to go out to the wind fields later?"

"In the dark?"

"In the moonlight, they kind of remind me of a Mercedes-Benz commercial. Besides, you can see the red lights on top."

It was sweet of him to want to take me out there, even in the dark, and I wondered if he didn't get a little strength from the whispering giants, too. I sighed, wishing I could magically become a windmill, standing quietly on the prairie while the breeze nudged me.

"You doing all right?" Clyde asked.

"I'd be better if I had more of that whipped cream."

He didn't smile. Didn't look away. Just kept staring, but I didn't care. It felt good. Almost as though he had crawled inside my brain, and surprisingly, I liked him there.

I cleared my throat, wishing I was as good at *not talking* as he was. "I'm okay now, but the bad thoughts still come over me when I'm home alone."

"Maybe you shouldn't live alone."

My face warmed, but Clyde pulled his gaze away from me to look out the back window. Probably he didn't mean what it sounded like he meant, but I vividly remembered last Friday night after the football game when he told me we were too old to fiddle around with dating.

"I heard a rumor about Hoby," Clyde said.

A dollop of whipped cream remained in my bowl, and I smashed it with my fork, swirling it until it looked more like milk than cream.

"They're saying there wasn't a body in the truck," he said. "You heard anything like that?"

I tilted my head and nodded twice.

"Did Hector tell you not to tell me?"

"He told me not to tell anyone." But I should have told Clyde. *Clyde doesn't count like everyone else.*

"It's all right, you know."

"Yeah." I shrugged. "Hector seemed confident Hoby's dead, but I don't know what he's basing it on."

"Everyone thinks it was suicide."

I let my eyes wander to the backyard, where the chain-link fence was disappearing in the light of dusk. "You ever thought about suicide?"

One of his shoulders bunched into a shrug. "In prison, sure. Everybody thinks about it."

"But not since you've been home."

"Naw, not in years."

"What made you stop thinking it?"

His eyes turned to slits as he formed an answer, but then they widened. "I just decided life was worth it. Whatever comes, I'll deal with it." He yanked his sleeve to expose his tattoo. "Joshua 1:9."

I shrugged a shoulder gently. "What is that verse?"

"Be strong and courageous. Do not be afraid. The Lord is with you wherever you go."

I chuckled. "Hoby needed that tattoo. Maybe then he wouldn't have killed himself." The breath in my lungs felt as if it might sap all the energy from my spirit, so I released it into the kitchen, feeling momentarily better because of it. I leaned my elbows on the table. "I can't blame him, though. Sometimes I think suicide might be nice."

Clyde took a deep breath, held it, and then let it out slowly. "Are you thinking on doing something?"

Sometimes Clyde could be so daft. "For crying out loud, I'm not going to kill myself." I stacked plates and bowls. "Besides, think what it would do to Velma. And Ruthie."

He spoke so quietly I barely heard him. "And me."

My mind had wandered as I thought about my sister and my daughter. "What?"

His eyebrows puckered. "Think what it would do to me."

"You?"

Then he stared at me again. No words. Nothing but that same unbroken eye contact, so intense I had to look away, but when I did, his hand reached up to my hair, and he pushed a strand over my shoulder.

Thoughts and phrases and arguments spun through my brain like towels in a dryer, but I couldn't think quickly enough to snatch a complete sentence. "You?" I repeated.

He ran the back of his fingers under my chin but still didn't reply. Instead, he leaned over in slow motion and rubbed his lips softly against mine. It wasn't really a kiss. More of a nuzzle. Nothing like Friday night at the football game when we were angry. Nothing like the kiss in the kitchen. And nothing about it seemed spontaneous or accidental. This action felt premeditated and determined and purposeful. This kiss felt like Clyde had been thinking on it for quite a while.

His mouth met mine once more, and I thought he would merely brush against me again, so I didn't move. But instead he pulled my bottom lip with both of his. Gently, playfully, clearly asking a question.

When he leaned back slightly and peered into my eyes, I realized I could hear him even though he wasn't speaking. He was telling me so much without any words at all.

CHAPTER
THIRTY-THREE

Clyde pulled away from his house, hoping Lynda would scoot over to the middle of the seat the way she'd done when he took her to the lake, but of course she didn't. He wondered if she was thinking the same thing and remembering the nightmare of watching Hoby's truck come up out of the water.

He felt like cursing that whole day. Why had he talked about it being their first date? Now she would forever tie negative memories of Hoby's death—or supposed death—to happy memories of their own time together. He wanted to give her another outing to remember. Something they could call their own.

He knew he ought to wait and give her more time to grieve, but he had waited a lifetime already, and now that he had experienced a few happy moments with Lynda, he couldn't bear to do without her much longer.

He coughed. "Seeing as how our first date ended up all strange-like, I decided we need a new first date."

She shifted, and Clyde worried that he had made her uncomfortable. "Thanks for dinner," she said. "It was nice."

"I'm not talking about dinner, Lyn. I want to do something to take your mind off your worries."

"That sounds good to me, but the windmills likely won't have the same effect, since it's pitch-black. There's not even a moon out tonight."

He smiled to himself. Clouds may have covered the moon, hiding the three-hundred-foot giants behind a blanket of darkness, but above their heads, where stars should have shone, was a sea of blinking red lights, which disappeared into the distance. Clyde slowed at a county road and turned off the highway.

"Where are you going?" she asked.

"Maybe we can find a road that'll take us to the base of a turbine. You said you've never seen one up close and personal, right?"

"No." She was quiet for a second. "No, I haven't."

Clyde wasn't sure why, but it suddenly felt like the space between them in the car had doubled in distance. "I thought it would be fun," he said.

"It's too dark to find a road, Clyde."

She didn't say anything else, good or bad, but his spirits fell harder than a mallard shot out of the sky on one of his grandpappy's hunting trips.

In the distance, a bolt of lightning illuminated a bank of clouds, and for an instant, the towering giants were visible. Lynda gasped, then leaned forward with her hands on the dash. "That was cool."

"Kinda creepy, if you ask me," Clyde said. "Like monsters sneaking up on us in the dark."

A flash swept the sky, revealing dozens of rotors surrounding the car.

"Now you see it, now you don't," Lynda sing-songed. "I can't believe I've never been out here in a lightning storm. This is fun."

Clyde laughed. "I was thinking it was sort of like a scary movie. You're thinking it's cool."

"It is cool. Wait … for … it." Another flash caused her to laugh. "This is better than a roller coaster."

"No, it ain't."

"Okay, maybe not, but it's a lot of fun for free."

Clyde caught himself before he said it was a cheap date, worried he would send her cannonballing into silence again. He sighed and smiled and listened to her laugh, and he was incredibly glad he had brought her out there. Not only that, but he knew from now on, he would be driving her down Highway 84 during midnight thunderstorms. He would do almost anything to make her happy, to hear her laugh and see her smile.

He slowed, watching for road signs until he finally found what he was looking for, and then he turned and stopped in front of a metal gate. He put the car in park and reached for the door handle.

"What are you doing?" Lynda asked.

"Opening the gate."

"But it's chained. And this is private property." She leaned across the seat and called after him, but he kept walking, slipping the chain easily from the metal-pipe gate and swinging it against the side fence. As he walked back to the car, he could see her in the glow of the dome light, her mouth parted in curiosity. "Does this have anything to do with Troy Sanders?" she asked.

He slid the gearshift into drive and eased off the brake, his headlights illuminating an arc on the white-rock road as he pulled forward, then stopped again. "Maybe." He got out to shut the gate, and when he got back in, Lynda peppered him with questions.

"Maybe nothing. What did he do? Leave the gate unlocked?" She looked behind them. "He could lose his job for something like that. He's so reckless."

"Troy ain't nearly as reckless as Pam makes him out to be."

"I think his wife would know. She said he's just as irresponsible with the turbines as he is with the volunteer fire department. And we've both heard stories about that."

Clyde held his next words. It would do no good to argue about something neither of them knew much about. Rumor had it that Troy was reckless, but rumor also had it that Pamela was a worry-wart, and Clyde figured both rumors were partially true. Another burst of lightning vibrated, but it was farther away now and didn't produce so much as a giggle from Lynda.

He followed the road straight back, and after a hundred yards or so, it curved to the right. His headlights shone starkly against the white base of a windmill, so close it was almost unrecognizable.

"Why are we here?" Lynda's voice monotoned as he killed the ignition.

He punched the headlights off, and the curved wall of the windmill disappeared. "Troy brought me out here and showed me around. He thought you might like to see inside."

"He thought so, or you thought so?"

Clyde scratched his ear. "Both of us, I guess. We don't have to stay if you don't want to."

He couldn't see her, but from the sound of it, he guessed she had crossed her arms and leaned against the passenger door. Resting his fist on the steering wheel, he leaned forward and peered high above the car where the rotors hummed mechanically, but he couldn't see them. From this angle, he couldn't even see the red light on top. If he hadn't known better, he would have thought they were parked in the middle of an empty field instead of directly beneath a two-million-dollar wind generator.

He reached for the ignition, then hesitated, confused. He had been so sure she would enjoy this little field trip, had thought it would be a happy memory to erase the bad one. He had even hoped for a few kisses, not to mention a lot more smiles. His hand dropped to his knee. "I don't get it, Lyn. Talk to me."

She huffed. "When you said you planned a special date, I didn't think you meant to bring me out here and show me your dream job. Are you going to give me a sales pitch? Because no matter what you say, I'm not going to think you should get a job as a stinking turbine cowboy."

Clyde's nerves settled instantly, and he almost laughed. "What are you saying?"

"Wind technician is one of the most dangerous jobs in West Texas, if not *the* most dangerous. Pam says Troy has to climb onto the very top of those blasted things and walk around up there, as high in the air as a football field is long, and she's terrified every single day." Her voice rose slightly. "I'm sorry, Clyde, but I can't live like that … always worried that you won't make it home in the afternoons. I know I have a lot of baggage that you don't necessarily take into account, but I cannot be the wife of a wind tech." Her voice got faster and faster, and more and more wobbly, and just when Clyde thought she might cry, Lynda shoved open the car door and climbed out, slamming it behind her.

In the brief time the dome light had been on, Clyde noticed her hands were trembling. He took a deep breath and tried to still his own hands. Most of what she had said had no effect on him at all, as though she were hurling cotton balls at him and expecting him to crumple. However, her last five words acted like a shot of adrenaline, peppering him with the possibility of a future. *Wife of a wind tech.* Had she really said that? In reference to the two of them?

He ran his fingers through his hair, then gripped the base of his neck, and an uncontrolled chuckle rose from deep in his throat, startling him into action. Surely she hadn't gone far. They were in the middle of a wind field, for heaven's sake.

He thrust the door open and then leaped to his feet, ready to scan the horizon, but she was leaning on the passenger side of the car, her back and neck glowing from the dome light.

"I didn't mean to say that," she snapped.

Clyde shut his door. She was so cute. So determined. So fragile. He walked around the sedan, letting his fingers trail across the hood, and when he got to the passenger side, he stood in front of her for a few seconds before saying, "I never said I wanted to be a wind tech."

She made a tiny sound but didn't speak.

"I guess I may have told you Troy was talking to me about it, but I never honestly considered it." He put his hands on his hips, still trying to calm his pulse. "You know how it is, Lyn. I've missed too much of my life to go taking risks like that. Besides, they probably wouldn't hire me to do electrician work, since I'm color-blind." He couldn't hold back a soft laugh. "Working the turbines ain't for me. Never was."

Still she didn't say anything, and he searched for what might be holding her back. Then he realized she was embarrassed. She had shown him a teeny part of herself that he hadn't seen before, a frightened, timid part that was desperately afraid of being abandoned. Then she had topped it all off by blubbering about marriage, something Clyde knew she would never deliberately talk about.

He took a step away. "So anyway. You want to see inside now? Troy left it open. We can't do any climbing, of course, but we could look around just the same. Here, I'll show you." He stepped around the front bumper, fumbled with the car door, and then pulled on the headlights. "The door's around at the side."

He walked away from the car, unable to hear her steps over the hum of the rotors, but when he opened the door, she was behind him a few steps, looking away from him like a scared rabbit. "Troy could lose his job for this," she mumbled. "Reckless."

"There's a light in here somewhere, but I don't rightly remember where it is."

Lynda turned on the flashlight app on her cell phone and lit up the circular interior of the tower. Instead of looking for a light switch, her gaze fell on the vertical ladder, and she shone her light straight up, revealing a fraction of the rungs disappearing into the darkness above their heads. "Now that's creepy," she whispered. "Knowing it goes on and on and not being able to see. I feel like someone's up there, spying on us."

"You watch too many scary shows." Clyde found the switch, and when the lights came on, they both startled, and Lynda gasped.

"Man, that's taller than I expected." She laughed. "I feel so small, don't you?"

"I reckon I do, for once in my life."

They stood side by side, Lynda gazing upward at the enormity of the monster's belly they had crawled into, and Clyde gazing downward at the smile on her face. When she noticed him, she blushed. "So did Troy let you climb?"

"He took me up to the first landing. See it there?" He pointed. "But I made sure that reckless rascal used all the appropriate safety precautions."

Her gaze bounced around the enclosure. "Like what?"

"Harnesses, lines, locks, hooks." He shrugged. "I'm not sure what all the stuff was."

She bit her lip, then timidly put a hand on the ladder. "Can I?"

"You're kidding me," he said. "How far?"

"As far as I can." She gripped the metal and started climbing up the rungs, one after another, hand over hand, not quickly but fast enough that Clyde got nervous. She seemed to be climbing up a swinging bell rope. Her giggles echoed to the top of the tower and back down again.

"Uh ... Lyn?"

She slowed to a stop, then looked down at him. "Whoa." She clung to the side rail. "I see why they say don't look down. I think that's far enough."

Her Converse sneakers were just above Clyde's head, and he moved to the other side of the ladder and climbed the first two rungs so he could rest his hand on her thigh. "Go slow." She stepped down, and his hand met her waist before they backed down together.

When Lynda was safely on the bottom rung, she stopped there and looked through the ladder where he stood opposite her. Their faces were level with each other, and she smiled. "This is a good date, Clyde. Thanks for bringing me here."

He shook his head, feigning exasperation. "I would've left you at the trailer if I'd known how reckless you were going to be."

She reached through the ladder, hooked her finger on the neck of his T-shirt, and tugged, and when she covered her mouth with his, he felt her smile again. Silly girl, what on earth had given her the impression he wanted to work with Troy? He had never told her that, but then again, there were a lot of things he had never told her.

She pulled away, then stepped off the ladder, and he felt the distance as if it were a solid wall of steel, but then she came to him and melted into his embrace. She pressed her cheek against his chest and slipped her arms around his waist. Even though he couldn't see her face, he thought she might still be smiling, because everything felt so natural, as if for once she wasn't holding anything back.

She looked up at him. "You know what I said before?"

He wasn't entirely sure which thing she meant, but he imagined it was the five words that were still exploding in his head. Or really just the one word. *Wife.* Because the others were irrelevant now. "Yeah?"

"Can you just forget I said that?"

Her eyes drooped on the edges, and she looked like a woman who had been through hell over the past week—exhausted, unsure, and afraid. But also happy.

Without a doubt, Clyde would remember those five words as long as he lived, but he pulled her close and kissed the top of her head. "I can forget you said it, Lyn ... but only for a while."

She nodded, and her body relaxed into his.

CHAPTER
THIRTY-FOUR

"You working today, Lyn?"

Clyde had persisted in asking me that, but now I could finally say yes. Three days off had stretched Dixie's bereavement limit, and she had gently but firmly told me it was time to come back to work. I didn't mind. Even though I felt more comfortable at home, I couldn't afford the time off without pay. "I'm working this morning, and the lunch shift tomorrow."

I sat on the passenger seat of his sedan, but I had no idea where we were going. He had knocked on my door and invited me to breakfast, but then he clammed up. Surely he wouldn't take me to the DQ or the diner, and other than the Allsup's convenience store, there were no other options. He had already passed his street, so the trailer house was out of the question, and he was headed north, the opposite direction of the wind fields.

He nodded. "Tomorrow, will you get off in time to go to the game in Tahoka?"

"Give me a break. You're lucky I'm going to work." He was lucky I was going to breakfast with him. Clyde had become a healing tonic to my nerves. Every time I was with him, the darkness lifted a tiny bit, and when he kissed me, my doubts were banished to the back side of my heart, where I could easily forget they existed. "Where we headed?" I asked again.

He didn't answer, just kept driving north, past the city-limit signs and on toward Lubbock.

"I have to be at work in an hour." We couldn't make it to town and back in that time, but surely Clyde knew that.

"Yep." He flipped on his blinker, and as it clinked, I cringed. He was turning east on the gravel road at the top of the Caprock, and I knew immediately what he had in mind. We meandered down the small lane, around the curve that inched too close to the drop-off, then parked in front of his grandpappy's old house.

My fingers clenched the seat cushions. Clyde hadn't brought me to his family's home place until I got all stupid and called myself his wife. What had come over me? He probably got the impression I sat around dreaming about white dresses, when actually my comment had startled me as much as it seemed to startle him. I didn't want to be his wife. *Did I?* Now it felt as if we were barreling toward marriage with the speed of an out-of-control locomotive.

But still … the property was breathtaking.

The house sat near the rim of the Caprock, and I looked across the rolling plains, hundreds of feet below us. The northern Cap, free of the windmills I loved so much, had an unpolluted beauty that I had always found mesmerizing. "This view is amazing, Clyde. You should be proud you own something like this."

"You like it?"

"Who wouldn't?" I turned to smile at him, surprised to realize his gaze was fixed on the run-down house. "No," I said quickly. "I was talking about the land and the view. You should tear the house down."

He snatched a paper sack from the seat between us, then opened his car door. "Funny."

The shack, originally built as a home for ranch hands, had seen at least a hundred summers. The weathered wood siding stood exposed to wind, rain, and insects, and tattered curtains—probably left there when Fawn moved—gently fluttered behind broken window panes.

I followed Clyde, high-stepping the tall grass and gingerly picking my way across the rotting plank porch. The house lay in stark contrast to the grandeur of the landscape, seeming grossly out of place.

"You're going in?" My nose wrinkled, but then I felt bad. This had been his grandfather's place. Surely Clyde had all kinds of memories here. Happy ones.

"Why wouldn't I?" He pushed the door open without turning the knob.

A few pieces of furniture had been left in the living room, but they did nothing to make the place feel homey. The cushions of a floral loveseat had been ripped apart and chewed, evidently forming a nest for an animal, and an odor radiated from the woven rug spotted with brown and white droppings. When I heard a rustling sound in the next room, I scurried back outside, and Clyde followed me.

We walked silently back to the car, and I nudged his shoulder. "Found any more rattlers out here?"

"I reckon a few are making their way back. It's been a year since we gassed the den."

"This place just gets better and better."

"It ain't that bad, Lyn." He looked back at the structure, his eyes following the roofline. "In fact, I'm thinking about moving up here."

I scrutinized his face to see if he was serious. "It's not fit to live in."

"Fawn was here just a few months ago."

"It was almost a year, and the storm that ran through last spring did a number on the place."

He crossed his arms. "It's still standing."

"Barely." I jabbed the word at him, but it did no good to argue with the man. He was as hardheaded as a Brahma bull.

He still held the paper sack, and now he set it on the hood of the trunk. "Homemade blueberry muffins and fresh-squeezed orange juice."

"Homemade?" I asked. "Fresh-squeezed?"

He ducked his head, and I stared at the covered plastic container and two travel mugs, *knowing I should have been flattered.* Instead, a twinge of panic returned as I calculated how early he would've gotten up to cook.

"Well … thanks," I said. "It's so nice of you to do this … for me."

He leaned against the bumper. "I know what you're thinking."

"What am I thinking?"

He took a drink of juice, and I could tell he didn't want to say whatever he was about to say. "It's too much."

I scooted back to sit on the hood next to him, then reached for a muffin. Yes, it was too much. Good grief, Hoby had only just died. *Sort of.* Maybe. But as I sat there nibbling the best blueberry muffin I had ever tasted, I wanted—more than anything—for it to not be too much, and I longed for the day I would be able to handle things. To handle Clyde. "It's just breakfast," I mumbled.

We ate in silence then, side by side, each of us lost in our own thoughts while the sun crept up the sky. I tilted my face to absorb its warm rays and thought what a perfect morning it had been. Beautiful view, sunny weather, and Clyde. Lifting a palm, I shaded my eyes so I could see him. "You should open up a restaurant here."

He laughed once, hard, like a bullet.

"You could have an outdoor deck for seating right on the rim of the Cap, and an indoor dining room with floor-to-ceiling windows. It would be perfect." I poked his leg with my fingertip. "You can't work at the DQ forever."

"Come on, Lyn."

"You have a dead-end job."

He leaned forward, intentionally shielding me from the sun, and when his shadow fell across my eyes, I could see the scowl on his face. "How is my job any different from yours?"

I started to spout off a retort, but nothing came to mind. Finally I shrugged. "I guess the only difference is I'm not content with mine."

"So you're thinking on looking for something else then?"

He was shoving the discomfort right back at me. "I don't know," I confessed. "I'm not sure what I would do. No reason to switch jobs if it's not a good fit." I reached down and tugged on a blade of tall grass, then slapped it gently against my thigh. "But think of it ... You could have a dining room, or a deck, right on the rim of the Cap. And you're a darn good cook."

"I can't even tell when steak is done." He glared at a prickly-pear cactus three feet away and ignored the expansive view that I couldn't pull my gaze away from. "I can't even tell the difference between bean dip and guacamole."

"You don't need to do those things. I googled it."

"Why would you google it?"

"Because you cook really, really good."

His frown deepened, but around the edges, I thought I saw a smile.

"Real chefs check steak by touch," I said, "not color."

"Naw ..."

"They touch it and see how firm it is or something." I slid off the hood. "There are even blind chefs. Famous ones. And if a blind person can cook, you ought to be able to manage it."

He rubbed his palm across his cheek and down his chin, making a scratchy-whisker sound. "What about vegetables?"

"You learn to tell the difference. Green tomatoes are bound to be more firm than ripe ones." I rolled my eyes. "Or you could just get someone to help you. You're using your color blindness as an excuse."

He gazed unseeingly at the cactus, and I imagined him mentally cooking a steak and checking to see if it was done. Then his eyebrows bounced, and a corner of his mouth inched upward. "I can't think of anyone who would help me."

I punched him on the shoulder, but after a few chuckles, he sobered again.

"There's not room enough," he said. "Not for parking and all that."

"There would be if you tore down the house."

"I can't tear down the house."

I inspected the shack one more time. The wasp nests under the eaves, the missing board on the porch, the holes in the roof. "You could just wait for it to fall down."

"If anything, I'll repair it."

"You can't be serious."

"Lyn, I've got a lot of memories here." He winced as though the statement caused him pain.

"Your grandpappy?"

He paused. "And Fawn."

"Fawn wouldn't get her feelings hurt if you let it go. It's not like she comes out here and reminisces about her unmarried pregnancy days."

He resealed his travel mug, then slipped it into the sack. "I'm surprised Neil hasn't torn it down already."

"What?" I asked. "Neil's all lovey-dovey with Fawn now. I think he's forgotten she was ever out here."

"There you go defending him again."

A bolt of lightning charged through my nerve endings. "I've already told you I can't stand him, and I wouldn't—"

"I saw Neil's letters, Lyn. Sunday when I made the sandwiches."

For a split second I couldn't think what he was talking about. *Letters?* But then I remembered him in my bedroom, and the letters had probably been on the nightstand. I wiped my hands on my pants, but they were so sweaty, they slid across the brown polyester like an ice-skater on frozen mud.

His eyes were pleading with me, begging for an explanation, but I didn't want to explain. I wasn't even sure I could. For years I'd guarded those old letters, kept them hidden from Ruthie, pulled them out of the trash dozens of times. I had no idea why. I certainly didn't want them, didn't want to need them.

But if I didn't answer, Clyde's gaze would suffocate me. "It's not Neil I'm hung up on," I said.

He let my response float on the breeze for a few seconds. "Explain?"

"Maybe it's the idea of him. Or the echo of a teenage girl's broken dream."

"Like … first love?"

If the earth had opened right then and swallowed me alive, I wouldn't have minded, but I kept looking him in the eye, determined to beat this part of my demon. "I guess so. First love is different from the rest, you know? It's like I had an image of what the perfect life would be, and then it shattered."

"And you think nothing else can be as good as your time with Neil?"

"No!" I glared at him. "It has more to do with me not letting go of the fairy tale."

He looked away from me then, back to his precious house. "Do you still love him?"

I couldn't breathe. "I don't know if I ever loved him. Neil is a selfish user, but I loved the way he made me feel—important, necessary, loved—so I'm just as selfish as he is. But those letters represent my life when it fell apart, and I keep them to remind myself that happiness is only an illusion."

Clyde studied the front window, his gaze tracing the outlines of the panes. Maybe he was unwilling to look at me. Maybe he no longer wanted to.

"There's another reason I keep them," I admitted, knowing Clyde might never look at me again once I explained it. "I wrote Neil a letter once. Pretty much like the one he wrote me."

Finally Clyde's eyes stilled, focusing on the front door. "When?"

"Right after he married Susan. I was insane with emotion. One week we were shopping for rings, the next week he was married and building a huge house on her father's ranch." I shook my head. "I thought I would die."

"So did I." Clyde hummed low in his chest. "I lost Susan and the baby and my life, all on the same day."

"But in the end"—words spilled from my lips like water gushing from a garden hose—"Neil couldn't give up all those material possessions and the status. He refused to get an annulment, yet he expected me to be there for him—in every way a man expects a woman to be there. But he didn't know me as well as he thought." I snickered. "My anger consumed me until I couldn't see straight, and to retaliate against him for what he had done … I married one of his best friends."

Clyde closed his eyes as though he didn't want to hear more, but so far I hadn't told him much that he didn't already know. "So you didn't love Hoby?" he asked.

"Not when I married him, no." I tossed the rest of my muffin in the paper sack and rolled the top down over itself, not really paying attention to what I was doing. "Most people marry for love, but I married Hoby because of hate. Hate for Neil. I wanted to hurt that man as badly as he had hurt me, and the only way to do it was to give someone else what he wanted for himself." My body trembled as I relived the emotions from all those years ago, but then I calmed, right along with my memories. "But something happened that I didn't expect."

Clyde smiled, as if he knew what I would say next.

"I fell in love with him." An uncontrolled, airy breath laughed from my lungs. "I didn't see it coming, you know? We had always been good friends, and we knew each other so well, I guess the love just came on naturally. It started right after I got pregnant, but by the time Ruthie was born … I loved him desperately."

"So why did he leave?"

"Neil lied to him."

"But why did Hoby believe him?"

My teeth ground against each other, and I deliberately relaxed my jaw, knowing I'd end up with a headache if I didn't calm down. "Apparently Neil kept my letter, too." I smiled at Clyde so I wouldn't cry. "When Ruthie was seven, he showed it to Hoby and told him I had just sent it. He told Hoby I'd been unfaithful and that Ruthie was his child, not Hoby's."

Clyde's head jerked as he looked at me.

"But I still keep all the letters. Isn't that moronic? Neil ruined my marriage with a letter, yet I cling to its twin like a crazy woman. It doesn't make any sense," I whispered. "I torture myself with them."

"It makes sense." Clyde pulled me against his chest. "They're like some kind of psychological token or something. You're scared to live, Lyn. You're scared of the risks, and those letters are your excuse to keep hiding."

CHAPTER
THIRTY-FIVE

Clyde dropped me off at the diner, promising he'd be waiting when I got off work. Even though I still regretted my *wife* slip, my anxiety had eased tremendously, just since breakfast. The speed at which my life was hurtling through the various stages of my comfort zones was enough to give me motion sickness, but all I could do was hold on tight and hope for the best.

"You doin' all right?" Dixie's chin jutted forward cautiously.

"I'm fine, Dix." I tied my apron. "Been a strange week, though."

She frowned, seeming to evaluate my honesty. "Well ... it's good to have you back." She flipped sausage patties on the griddle. "I'm about ready to thrash that new girl. She doesn't know the difference between tater tots and hash browns, and when I asked her to work an extra shift, you'd have thought I was forcing her into slave labor."

"She'll get the hang of it soon enough."

"Actually, she won't." Dixie's eyebrows lifted like two hot-air balloons. "She got all huffy last night and quit on the spot."

"That right?"

"I say we're better off without her. Might take a few days to find a replacement, though."

I squirted soap in my palm, then paused before I turned on the tap. "Put me down for extra shifts till you hire someone."

"Aw, Lynda. You sure about that?"

"It'll be good to stay busy right now. Too much to think about." Clyde would say I was hiding—and Clyde would be right—but he would undoubtedly agree that hiding at my workplace was an improvement from hiding in my house.

He knew me well, and I felt like a teenager with a crush. Last night when Clyde cooked dinner at his house, I had still felt awkward with him, but when we went to the wind fields after dark, his gentle ways put me at ease. And during breakfast this morning at his property on the Cap, I had felt like I was returning home after a long absence. It was ridiculous, really. Less than twenty-four hours after our enchiladas and guacamole, I couldn't imagine going a day without seeing him. But I wasn't ready to tell him that. I was ready to do some other things, though.

Like change.

Like grow stronger.

Like become the person a wife should be.

The cowbell on the door jangled, and I glanced into the dining room to see the same three Rangers who had been in before. This time they had twice as many eager-eyed Scouts with them, banging chairs and pulling tables together. "Better put on more sausage," I called to Dixie.

I pulled a mixing bowl down from a shelf and began cracking eggs into it. I would add a touch of milk plus salt and pepper, then whisk it before scrambling them. I wondered how Clyde cooked eggs. All I ever did in the kitchen was exactly what Dixie had taught me the first week I started cooking for her. Never once did I consider changing her recipes or trying something new. I had no inclination to do that at all, but it was different with Clyde. The man had a knack for cooking, and he didn't even seem to try. I reached for the salt.

"Hey, there! Lynda, isn't it?"

I startled so badly, I dropped the shaker in the bowl of eggs.

The Ranger with the raccoon tan around his eyes was leaning through the pass-through window. A spray bottle of vinegar water sat on the Formica ledge, and he scooted it over so he could lean on his elbows. "Where you been hiding?"

With my thumb and forefinger, I fished the plastic shaker out of the runny mess, wondering what made the idiot think he was welcome behind Dixie's counter. "Oh, you know ... here and there."

"You working all day?" The way he was leaning caused his shoulders to bunch around his ears like a turtle.

Dixie bustled to the window and stood protectively between the two of us, her eyes level with his, since the man was leaning over. "Looks like you boys have a crowd working with you today," she said.

"One more weekend out here." Raccoon Man stretched to peer at me before focusing on Dixie. "We're making a last-ditch effort to find the rest of those bones, or a grave, or something. Without the rest of them, there's no murder case, I reckon. They can't make a positive ID leastways, even though the sheriff has his suspicions."

I walked to the sink, out of sight of the window, and rinsed my hands. The egg felt slimy on my skin, and I tossed the shaker in the trash instead of washing it.

Dixie continued to probe for information. "How will it make a difference? I heard there wasn't enough DNA because the bones were too old."

He chuckled, and from the sound of it, I imagined him thrusting out his chest like an overconfident wild turkey, just before a hunter fills him full of shot. "We've got an anthropology team down in Austin, and if we find the skull, they'll be able to extract DNA from the teeth."

"But don't they have to have something to match it to? Hair from a hairbrush or something?"

"Oh, they've got something to match it to, believe me."

"No kidding?"

"Now, see there? You made me tell a secret." His voice lilted, and I realized he was flirting with Dixie now, regardless of their age difference. "They're just figuring it to be the fella that owned that truck in the lake. Most likely a suicide, but I speculate his old lady could have knocked him off. Like maybe she got him good and drunk, then sent his truck off that cliff with him in it. But that's just between you and me, 'cause—"

Dixie snatched the spray bottle from the ledge and squirted the Ranger full in the face. "You best get on back to your table, young man."

He coughed and sputtered. "What the—"

She sprayed him again. "Go on now. Git!"

Suddenly I wasn't so glad to be back at work.

Dixie slammed the bottle on the counter and glared through the window. "Don't pay him no mind, Lynda."

From where I stood at the sink, I was hidden from the dining room, but if I took a step in either direction, I would be exposed, and that man would be talking about me—even if he didn't know I was the *old lady.* I felt cemented to the sink, unable to move in either direction. Maybe others in the dining room had already heard his accusation. *Am I a suspect?* Would they arrest me just on suspicion? I didn't know what was reality and what was drama from the television shows I watched.

I rinsed my hands one more time, wishing I could wash away the grime of gossip that seemed to taint me no matter what I did, and then I slapped them against my thighs to dry, trying to mask how badly they were shaking. "Another day, another difficulty."

"The man's a cockroach," Dixie growled.

"Clearly." Returning to my scrambled eggs, I did my best to go about my work as if nothing had happened. A lot of good it would do if I crumpled into a frazzled mess right there in front of my boss. I considered tossing the eggs and starting over with a fresh batch that hadn't been tainted by a salt shaker, not to mention my hands, but when I remembered they would be going to the Rangers and Scouts, I changed my mind. The eggs were good enough.

I poured the thick liquid onto the griddle and busied myself, stirring with a spatula.

"Are they really saying I killed him?" I asked Dixie.

"Most people are banking on suicide." She lowered her voice almost apologetically. "But I reckon a few people around town have wondered as much."

Maybe Dixie had wondered as much.

I scraped the eggs and flipped them over, but without thinking, I kept slicing and chopping until they looked more like rice than eggs.

"Dixie?" A tentative voice called from the doorway between the kitchen and dining room. "My cinnamon rolls ready?" Pamela Sanders stood in the doorway between the kitchen and dining room.

"Sure thing, Pam, come on back."

"I don't want to bother you girls, but ..." She came at me with palms outstretched, giving me a thorough hug. "Lynda, I didn't know you were back at work. Good for you, girl."

I smiled. At least it felt like a smile.

Dixie pulled the cinnamon rolls from the oven. "Say, how are things over at the Trapp Door?"

"Couldn't be better." Pam stuffed herself into a corner near the dining-room doorway, settling in for a talk with her old friend. "Just got the coffee bar going yesterday, and last night I programmed the Keurig to start this morning, so when I open up at ten o'clock, the place should smell like hazelnut." She giggled. "Corky Ledbetter and a few friends have planned a mothers' get-together, and they asked me to pull out all the books I've got for preschoolers. Won't they be surprised? Coffee and cinnamon rolls."

For a moment I mentally abandoned my scrambled eggs and the humid kitchen of Dixie's Diner, where everyone might or might not have been talking about me. Instead, I was sitting on the soft couch in the back room of the Trapp Door. The scent of hazelnut coffee blended with the mustiness of the old books, and I bit into a warm cinnamon roll. I decided Pam might be onto something.

My cell rang in my pocket. "Sorry, Dixie, I forgot to turn it off."

"No worries." Dixie sounded funny, as if she could undo the weirdness of the Ranger's comments simply by raising the pitch of her voice to a level of fake.

I pulled my phone out to silence it but then noticed it was Velma. I glanced at Dixie.

"Sure, hon." She waved a pot holder. "Go right ahead."

Lifting the phone to my ear, I asked briskly, "Hey, what's up, Velma?" My sister rarely called me in the mornings anymore, since Ansel stayed home now, keeping her company.

"Can you come?" she asked quietly. "I need you to come."

"Um ..."

Pam's eyebrows bunched together as she listened to my side of the conversation. She mouthed the words "Everything okay?"

I shrugged. "I'm at the diner, but I can come by when I get off."

Velma didn't answer, but Pam waved her hand and bounced a little, as if she needed to go to the bathroom.

"Velma, do you want Pam to come over and sit with Ansel for a while?" I cut my eyes toward Pam, and she gave me a thumbs-up.

"Pam?" Velma asked. "Pam's a sweet girl."

Through the doorway, I noticed the Boy Scouts crowding around one table as two of them arm-wrestled. Chairs scraped against the floor, creating a momentary ruckus. I shoved my finger in my opposite ear and lowered my head so I could hear her. "Velma, is something wrong?"

"Ansel's gone." Her voice held a tinge of a whine.

"He's what?" Surely I hadn't heard her right. "What do you mean he's gone? Where did he go?"

The noise level increased as a skinny boy outwrestled a stocky one, and then there was a quiet lull.

"He's dead," Velma said.

I pressed my fingers to my lips, and Pamela and Dixie came to stand in front of me as I swallowed a sob.

Velma whimpered on the phone. "I don't know what to do, Lynda."

A mere twenty minutes ago, I had told myself I wanted to be more brave and bold, but now I changed my mind. Velma didn't know what to do. My sister, who had raised nine children and easily managed a farmhouse at the same time, was suddenly at a loss.

She sounded calm but deceivingly so. "He's just ... *here.*"

The room seemed to close in, darkening around the edges like an old photograph. Ansel couldn't be dead. He had doctors' appointments scheduled. And treatment options to consider. Home health hadn't even scheduled a preliminary consult.

"I'll be right there." I pulled my phone away from my ear and held it at arm's length. I stood dazed before Pam and Dixie, my eyes focused on Pam's concho belt. "She said Ansel's just *there*, and she doesn't know what to do. But of course she doesn't know what to do. It's a dead body ... probably lying in the recliner ... and it's *Ansel.*"

I couldn't think or reason or move, but then Pam's gentle arm went around my shoulders, pulling me into one of her side hugs, but this time, it didn't bother me nearly as much as before. "Shh. It's all right, Lynda. It's natural."

I shivered. "It's not natural for me. And not for Velma."

"I know, sweetie. Dixie and me? We'll call nine-one-one, and the volunteer fire department will meet you there. They'll know how to handle it. They'll tend to Ansel, and you can take care of Velma."

"Okay, Pam." I wiped wetness from my cheeks, and my gaze swept the kitchen. "I can't leave the diner. The new girl quit." The statement sounded absurd yet sensible at the same time.

"I'll help out here." Pam's head jerked toward Dixie, who nodded firmly and pulled her phone out of her apron.

"But Corky's coming to the Trapp Door," I mumbled.

"That's not your worry, hon," Pamela said. "I'll call Corky, and she'll call the other mothers. They'll understand." She squeezed my hands. "Go take care of Velma. She needs you."

It felt as if I had rusty gears in my brain that wouldn't allow my thoughts to flow, but in spite of it, I knew I needed to get to Velma, and I needed to hurry. I stumbled toward the doorway, pulling at my apron, which seemed to be knotted.

Dixie talked into her phone, telling the dispatcher that Ansel Pickett had died out at his home place. Pam walked with me toward the front door, patting me and speaking soft, soothing words. The Boy Scouts kept arm wrestling as if the world hadn't just ended.

Ansel couldn't be gone.

My feet stopped working before I got to the door, and I turned to Pamela, hating the tears that streamed down my face. "I don't even have a car," I said. "Clyde dropped me off."

Pam thrust her keys into my hand. "You can do this, Lynda. You can." She waved me away, wiping the tears in her own eyes. "Go, now," she said. "Just go."

CHAPTER
THIRTY-SIX

Clyde couldn't believe Ansel was dead. He had seen the body yesterday, stood by as paramedics covered it with a sheet. He had felt the stark emptiness in the house, and still he couldn't believe it. *He couldn't believe the timing.* The Pickett family, Lynda and Ruthie in particular, were already devastated by troubles, and they didn't need a death to deal with. They needed Ansel. Everyone had always said Velma held the family together, but now Clyde could see that Ansel himself had been the Krazy Glue. He had been Velma's strength, and together they had formed an unbreakable unit of family love.

A scorpion crawled past Clyde's boot as he leaned against the hood of his sedan. In the fading sunlight, he sat in the parking lot of the Tahoka High School football stadium among a sea of cars painted with festive shoe polish and window paint. But Clyde felt no excitement for the game. Even as he listened to the announcer blare details of the Panther-Bulldog showdown, he found his mind wandering.

He nudged the scorpion with his toe, causing it to curl its tail until it resembled a ballerina holding a pistol above her head. The scorpion froze, held a threatening pose, and waited for him.

Clyde didn't want to be at a football game a day after watching Ansel's body being taken away from his home and his family. He wanted to be with Lynda, holding her, sheltering her, keeping anyone else from hurting her ever again. When Velma's kids had started arriving in town, Lynda had gone back to her own house, and Clyde wanted to go there now, but JohnScott had asked him to go to the game. Even though the assistant coaches were sure to text JohnScott the stats, the coach still wanted a closer connection to his team.

He wants you to go because he can't, Lynda had said softly.

Yep.

Clyde had mentioned that she could come, too, but she had been understandably distant. She could barely muster the strength to eat her dinner, much less get out and go to an athletic event. She wasn't hiding this time, though. She was just tired.

He pulled his boot away from the scorpion, giving it the same distance Lynda needed, and gradually the ballerina lowered her pistol. But she didn't fully relax. Instead, her eight legs picked across the gravel until she lay positioned toward Clyde with her pincers lifted. If scorpions could sniff the air, then that one was doing it.

A movement at the gate of the stadium caught Clyde's attention, and he noticed Susan making her way toward him. She inched past the cars next to him, moving sideways, then took two long steps and stopped at his side.

"Susan."

When she didn't speak right away, Clyde felt the urge to get in his car and leave. No telling what she was up to, but whatever it was, he didn't need it.

"I'm sorry about Ansel," she muttered.

"Yeah, it's no good."

"And I'm sorry about the way Neil's been acting."

Clyde felt foolish. As if they were some sort of secret-service spy team meeting in a darkened alley and speaking in code. He didn't answer.

"He's obsessed with keeping you away from Fawn, to the extent he's not even thinking straight."

"Okay."

"He's never been able to share. I'm not sure it even has anything to do with Nathan. He just doesn't want you to have anything to do with his daughter."

Clyde frowned at Susan's strappy high-heeled sandals, then ground the heel of his boot into the scorpion. "Whose daughter?"

One of her sandals crunch-crunch-crunched the gravel. "You're right. She's not his daughter, but you've got to admit, he has a bond with her, even if it's weak. He figures if he keeps you away from the baby, you won't have any reason to be near Fawn." She hesitated. "But he's always underestimated you."

Clyde shifted his jaw. "He didn't want a relationship with her until I came home."

"Neil never does anything without being provoked. If he doesn't feel threatened in some way, he can't make a decision to save his life."

He glanced at Susan with her too-big hair and suddenly felt a mixture of disgust and pity. How had he ever thought he loved her?

It seemed so long ago, and his memories were as dark and foggy as a reflection in an antique mirror, but it was high time he made things right. "Susan, I'm sorry for the trouble I caused you back then."

Her hand fluttered to her throat like one of those helpless Civil War ladies in a big hoopskirt, but she shook her head as forcefully as a modern teenager. "I'm the one who should apologize. I was too weak to stand up for myself, and I did just what my father told me to do. My actions were deplorable, as were my family's."

"We were both at fault, I reckon."

A lone trumpet from the stadium blared a few notes, and Clyde's thoughts were momentarily overpowered by the brassy tune. Maybe his memories were overpowered, too. Twenty-two years ago, Susan hadn't been what he thought—she was weak—but life had dealt her a hard hand, and she had grown stronger because of it.

"Since my wedding day," she said, "I've learned a lot about my husband." Her unblinking eyes became two black olives floating in cups of milk. "He was raised in a stiff environment, and I'm not sure he knows how to be civil." She flinched. "I mean … most people don't know him, really. Underneath all the pain."

"Pain?"

"I think he feels enormous guilt."

"You think or you know?"

She flicked her wrist. "After years of counseling to deal with my own guilt, I think I recognize the symptoms."

Clyde lowered his gaze to the gravel.

"Think about it," she said. "You and I made one mistake when we were young, and it changed our lives forever." She glared at him. "How is Neil any different? He made one decision when he was young, and every other bad decision he's made since then was connected to the first one. All because guilt can influence a person's choices and corrode his mind."

Clyde wasn't sure he liked where her train of thought was leading, but he didn't say as much.

"And of course his mistakes have affected you and me," she said.

"And Fawn and Nathan."

"And JohnScott and Lynda and Ruthie, and the list goes on, but back when he was twenty-one?" Susan shook her head. "He had no way of knowing the chain of events he was setting in place—the domino effect. When he took my father's money and let them send you to prison, he felt more guilt than one person can bear. Trust me."

"Are you saying he has no choice now?"

"No," she said swiftly. "I'm just saying I understand, and … I'm scared for him, Clyde."

He squinted at her, wondering.

"He's not been himself lately." She looked over her shoulder. "I think he may be in trouble."

"What kind of trouble?" Clyde wouldn't doubt it if she told him Neil was guilty of tax evasion or embezzlement or some other white-collar crime his lawyers could cover up for him.

"It's probably nothing, really. He just seems nervous and sort of paranoid." Her thin shoulders lifted and fell helplessly. "Sometimes I think he's having a breakdown."

Clyde peered down at the dead curls of the scorpion, so small and helpless now, but he could think of nothing to say to Susan. She had ignored him for two years, and he had avoided her right back.

Now her openness and determination caught him off guard. "You understand him." Clyde nodded. "And you stay."

"I stay?"

She sounded surprised, but she shouldn't have been. She stayed. She cared. She understood Neil.

"I love him." Her confession whooshed from her lips like a quickly deflating balloon, but as she continued, the airflow got slower and slower until it petered down to a near whisper. "I couldn't tell you why or how or even when, but I love him." She bowed her head. "Sure, there have been times I almost left. Times when I should have for Fawn's sake. Back then I stayed out of fear or obligation or piety. But now? Now I simply stay."

"I'm glad for you." *Maybe.* "Is that why you came over here?"

"No." She peered at the top row of bleachers, to the flags of the Bulldog band. She studied them as though they might blow away in a windstorm, and then she shivered. "Clyde"—her voice was scratchy and faltering—"I heard something up in the stands."

"Yeah?"

"There's a troop of Boy Scouts up there. They've been working with the Rangers out at the lake." She lowered her voice. "They found the rest of those bones at Picnic Hollow."

Clyde shifted, gripping the edge of the hood. "Picnic Hollow? We were just out there." His eyes were trained on Susan, but his mind was racing with thoughts of Lynda. He had to get back to Trapp before she heard this from someone else, but something occurred to him. "So it's not Hoby. That's way too far from the truck site." Relief eased his mind. Relief that Lynda wouldn't have to deal with another visit from Hector, wouldn't have to wait for the results of DNA tests, wouldn't have to be the center of any more of the craziness. But then he faltered. This meant she was still married. He pushed away from the car, shoving the thought from his mind. That didn't matter right now. He dug in his pocket for his keys.

"No, Clyde." Susan's hair-sprayed fuzz quivered as she shook her head. "The Rangers are still running tests to see if it's him."

He blinked, trying to make sense of what she was saying. "So these bones don't go with the others? These are out of the truck?"

"They go together," she snapped. "They found everything except the thigh and pelvic bone."

He shook his head. "There's no way an animal could have dragged the bones that far. It's miles away from the truck."

"Clyde." She dragged his name out, grating on his nerves. "They said the body was wedged in a deep crevice and covered with rocks."

He frowned. "Well, it ain't Hoby, then. He drove his truck off a cliff."

"You don't understand." Susan's entire body shook from shoulders to knees, and her voice took on an annoying whine. "They're saying Hoby may have been murdered."

A dull ringing in Clyde's ears overpowered the sounds of the game. "Murdered?"

"I think I should go to the sheriff. I think I should talk to him."

"What would you have to say to Hector?"

She paced the length of the front bumper, her ankles wobbling in her high heels. "Hoby came back once," she blurted. "Years ago. He showed up on our doorstep asking for Neil." She stopped in front of Clyde again but kept her gaze on the windshield of the sedan. "They left the house together."

A knot formed in Clyde's stomach, and he felt even more desperate to get back to Lynda. "Where did they go?"

"Neil said he followed him into town, and they got a cup of coffee and talked." Her hands fluttered again. "But Neil was gone for hours."

Clyde paused with his hand on the door handle. "Are you accusing Neil?"

"I don't know what to think. They don't even know if that's Hoby out there, so maybe I shouldn't go to Hector. Neil's already stressed, and I don't know how much more he can take." She nibbled a painted fingernail. "I'm afraid for him, Clyde."

He stared at her, disgusted and itching to get away where he wouldn't have to listen to her self-centeredness, her ever-present tendency to look out for herself, her inability to see past the end of her nose. Susan may have grown stronger through the course of her marriage, but she would always have a selfish streak. Even while she accused her husband of murder, she couldn't fathom that he might be a danger to someone else.

"Susan?" Clyde opened the car door. "You should be afraid for all of us."

CHAPTER
THIRTY-SEVEN

"Lyn? You here?"

"In the kitchen." And I didn't have the strength to open the door for Clyde. He let himself in and followed my voice to where I sat at the kitchen table with my head resting on my arms. My life was spinning out of control, and I couldn't catch my breath.

He touched the middle of my spine.

"Pam called." I held up my cell phone, then let my hand fall back to the table. I sat up slowly. "What did you hear?"

Clyde sat hesitantly in the chair catty-corner from me, and I remembered the last time he had sat there. The night I told him he was moving too fast. He glanced at the oven, and I wondered if he was thinking the same thing. Frozen pizza, ranch dressing, and our first kiss.

"They found the rest of the skeleton," he said, "and they're testing it to see if it's Hoby. From the sound of it, they're assuming it's him." Clyde studied me. "Are you okay talking about this?"

Of course not. I hated hearing Hoby's name attached to such a gruesome conversation, but in the past week, I'd had so many gruesome conversations, it almost seemed routine. "I'm fine."

He leaned back in his chair. "I don't understand why they can run DNA tests now, but they couldn't on those other two bones. Do you think this is all just gossip?"

"I heard they use the teeth." My shoulders trembled as I thought of the small gap between Hoby's front teeth, as well as the chip in his incisor from when he took a hard fall during a basketball game.

Clyde stood and paced to the window above the sink, then back. "I can't believe we're even talking about this. It's crazy."

"Maybe it's not him." I lifted my chin. "Everybody's assuming it's Hoby, but maybe it's not. Maybe his body is still in the lake." My imagination took me deep into the dirty lake water, where a pale body bumped and banged its way through the open windows of a wrecker. When the body swirled and turned in the wake of a fishing boat, the face smiled at me, with a gap between the front teeth. I shoved away from the table and lunged down the hall, barely making it to the bathroom before I vomited.

Clyde was right. Things were crazy. For so many years, I was the only one thinking about Hoby, but now the entire town revolved around those missing years. I felt as though my life had derailed, but maybe finding the answers would help me make peace. After splashing cool water on my face and brushing my teeth, I opened the bathroom door and only paused in front of my bedroom for a few seconds. Lord, it would feel good to go in there, shut the door, and hide myself beneath the blankets, but if those bones belonged to Hoby, then this was the answer I had to face. For my sake, and Ruthie's, and now Clyde's. Hiding was no longer an option.

I didn't want to be that woman—the one who badgered herself with regrets and bitterness and shoved away the people who cared about her. No, I wanted to be the girl who climbed ten feet up the ladder inside a wind turbine, who started reading again for the first time since high school, who challenged an ex-convict to better himself and swore she would do the same. I wanted to be a healthy person who could live life, and I wanted to live it with Clyde Felton.

In the meantime I needed to deal with these disgusting rumors. I returned to my seat in the kitchen, more hopeful and determined than I'd been when I left it.

"I hope you don't mind." Clyde was standing next to the stove. "I'm making tea."

"Sure. Tea bags are in the cabinet to the left of the sink."

He cleared his throat. "I'm sorry this thing is happening."

I didn't answer.

The water on the stove boiled, and Clyde dug out two tea bags, then held them by the paper tabs and dunked them up and down in the water. "I left the football game during the first quarter. We were down by six."

"Who told you about the bones?"

He let the strings slip through his fingers. "Susan. She heard it up in the stands, and I reckon she figured I could use a heads-up." He measured sugar into the pan and stirred it several times before he continued. "She thinks Neil might be involved in it."

"Involved how?" Neil hadn't seen Hoby since before he left, and I didn't see the connection.

"She's just speculating is all. Said he's acting quirky. Feeling a lot of guilt."

"He deserves to feel guilty, but what is Susan speculating about?"

He poured the tea into a pitcher, then looked at me. "Well, if they found the skeleton all the way up at Picnic Hollow, on the opposite end of the lake from the truck …"

"I don't understand what you're saying." And I was getting frustrated with him.

"The bones were found in a shallow grave, Lyn." He held the pitcher over the sink, then hesitated before saying, "For some reason, Susan thinks Neil may have had something to do with it."

Whatever normalcy remained in my imagination evaporated. "Seriously?"

Clyde shoved the pitcher under the faucet and turned on the water. He left his back to me until the pitcher was full. "I reckon."

I picked at a speck of food stuck to the table. The gossip was already flowing, but I didn't want to admit that Pam had mentioned the same possibility when she called. Even though I despised Neil, I couldn't picture him killing someone. Especially Hoby. They had been friends once. We all had.

Clyde dropped ice cubes into a glass, filled it with tea, and brought it to me. "You should drink."

The cool wetness felt good as it ran across my throat, cleansing my palate and quenching my thirst, but not coming close to washing away the filth that smeared my mood.

A knock sounded at the front door, and when Clyde raised his eyebrows, I answered his unspoken question.

"Probably Ruthie. I'll get it." I stepped across the living room and flipped on the porch light at the same time I opened the door, but then my stomach tightened.

Neil leaned against the iron porch railing, leering at me through the screen door.

"I figured the two of you would be holed up in that love nest up on the Cap." He motioned to Clyde's sedan at the curb. "Neither of you have enough sense to get out of town."

"I don't—" I glanced over my shoulder as Clyde followed me to the door.

"What can we do for you, Neil?" Clyde put his palm in the small of my back.

"Just stopped by to make sure you were all right, what with the ruckus over at the stadium in Tahoka." He peered down the street, and I expected him to loll his eyes lazily, but instead they skittered back and forth.

"I was there less than an hour ago," Clyde said. "Things seemed peaceful enough to me."

"Did you hear what the Rangers found?" His voice broke on the last word. "They think it's the rest of Hoby's body."

Suddenly I grew cold, but my head felt clearer than it had moments before. "They don't know that for sure," I said.

"Oh, it's Hoby, all right." Neil's lips drew back to show his teeth, but it seemed more like a grimace than a smile.

"What makes you think so?" Clyde's fingertips dug gently into my side.

Neil backed away, lowering one foot to the second step. "The Rangers sent those teenage boys away as soon as they found the body. I heard there were details they didn't want the Scouts to spread around."

I felt as if a housefly were buzzing around my head, and I had the overwhelming urge to slap it with a plastic swatter. Neil always tried to push my buttons, but if he thought he could rattle me this time, he was wrong. With a strength I didn't feel, I snapped, "Why did you come here?"

"To warn you."

"About what? So far you haven't told us anything we didn't already know."

"People are talking, Lynda, and they're figuring things out. Before morning they're going to know what you did."

Clyde's fist gripped the doorframe.

"What are you accusing me of?" I asked.

"I'm not accusing you of a thing. I'm just saying I know Hoby was suicidal before he left—he was always weak like that—but the town never knew everything you did to drive him there."

His statement sounded like a rehearsed monologue. Empty.

Clyde thrust the screen door open, and it slammed back against the house. "You should leave." He towered over Neil, who seemed much smaller on the second step.

I remembered Clyde's explanation about his anger, and I put my hand solidly on the inside of his elbow and tugged. If Clyde couldn't handle seeing a puppy get kicked, I had a feeling we were about to have an explosion.

"Now, Lynda." Neil looked past Clyde and shook his head. "You just lost one pitiful husband. Are you already working to get another one?"

Clyde shook his head as though he thought Neil was the pitiful one, and I felt him yield slightly to my tugging.

But then Neil clucked his tongue. "Well, loose women can't attract anything else."

In one swift movement, Clyde shoved Neil backward down the steps, and Neil stumbled before falling hard on the front walk.

"Don't, Clyde!" I clung to his arm with both hands, but Clyde was already backing away. He lowered his head and rested a hand on the post, then took a deep breath.

Neil scurried backward on all fours. "No!"—he raised his voice— "I didn't do anything to you." He stumbled to his feet. "Don't hit me again!"

I stepped onto the porch beside Clyde, wondering if Neil were having a nervous breakdown right here, right now, in my front yard. He had seemed tense before, but his behavior had just spiraled toward erratic.

Neil clambered into his truck, but instead of driving away quickly, he lowered the window and pulled slowly past the neighbor's house while he rubbed his neck.

"Has he lost his mind?" I mumbled.

The two of us stood on the porch, staring after the truck as it drove away, but suddenly Clyde made a guttural sound, almost like a growl. "Good God!" His arm caught me at the waist, and he guided me back in the house. Just as he slammed the door, I saw what he had seen.

A news camera was pointed at us from behind the neighbor's carport.

CHAPTER
THIRTY-EIGHT

By Saturday morning Clyde and I were on every local channel. Besides the clip of Hoby's truck being pulled from the lake—a video they had aired every day for the past week—they now had footage of Clyde shoving Neil off my porch. Channel Eleven even ran exclusive coverage of me kissing Clyde just before the truck was pulled out of the lake … and fainting afterward.

I recalled Neil's suggestion that I move away from Trapp, and the idea now sounded blissful, even though it was clear he had hoped to make Clyde and me look guilty.

"Can't we just keep driving and not stop?" We were headed down Highway 84, and the hum of Clyde's sedan soothed my nerves.

He laughed lightly, but it didn't sound like he thought anything was funny. "Might look bad, huh?"

I nestled my chin in my hand, and my hair fell across one eye, causing me to feel half hidden, half exposed, half clothed, half naked. I peeked from behind the locks and stared at the windmills just coming into view. Today they were scarecrows stomping across the cotton fields, flailing their arms as we passed. Hundreds of pumpkins with thousands of arms spiraling endlessly day and night. Mocking me.

My gaze landed on a slow-moving windmill whose arms needed oiling like the Tin Man. He moved slowly, trying to keep up, but was inevitably headed toward an early death. And far ahead, on the edge of the cliff, one windmill stood completely motionless, its rotors set at the wrong angle to catch the wind. The frozen structure appeared deformed compared to the rest, and I looked away from it, forcing my eyes to the machines that were still alive, still moving, still toiling on and on.

After a few minutes, Clyde pulled over and killed the ignition, but he didn't break the spell. He didn't invade my time. He just sat with me. Without his saying so, I knew Clyde didn't want me to fall back into depression. He didn't want me to hole up in my house again, not for three days and not for three years. He had brought me out here to remind me of that, and his presence comforted me even though I felt like a fragile leaf blowing on a raging wind.

"When's the funeral?" he asked.

At first his question confused me because *they hadn't even identified the body*, but then the nightmare before this nightmare flashed across my mind, and I remembered Ansel was gone. "Tuesday."

"I guess Dixie's closing the diner?"

I nodded, but the *mm-hmm* I tried to add got stuck in my lungs.

"You handling it all right?"

"I'm not handling it at all." My mind, my thoughts, my heart were all neatly distracted from the pain of Ansel's death, held captive by a greater urgency. The fear of being accused, possibly even convicted, of something I didn't do.

I once heard about an infant picked up by a tornado and carried away, but when the storm blew over, that baby had been found in a bar ditch half a mile away, safely settled in a bed of knee-high johnsongrass. I felt like that baby. If everything happened just right, I might survive the chaos, but if one little thing went wrong, I might get slammed against a brick wall and die before the storm settled.

Without turning toward me, Clyde reached out, and I took his hand.

"Do you think they really suspect me of murder?" I asked softly, knowing the answer.

"Depends on what evidence they have. No telling what the Rangers will find once they get the lab results back from Austin."

"It'll be Hoby." I gazed blankly at the arms of the turbines turning, turning, turning. Life was like that. Never ending. Always pulling something away from me. Always coming back around to slap me across the face. I squinted at Clyde. "I didn't drive him to suicide like Neil said. He was coming back to talk to me. He was better, and we were going to work things out."

"Don't you be thinking about anything Neil said. He's half crazed right now."

I knew I shouldn't think back over the conversation, but there was no way not to. Neil had seemed so nervous and desperate and—I chuckled—*antsy*. But there wasn't anything to laugh about. Hoby might have been murdered, and Neil might have done it, but I looked the most guilty.

Everything seemed so absurd. "Do you think he set up the camera crew at my house?"

"I do, Lyn."

Leaning my head against the headrest, I suddenly recalled something Neil had said that seemed strange. "Why would he refer to your shack as a *love nest*? He said we should hide there."

When Clyde didn't answer, I turned to look at him, but his gaze was focused on the rearview mirror. "Here comes Hector."

The highway patrol car pulled to a stop behind the sedan.

"Maybe he thinks we're stranded." My words sounded unconvincing, even to me. "Right?"

Clyde rolled down his window. "Hey there, Sheriff."

"Clyde."

I leaned across the seat. "Hector, what's up?" I asked.

"I'd like to ask you a few questions. Sort of off the record."

"Off the record?" I asked dumbly, as all feeling left my arms and legs.

"The Rangers are starting to wonder about some things. They'll probably bring you in for questioning Monday morning." He looked up and down the highway. "But since I happened to bump into you, I can ask you a few questions of my own."

"Do you want us to meet you somewhere?" Clyde asked.

"Lynda, would you mind riding with me?" Hector waited until I nodded. "And Clyde, can you meet us at my office?"

The demon I had managed to shove from my life now snickered in triumph. Hector was separating me from Clyde, and I could only imagine it was because he thought I was guilty. Guilty of murdering my husband. I took a deep breath, trying to fill my lungs, but the effort seemed too great.

A sudden pressure caused my gaze to fall to the seat, where Clyde still held my hand in his. My fingers were so tightly clamped around his thumb that my knuckles were white. He slid his other hand over mine and drew them to his lips. He didn't kiss my fingers, only brushed them against his cheek, but the action—so bold of him right in front of Hector—gave me the strength to press through one more trial.

I slipped my hand from his, and Hector met me at the back bumper. The sheriff shuffled his feet, wiped a fist across his lips, then squinted at me as though he had just bitten a lemon. "Lynda, I don't want to be saying this to you, but"—his gaze swept the sky—"you have the right to remain silent."

CHAPTER
THIRTY-NINE

I expected Hector to lock me in the back of his cruiser like a regular criminal, so when he ushered me to the front passenger seat, confusion filled my mind. Maybe I wasn't about to be arrested for murder. *Good Lord.* That sounded insane.

As we drove to the turnaround that would allow us to head back to Trapp, the windmills crept past the passenger window. I cut my gaze to the speedometer to verify the sheriff was driving as slowly as it seemed. Did he dread having to lock me up once we made it back to his office?

Clyde's sedan passed us, and our eyes met briefly before he went ahead of the cruiser.

"Lynda?" Hector took off his cowboy hat and set it on the seat between us. "I figure if I drive slow enough, you and I may have this thing settled before we get back to town." He shrugged. "Not that I have anything against the Rangers. They're a regular bunch of guys."

I uncrossed my arms and let them wilt into my lap. "You just read me my rights, Hector."

"Had to. Otherwise your comments wouldn't be admissible in court." He sighed. "For what it's worth, I'm sorry. I know this has got to be hard on you, dredging up memories of Hoby and all."

"It was a long time ago."

He nodded. "It's like this ..." His voice rose to a confident volume, but when he faltered, I remembered that he had memories of Hoby, too. He swallowed. "The rest of the skeleton has been found *on my daddy's property*." He shook his head. "What are the odds of—"

"Was it Hoby?"

Hector sighed. "They won't know for sure until the DNA tests are completed—probably sometime Monday—but even then, they're going to need a sample to match in order to determine if it's him."

"If you mean something like a hair out of a hairbrush, it'll be impossible."

His eyebrows quivered for a moment, and I imagined he almost smiled. "They can just match it to Ruthie since she's his daughter."

It felt like ice water piercing my heart. The last time I saw Hoby, he had questioned me about whether or not Ruthie was his daughter. Nothing I could say would convince him, and now it was the only thing that could identify him all these years later. We crawled past a herd of Angus cattle, solid-black animals scattered among the mesquite trees, but in the midst of them, one red-and-white Hereford cow munched quietly on grass, oblivious to her differences. "So ... this is Saturday. That's two more days of not knowing?"

Hector tilted his head and scratched the side of his neck with his thumb. "That's when they'll know something with a hundred percent certainty, but really, I think we can be safe to say it's him, Lynda."

"Why?" A flash of indignation flared in my gut. "Your daddy's place is nowhere near where they found Hoby's truck, so it could be a horrible coincidence the two things happened at the same time. If the truck hadn't been found, you never would have considered the possibility of that skeleton belonging to Hoby."

Hector slowly raised his palm to silence me, and I hushed. "Actually ..." He peered across at me before returning his eyes to the road, and I figured that was another reason he wanted to talk to me while he was driving—so he wouldn't have to look me in the eye. "Even from the first two bones, they could tell it was a tall, athletic male in his late twenties ... slightly bow-legged."

At Hector's description, a memory picture surfaced in my mind. Hoby, dressed in boots and Wranglers, walking up the sidewalk to the church building. He held Ruthie's baby hand, and as he bent to smile down at her, his bowed legs looked even more curved.

"Not only that," Hector continued, "but the thigh bone had been broken at some point and healed." He paused as though he were admitting a great sin. "I had the Rangers checking on Hoby right from the start."

He didn't look at me again, and I was glad of it. He knew as well as I did that Hoby broke his leg the spring of his freshman year of high school, riding on the back of Eldon Simpson's dirt bike. He sat out of track that year and spent all summer building up strength so he could play football in the fall.

"Dental records?"

"They're working on that." He shivered, then shook it off, seemingly embarrassed. "I've seen the skull, and ..." He swallowed, then turned his head as far away from me as he could while still being able to see the road.

It didn't matter if he finished his sentence, because I knew what he was trying to tell me. The skull had a gap between its front teeth, and that detail combined with all the other forensic markers positively identified the corpse, at least to Hector and me and anyone else who knew Hoby.

The indignation in my gut dwindled to indifference. "I don't understand how the body got that far away from the truck, though. That's what? Ten miles? No animal would … you know."

Hector didn't answer me right away. "When did you last see him, Lynda?"

We passed the city-limit sign, and as Hector slowed the car, his cowboy hat shifted toward my thigh. I fingered the edge of the gray felt. "The day he left town. I don't remember the date. It was a weekday, I think, because he was headed to the garage."

"Around Thanksgiving?"

"I guess so. Why?"

"And you never saw him again after that, right?"

"No …" I squinted at him. "But I heard from him once."

"He called you?"

"Sent me a letter."

"Do you still have it?"

"Why do you want to know?" I snapped. "What are you not telling me?"

His shoulders drooped. "I'm sorry, Lynda. I don't know what I'm asking. I'm just fishing for some nugget of information that will clear you."

I turned in the seat and glared at him. *"Clear me?"*

He flashed his palm in front of my face again, then stated firmly, "Work with me, Lynda. I'm trying to help you."

So I really was being accused of killing my husband. I slumped against the seat. There were a few years, way back, when I felt like killing Hoby, but that rage had long since been replaced by bitterness, and finally apathy when he had left and never returned to me and his daughter. "I have the letter."

He stopped at the flashing red light in the middle of town, waited for traffic to pass, then continued down Main Street. "What does it say?"

"Hoby said he was sorry, and that he'd had time to think about it, and he wanted to talk things over."

Hector's face wadded like a crumpled piece of aluminum foil, but still he didn't seem to have the nugget he was looking for. "That all?"

"He said he would be home soon, and that he'd make it up to me."

"Did he mention Neil Blaylock?"

I huffed. "Of course he did. How could he not?"

Hector's eyes widened in exasperation. "Well, what did he say about him?"

"He called him a few creative names and said he had a thing or two he wanted to say to him."

"Is that all?"

"Basically, but the letter is a full two pages."

"Do you have the envelope with the postmark?"

I shrugged. "I'm a bit of a hoarder."

"Thank God for that."

He turned onto my street, and I realized he wanted the letter immediately.

"So is that the nugget you needed?" I asked.

"That's the nugget we both needed."

He pulled to a stop at the curb, but before I went in the house for the letter, I turned to look at him straight on, now that he couldn't avoid me. "There's something more, isn't there?"

He slid the car into park and reached for his hat. "What do you mean?"

"I've known you since kindergarten, Hector. I was there when Mrs. Sanchez asked you if any of the other boys were naughty when she was out of the room, and you said *I don't think so, ma'am.*"

Hector shifted. "I don't see where you're headed."

"You had the same look on your face back then. You didn't mention to her that three of your friends stuck gum under their desks. There was more to it, just like there's more that you're not telling me right now."

"Aw, Lynda, come on, now. Can't we just get the letter and be done here?"

I crossed my arms.

"You are so—" The sigh that crossed his lips sounded hollow and exhausted, and I almost felt sorry for pushing him. But not quite. "All right. I didn't want to be the one to tell you. Then again I didn't want to be the one to handle this case at all."

I bit my lip. "Thank you for that, Hector. I do appreciate it."

He squinted at two joggers, waiting till they had passed. "When they found the rest of the skeleton?" His gaze cut to me, then away again. "There was a bullet in the skull."

CHAPTER FORTY

When Hector finally left, I stood in the middle of my living room. Alone and empty. But the solitude no longer refreshed me, and my emotions slunk through my heart like the wispy clouds of an early morning fog. Gray and silent, they obscured all that was real in my world, and the details of my life blended together into a haze of uncertainty.

I blinked, chiding myself for being melodramatic, and then I padded into the kitchen and opened a bag of pretzels. My shift at the diner started in an hour, and Dixie was running out of options. So what if I was suspected of killing my husband? More than likely he was murdered by my ex-boyfriend. But either way, I still had to go to work. I snickered at the absurdity of it and shoved a pretzel in my mouth. I chewed, but the salt had little or no taste, and the gummy texture on my tongue repulsed me. Spitting the pretzel in the sink, I cupped my hand and drank a swallow of water to wash it away.

I stomped to my bedroom, sick and tired of feeling sorry for myself, fed up with wallowing in pity, and past ready to get on with life. I jerked the remaining letters from the drawer of the nightstand, then fell to my knees and reached far under the bed for the metal fire-box, whose contents I dumped on the rug. I shuffled through papers and trinkets. A tiny card that had come on a delivery of flowers from Neil when we were dating in high school. A newspaper blurb from the *Lubbock Avalanche-Journal* about a little-known citizen of Trapp who had been convicted of rape and sent away to prison. A paper lunch sack on which Hoby had scrawled a love note one morning before he left for work. The bulletin from that Sunday morning, the week the church asked me to worship someplace else. And one more item that I fingered carefully. The program from my parents' funeral.

When I had it all piled in front of me, I realized I was breathing hard. I settled back against the side of the bed and stuck out my tongue at the pile. Clyde was right. I had been holding on to this junk too long—*psychological tokens*, as he called them—to keep myself locked away from the world. I nudged the papers with my tennis shoe. Maybe I didn't deserve better … but maybe I did.

Pushing the box back under the bed, I lifted each of the papers, one at a time, and laid them across my palm. Then I stood, walked to the kitchen, and dug through a drawer for a lighter. Such an obvious thing to do, and I wondered why it had taken me so long to think of it. It wasn't as if destroying these tokens would erase my past, but in a crazy way, it might release my future. Or at least open my mind and my heart.

I stepped onto the back porch, closed the door behind me, and eased down to lean against it with my bottom on the cement. Stretching my legs out in front of me and crossing my ankles, I peered at the sky. Cotton-ball clouds dotted a blue background, but I knew it wouldn't last long. Clyde had said another storm would be blowing in tomorrow, but that was Texas weather for you. Calm one day, wild the next.

Sort of like my life.

I reached for the paper sack and held it by its bottom edge, and then I cranked the lighter until a flame leaped forward and nicked at the bag. Soon the rich gold ate away at Hoby's words, leaving a line of black ash that gradually gobbled the memory and dropped it in pieces to the ground. I released the last corner to the porch before the heat touched my fingertips. And Hoby's love note was gone.

Seven years of my life—rocky, beautiful, married years—were now placed in a closet in my heart. A closet I could visit occasionally, but not one I would ever want to hang out in. It wasn't warm or welcoming, not a home, merely a functional storage space for items I no longer needed. I reached for the funeral program.

That one was harder. A part of me felt as if I was denying my feelings for my parents, rejecting them. But a bigger part of me—a healthier part—knew I would never forget them, never completely let them go, and my mind would be cleansed by this simple action. That's all it was. An action. An exercise. A way to grieve and heal and move on. More ashes fluttered away on the breeze.

Already I felt release, but the feelings of liberty were so foreign, they frightened me. I pulled my knees up to my chest and wrapped my arms around my shins. That felt better. Safer. And I knew if I rolled tightly into a ball, it wouldn't seem as though I were about to crack. But I had more work to do.

As I watched Neil's letter disappear, I heard a muffled knock in the house, and then the doorbell. It would be Clyde wanting to know what had happened with Hector, wondering why I had never made it to the sheriff's office. I started to boost myself up but changed my mind. I didn't need him right then. I needed to finish this once and for all, a personal funeral for all my regrets.

As the front door opened, the back door rattled from the suction, and I heard Clyde's heavy footsteps creaking through my house as I held his burning newspaper article in my hand. It sounded as though he opened and closed a few doors during the time I calmly destroyed a short note Neil had written, and by the time I held the last corner of the florist's card, the door rattled again, and Clyde had gone.

My gaze returned to the sky, where the cotton balls had shifted to the right, constantly moving, floating, changing, and I wondered if I would ever feel normal again. Whole.

Without looking, I reached for the last item in my stash. The bulletin from the church. My fingers automatically worked to open the fold, as they had done so often in the past, but I stopped myself before my eyes scanned the words. I had read that blurb too many times already. Good grief, the wording and the font would be etched in my brain until the end of time. The folks at church had turned their backs on me when I needed them most. They had hurt me almost beyond comprehension, but maybe … just maybe … I could forget.

Ruthie forgave them, and she had read that stinking bulletin more than I had. She used to keep it in her room, but she threw it away after she married Dodd. When I found it there, what once had been her token then became mine.

I cranked the lighter again. For all I knew, this was the last remaining copy. The last physical proof that those people had done such a hurtful thing. The last evidence justifying my bitterness toward them. But wasn't that what all these papers had been?

I waved the bulletin slightly, and the flames flared up, engulfing the folds of paper, then dwindled down into nothingness. Along with the words. They were nothing now.

My head thunked against the door behind me, and I tapped it twice, a gentle reminder of the sturdy things in my life. Like Clyde. Clyde Felton was solid.

I considered the men I had loved in my lifetime. All three called themselves Christians, yet each was so very different from the others. And each had treated me differently, too. Neil and Hoby had hurt me. Would Clyde eventually do the same?

I didn't want to think so, and I shoved the thought high above my head toward the cotton-ball clouds. Clyde was a good man, and he loved me. He wanted to make something better of himself, and he said he wanted me to tag along while he did it. But even if he never changed a thing, even if he worked at the Dairy Queen for the rest of his life, even if someday he hurt me … even then … I would want to be with him.

I shook my head and smiled. He was such a fool about that old shack of his. The thing was worthless, but he hung on to it because it reminded him of Fawn and his grandpappy. But mostly Fawn. It was silly, because the girl had lived there less than a year and never fully moved back up there after Nathan was born, but Land sakes, the place must have been nice in its day. Even though the house was small, the views from the front windows would have kept anyone from caring about the cramped living quarters.

I found it ironic that Neil, one of the wealthiest men in Garza County, had clearly been envious of my boyfriend's real estate. Then again, Neil Blaylock had always scorned anything he couldn't get his hands on. In fact, Clyde had said he was surprised Neil hadn't torn the place down already. I squinted, remembering Neil leaning against the porch railing on the other side of the screen door, and then my mood faltered.

Neil had called Clyde's old shack a *love nest*. He had said Clyde and I should be hiding out there. That seemed strange. The house had been abandoned for a year, and Clyde and I had only been up there one time in the past two weeks.

Two weeks. Had everything between Clyde and me happened in only two weeks? A charred paper fragment tumbled across the porch, the words still visible in the black ash, and I smashed it with my thumb, marveling at the way my opinion of Clyde had changed in such a short time. When he came back from prison, he was little more than a pitiful drunk, and at that time, I wasn't even sure I wanted to be his friend. But he had proved himself to the people down at the church, to me and his other friends, and most important, to his daughter. Now Fawn needed him more than he knew.

He was hanging on to the shack because of her, so I could hardly ask him to tear it down, even for something as life changing as opening a restaurant. Pushing myself to my feet, I brushed my hand across my bottom, hoping I hadn't dirtied my work uniform. I reached for the door handle, but then I froze, piecing together tidbits of memories not unlike how Hector was piecing together evidence from my past. Both of us were working our own jigsaw puzzles.

The sun must have gone behind one of the cotton balls, because a shadow swept across the porch, darkening the steps where ashes had made their way to the ground. My body went cold as all the pieces came together to form a complete picture, a vision from the past. I realized I wasn't the only one who had been hanging on to a psychological token.

I lowered myself slowly to my hands and knees, and then lay down on my side and curled into a ball.

But only for a minute.

CHAPTER
FORTY-ONE

When Clyde got off work that night, he drove straight to the diner, anxious to talk to Lynda about her discussion with Hector. That morning when the sheriff had placed her in his car, she looked so lost, terrified of getting arrested and being convicted of a crime she didn't commit. He could imagine her sing-song voice. "This is Trapp, Clyde. No matter what you do, the town will gossip a different version of it." And she had been right again.

He saw her through the windows of Dixie's Diner, sweeping the dining room, and he realized how worried he had been. He wasn't at all sure he wanted her going around town alone. The sheriff had stopped by the Dairy Queen earlier and said enough to let Clyde know that they were searching for Neil and that they considered him armed and dangerous. Clyde never figured Neil to be brave enough to kill another human being, and Clyde had met a few murderers in his lifetime.

But he had no intention of taking chances. Clyde tapped on the locked door.

Lynda startled as though she'd heard a gunshot, but when she saw that it was him, her shoulders relaxed and she flipped the lock. "What do you want?"

It was a strange greeting, but he let it go. "Thought I'd follow you home. They still haven't found Neil."

"Blue and Gray figure him to be well past the border of Mexico by now." She laughed, but it didn't sound real. "Crazy, huh?"

She propped the broom against the counter and turned a chair upside down on a table. Clyde hurried to help.

"I talked to the sheriff," he said. "Susan confessed that Neil has been liquidating assets." He paused with a chair lifted waist high. "I have to agree with the Parker sisters, Lyn. I bet he's long gone."

"I don't think so. Susan's still here. And Fawn and Nathan."

A pickup crawled past the front windows, and Clyde studied it before continuing to flip chairs.

Lynda dragged the broom slowly beneath a table, forming a small pile of dust and bits of food, but then she paused. "When Neil suggested we leave town together, do you think he was trying to make us look guilty?"

"I reckon so."

"It doesn't make sense," she said. "It's like he staged the whole thing to exploit your temper and make you look guilty, but you have the most solid alibi a person can have. The Texas prison system."

"He's desperate, Lyn, and thinking crazy. Like threatening to have me arrested because of Nathan. There was never anything to that. Just trying to make me look bad."

She continued sweeping. "And if we ran off together, I would look more suspicious."

"Yep."

"Is it all right if I hate him now?"

He flipped the last chair over and leaned against the counter. "Hate's too strong."

"Yeah, I suppose." She sighed, seeming lost in thought. Clyde couldn't get a feel for her mood. She'd had such a strange few days, her emotions were surely in a jumble, but she seemed detached, emotionless, numb. Maybe that was self-preservation. She gave a short grunt of a laugh and glanced at him. "Those stinking letters of mine came in handy after all."

"How so?" Clyde rubbed a palm over his mouth, not sure he should admit he had seen her burning them out on her back porch. Without a doubt, she had heard him calling her name, and she hadn't wanted to be disturbed. This time he had let her be.

"Turns out an old letter of Hoby's put Neil and him together around the time of the"—she cringed—"accident."

"How do they know when it happened?"

"Hoby got a speeding ticket on I-20 toward the end of December, but he never paid it. Hector says that could have been about the time it happened."

"But if you're the one that got the letter from him, why are they looking at Neil instead of you?"

She shrugged and swept under another table before she answered him. "I was in the hospital in December."

He leaned forward. "I never knew that."

"I was treated for psychological problems. You know, depression and all."

He studied her for a while, wanting to hold her but sensing she wouldn't accept it at the moment. "You were suicidal."

"Yes." She said it loudly. "Anyway, I have almost as solid an alibi as you."

The sound of her laughter, uncontrolled and sinister, forced him to move toward her, approaching as if she were a cottontail rabbit hiding in the brush. He took the broom in one hand and pulled her into his arms with the other. "I wish I had been there, Lyn, and I wish I could erase all the pain from your past."

"I do, too." She pulled away from him, and her eyes looked lost and abandoned. She took the broom from him and swept the debris into a dustpan.

Something didn't feel right. She was closing herself off again, and Clyde scrambled for a way to bring her back. They'd had such a good time before everything fell apart. Cooking together, exploring the turbine, making plans at his property on the Cap. He stepped toward her. "I don't have to work till late tomorrow. I was thinking maybe you'd come over and let me cook for you. I could make you a little batch of homemade ice cream."

She dumped the dirt in the trash and stored the dustpan with the broom on a hook in the corner. She didn't answer.

"Or we could just head out to the turbines again ..." His spirits fell as she stopped, exhaled, didn't look at him. "Or just whatever," he finished softly.

She stared at the side of the cash register for so long, he began to think she hadn't heard him. But no, of course she had. He shoved his hands in his pockets to wait her out.

"I guess I better not," she finally said.

Better not what? Talk to him? Sit with him? Love him?

She shook her head. "I can't do this."

His stomach sank to the floor beneath him. *She didn't want him anymore.*

"It's not that I don't care about you. Of course I do, but I'm not up to any more drama right now. What with Hoby and all. And Ansel dying. And I haven't even had time to think about Ruthie and what she must be feeling through all this."

She was telling him she was too busy? She still hadn't looked at him, but Clyde kept staring at her, not believing. "You must be tired after all you've been through today," he said. "Why don't we talk about it tomorrow? I'll pick you up, and we can take some muffins to the Cap again. Get away from everything down here in town."

"No." Her eyes met his then, and her chin quivered. "I'm not going up there with you."

The hatred in her eyes matched any glare she had ever leveled at Neil Blaylock, and it shook Clyde's confidence to have the same look directed straight at him. But it irked him, too. "What's up, Lyn? Talk to me."

Her hands locked together loosely on the counter, giving the impression she didn't care much about the outcome of the conversation, but Clyde doubted that was the case.

"I know about your house on the Caprock." Her eyebrows lifted slightly. "I figured it out."

Women had always been confusing to Clyde, but right now he thought Lynda was a complete mystery, and he had no earthly idea what she was talking about. "Do you mean my plans to move up there?" He rubbed the side of his jaw with his thumb. "I don't mind reconsidering that notion. That's something we can figure out together. But there's no rush," he added quickly.

"You don't even understand it, do you?" She looked at him then, with exhausted eyes. "You told me you wanted to keep the house because you had memories of Fawn there. I assumed when she lived there last year, but that's not what you meant." Her eyes narrowed. "Is it?"

Clyde felt as if he were falling down a dark tunnel, three hundred feet above the ground, with nothing to cling to and no hope of release.

Lynda's lips curved upward ever so slightly, but her eyes remained empty. "You don't have memories of Fawn living in your grandpappy's house. You have memories of her being conceived there."

CHAPTER
FORTY-TWO

"Clyde Felton is making me crazy."

"Aw, Lynda." Velma tittered softly. "You were already pretty loony."

Sunday evening we sat alone at the rickety picnic table in her backyard, watching the sky darken. "I don't need any more loony in my life, Velma. I've had enough of it to last awhile."

"I'm beginning to think crazy is the new normal." She picked at a chip of flaking paint on the tabletop. "Just when I think things will settle down, something happens to stir them up again. Makes me wonder what's next."

It was strange to hear Velma talking so pessimistically, and it reminded me that I was supposed to be comforting her, not whining about Clyde. "Sorry I brought it up."

"No matter." She peered far across the pasture, where all the cedars leaned slightly to the left, pushed over the years to the same angle by a gentle yet persistent wind. "Storm's blowing in."

"They said the worst of it will pass us by."

"Good," she said. "It's nice out here. Calm."

At that moment Velma's backyard was the only place on the property that wasn't crowded with family members. Her grandchildren had been put to bed on pallets, air mattresses, and roll-away beds—both in her house and in Fawn and JohnScott's double-wide fifty yards down the fence line. Her children and their spouses were congregated in her living room, talking and laughing, remembering good times with their dad.

All except JohnScott. He and Fawn had decided to go into town for worship, since they had missed services that morning. JohnScott had told his mother and sisters he needed the strength that would come from meeting with the saints, and even though they silently clucked their tongues in speculation, I got the impression that a few of them were envious of his connection to the church … even if they didn't understand it.

"How you holding up?" I asked.

Her mouth curved downward in a facial shrug. "I'll be all right."

In the past three days, I had seen Ansel's family—my family— slip back and forth between grief and joy, one minute crying from their loss and the next minute laughing at a recollection of happy times. But through it all, they bolstered each other up, and even though Velma didn't realize it, they were all being extra careful of their mother's feelings. "You can be sad, you know," I said. "Your kids expect it."

"I know they do." She peered at a bank of clouds far on the horizon. "But with all of them here, I've got other things to think about—Lilly's lost tooth and what's for dinner and will the toilet paper last through the week—so my grief is on hold for a while. You know what I mean … the hardest part of it." Her plump arms wrapped across her abdomen, and she patted both elbows. "It's sure nice having them here, though. They're reminding me of Ansel's life, and it don't leave much time for me to harp on his death."

"That'll come later?"

"And then some." She slid off the picnic bench and hobbled to a flowerpot, which she picked up and set beneath the faucet on the back wall of the house. She eased the water on. "Sometimes I wish Momma was still around," she said, "just for her hugs."

The cloud bank was rolling in, and a cool breeze came with it. "I had forgotten how much she did that. Her hugs were long and lingering, weren't they?"

"Annoyingly so," Velma said. "I've never been one for physical contact, but now I'd give anything for her touch."

Ansel's blue heeler, Rowdy, trotted around from the side of the house and stopped to lap water from Velma's overflowing flowerpot. She scratched his head, then bent to turn off the water, leaving the pot where it sat.

"Daddy's the one I miss most." I surprised myself with this declaration. "When he died, I felt lost without him."

Stepping past the table, Velma picked up a football one of the kids had left outside. "We all need someone to take care of us."

For years I had fought to keep people at a distance, not wanting to admit I needed them. "I never really got that, did I?"

She held the ball under her elbow like a running back. "But now ... Clyde?"

"I guess he could take care of me." *Maybe.*

"You could take care of each other."

Turning slightly I let the wind blow me straight in the face. "Is that how it's supposed to be?"

"Ideally." She set the football on the table, then sat down. "Men need just as much taking care of as women do. But in a different way."

"It just seems like everyone leaves me, but I guess if Momma and Daddy hadn't left, I would've handled it better."

"Don't say they left. That sounds like they had a choice in the matter."

"Okay, when they *died*."

She nodded emphatically. "They died."

"That's all they did." My voice trailed off. "They died."

She gave the dog another pat. "How's your grieving coming along?"

"All right," I said. "It's not as bad for me, since Ansel was my brother-in-law."

She clucked her tongue. "Land sakes, girl. I wasn't talking about Ansel."

For a moment my thoughts swirled, and when they settled, I mumbled, "You mean Hoby."

"We're both widows now."

My chest expanded, but then it fell back into its normal pattern of intake and exhale, and I thought I knew a little how Velma felt. With the investigation and Ansel's death and Clyde's … *whatever*, I had too many things distracting me from my grief, but I could figure it out later. And then some.

Velma squinted, and her nose scrunched slightly. "Will they bury him? I suppose they'll have to."

"Eww. There have been way too many gross thoughts associated with that husband of mine."

"It's been a bizarre week. That's for sure. By the way ..." She studied me for a second while she pursed her lips. "Sophie Snodgrass was out here earlier today. Supposedly to drop off a casserole, but it seemed more like a ploy to dump gossip on a slew of out-of-towners. Anyhoo. She was blabbering about that old pistol of Neil Blaylock's. You heard anything?"

I felt relief at the change in topic. "Hector explained it, but it still seems sketchy. He thinks Hoby was killed around Christmas, which would have been handy for Neil, because his gun was stolen the first week in December."

Velma frowned but nodded.

"The problem with his story is that he didn't file the insurance claim until January. So according to Hector, Neil looks like he's lying about the gun being stolen."

"So if they can find the gun, then they can match the bullet?"

"Apparently."

"But what good will that do if they can't find Neil himself?"

I shrugged. "I can't picture Neil ever leaving Trapp. This place is in his bones." A shiver raced up my spine and down my arm. "I can't believe I said that. It's creepy."

"Sure enough. Bones are creepy." She said it as though it didn't matter one bit, and I began to think it didn't.

Rustling movements came from the house, and through the sliding-glass door, we heard the weather radio blaring. The laughter in the living room increased in volume as the monotone voice described the coming storm.

"Time for me to go home."

"You're welcome to stay."

I chuckled. "Velma, if a storm hits, you don't have closet space for all your grandkids, much less me."

"Aw, Lynda. We're a couple weeks past tornado season. Besides, nothing ever comes of those radio alerts … except to get the young ones excited. Now they'll be asking for flashlights to play with." We stood, and Velma snapped her fingers to get the dog to follow her to the mudroom.

I pulled my car keys from my pocket and turned toward the hatchback. I'd go home and wait for the storm to pass, then find Ruthie and try to comfort her like Velma comforted me. After that, I'd call Clyde and make peace with him. If I could give up my memories, he just might be able to give up his.

Velma wasn't the only one who could have a family that laughed and talked together. She wasn't the only one who deserved it.

CHAPTER
FORTY-THREE

Clyde didn't mind working an extra shift on Sunday. *The Lord's Day.*
Lynda made it clear she didn't want to see him, but he hadn't figured
out what to do about it. Throwing himself into his work felt thera-
peutic, a distraction from his problems. Besides—like she said—he
enjoyed cooking. He flipped the switch to darken the Dairy Queen
sign, then hurried through his cleaning chores, hoping to make it
home before the storm hit.

The water was hot on his skin as he rinsed the sink. Lynda had
seen into his heart in more ways than one, and a gentle apprehension
settled over him as he thought about how badly he had hurt her. All
because of his shack on the Caprock. The place had always pulled
at him, but he told himself it was because of his grandpappy and
the memories before Clyde went away. If he had been honest with
himself, he would have known it was more than that.

Lynda had seen it.

But what she didn't understand—and Clyde hoped she would
let him explain—was that it wasn't the memory of the sex itself. It

wasn't his feelings for Susan. It certainly wasn't love or longing for what might have been. The pull of that property hit him deeper, more personally, like a self-inflicted wound. Clyde held on to the house as a means of keeping himself right where he belonged, working at the Dairy Queen, living in a trailer house, sitting on the back pew at worship.

He picked up a case of Fritos and emptied it onto a metal rack by his workstation. *Frito pie.* He shook his head. If he ever opened a restaurant, he'd serve something that took longer than forty-five seconds to prepare. Several hollow popping sounds came from the dining room, and he looked up to see paper cups and other trash blowing across the parking lot and knocking against the glass door. He paused with his hand on a bag of corn chips as lightning flashed behind the roof of the Allsup's across the street and, a few seconds later, a crash of thunder boomed. There had been a lot of talk about the weather—customers going on about the forecast and the intensity of the high winds—but the brunt of the storm was due to hit south of Trapp, so he wasn't overly concerned. Clyde had lived in Texas forty-three years and had never seen a tornado. Most people hadn't.

He glanced around the kitchen, checking to see if anything else needed tending to before he left, and he realized he didn't want to go home. He wanted to go by Lynda's house and explain, make her listen, tell her everything would be all right. See if she would smile again.

He reached for his matches and slipped them into his pocket. Someday he would have to try Lynda's suggestion of chewing spearmint gum when he was slicing onions. He turned out the lights, picked up the trash bags, and slipped out the back door, letting it lock behind him. The force of the wind surprised him, and he gripped the bags tightly so they wouldn't slip from his hands.

He was halfway to the Dumpster before he noticed Neil's truck in the lot. Supposedly the man was armed and dangerous, but obviously he wasn't halfway to the border yet. Clyde tossed the garbage into the Dumpster, slammed the metal lid, and turned toward his sedan, steeling himself for whatever his old friend might do. Maybe Neil would be angry. Maybe he would pull out a gun and shoot Clyde in the head. Maybe he would simply run him down with his truck. None of those scenarios frightened Clyde nearly as much as the possibility that Neil would go after Lynda.

Lightning shot sideways across the sky and the resulting thunderclap vibrated the ground. The truck was parked three spots past his sedan, so Clyde could have slipped into his car and taken off, but he didn't. Instead, he leaned into the wind, walked past his own car, and stopped just on the other side. He was near an overhead light, and its glow spread an arc two yards past his feet, but Neil's truck lay in shadows.

Lightning illuminated the cab, and Clyde could see Neil's outline, hunkered over the steering wheel. He thought the driver's window was down on the truck, but if Neil spoke to him, Clyde wouldn't be able to hear over the wind and thunder. The pickup door opened, and the dome light behind Neil transformed him into a gray silhouette, and Clyde couldn't see the expression on his face. He could tell Neil's hands were empty, though.

The rancher slid off the seat and stood with his hand on the door, appearing shorter than usual. Neil's shoulders slumped uncharacteristically, and when he shut the door, Clyde could tell it didn't close all the way, as if Neil didn't have the strength to slam it.

Clyde lifted his hand in a half wave, not knowing what else to do, and Neil took a few steps, bringing himself under the glow of the light. Clyde wasn't prepared for what he saw. Neil's hair was mussed, and his clothes were wrinkled, his shirttail wadded behind his belt buckle. He seemed to be wearing some sort of loafers. Outside of football practices years ago, Clyde couldn't remember ever seeing Neil wear anything other than starched Wranglers and polished boots, but the biggest difference lay in his face. His pale skin contorted beneath the glow of the lamp, and with every crash of thunder, his cheekbones became skeletal. If Clyde hadn't seen this person get out of Neil's truck, he might not have recognized him at all.

"About time you got out here." Even the sound of Neil's voice was strange, high pitched and warped by the wind, yet still demanding.

Clyde felt as if he were standing in front of a wild stallion that might rear back at any moment, crushing him under his hooves. An unpredictable beast. A jolt of fear raced through Clyde until he realized Neil had always been unpredictable. He'd always been a little bit of a monster. Clyde's nerves settled. Not only were Neil's hands empty, but they fell down to his sides—limp. At the moment Neil Blaylock didn't seem capable of hurting anyone.

"You all right?" Clyde asked.

Neil pointed at him. "You never should have slept with my wife."

Clyde expected Neil to say something about Hoby, or the investigation, maybe even Fawn or Nathan, but not Susan. Neil rarely mentioned her except in reference to her being Fawn's mother.

Clyde raised his voice to be heard over the increasing wind. "You're right. It was wrong of me, and I'm sorry." Clyde could have argued with him about Susan—*It was years ago. She was just as guilty. Susan wasn't your wife then*—but he had long since had the defensiveness sapped out of him. He looked down at a plastic drinking straw bouncing across the asphalt. "I should have apologized before now."

The temperature suddenly dropped several degrees, and Clyde inhaled deeply, invigorated by the coolness even under the circumstances, but Neil wrapped his arms around himself. He took three steps toward the light pole, then three steps back. "She's yours now."

Clyde frowned. "I've got no hold on your wife, Neil. She loves you, and she'll stand by you through this thing." A bolt of lightning shot down, striking a telephone pole a block away, but Neil didn't seem to notice.

"You ruined her life, Clyde, and you owe it to her to see she's taken care of."

"What about you?" If Clyde hadn't known better, he would have thought Neil had been drinking. He certainly looked the part, and his reflexes seemed delayed, but Neil had never been one to lean on the bottle, and he didn't smell like it now.

"Don't worry about me." Neil took a step toward his truck. "My dad is meeting me at the border tonight."

Tension gripped Clyde, but it had nothing to do with the storm and everything to do with the fact that Gerald Blaylock had been dead for years. Clyde bent at the waist, fighting the wind and growing more concerned about Neil.

Neil's gaze bounced to the Allsup's, where an RV swerved into the parking lot, and two people bounded out and ran into the store.

"Susan's set with enough money to last the rest of her life, but she'll need help managing things. She couldn't run a ranch to save her life, and my foreman's likely to take advantage of her ignorance. You'll do well out there. The guest bed is made up."

Clyde got a sick feeling in his stomach just as the weather siren down at the volunteer fire department went off, sounding as though it had to work its way up to full speed.

"So you're headed south?" Clyde's gaze roamed the sky. Something felt wrong in the air, and the light from the streetlamps seemed to glow with a greenish tint.

"Take care of Fawn and Nathan, too. You owe it to them." Neil swayed as he struggled toward his truck, and Clyde followed, trying to get in front of him.

A clatter of thunder echoed and a simultaneous burst of lightning lit up the sky half a mile beyond the Dairy Queen, and as it flashed, Clyde glimpsed a funnel cloud in the distance, so large it looked like a wall of fury. His heart beat hard against his rib cage, and he lunged after Neil, grabbing him by the arm. "We've got to get inside. There's a tornado!"

Neil jerked his arm away. "Get off me. My dad will be furious if I'm late."

"Neil! Look around you. There's a storm!" Clyde was shouting now, the only way to be heard over the increasing roar of a hundred jet planes speeding past them.

Neil yelled something Clyde couldn't hear, and then he reached for the door handle of his truck. On the other side of the street, the lighted sign at the Allsup's swayed, and the outside trash bins tumbled between the gas pumps and rolled down the street and out of sight.

A sudden surge of wind slammed both men against the truck.

Neil's eyes grew wide, crazed, and he shoved against Clyde. Another flare in the sky showed the tornado coming closer, and in the second it took Neil and Clyde to turn their heads and look, the Allsup's sign fell and slammed against the pavement among a flurry of sparks.

Finally Neil yielded to Clyde's tugging, and both men raced for the back door of the restaurant, Clyde fumbling for his keys. Just as he pulled them from his pocket, the power went out through the whole town, leaving them in violent darkness, broken intermittently by enraged strobe lights.

Neil didn't wait for Clyde to unlock the door, but reared back and slammed his shoulder against it. The second time, Clyde joined him, and the door broke open, banging against the time clock.

The kitchen alternated from darkness to light as the storm flashed through the dining room windows, and just as the two men scurried through the kitchen, Clyde saw his sedan slide across the lot.

"What can we get under?" Neil called over the moan of the storm.

"Walk-in freezer's our best bet. Get inside."

"Don't be an idiot!" Neil started to crawl beneath the front counter, but just then the windows shattered, and nuggets of glass shot past them. Neil cried out and bolted toward the freezer door.

The kitchen seemed to lift a foot off the ground, hovering around them, and Clyde had a feeling of weightlessness just before something big and heavy slammed against him, pinning him to the back wall. "Help me!"

Neil had fallen, but he lumbered to his feet, and together they shoved the metal appliance far enough for Clyde to slip from behind it.

Neil opened the freezer door and yelled something, but the shrieking of the storm drowned out his voice. Clyde tried to follow, but when he put weight on his left leg, he fell to the ground. He struggled to stand, but the leg wouldn't hold him, and he ended up crawling.

Hand over hand, Clyde worked his way across the floor, but then Neil grabbed him under the armpits and jerked him the rest of the way into the freezer. Just as the door closed behind them, Clyde heard ripping and pounding as though the kitchen were being trampled by a herd of angry longhorns.

He said a silent prayer.

CHAPTER
FORTY-FOUR

Lynda's Makeup and Stuff.

The stenciling on my cosmetic case had faded, but I could still make out Velma's handwriting. When I was fifteen, she had labeled it for me with blue-and-yellow marker so my nieces would leave it be. The case sat high on the shelf above the toilet, and I frowned at it, wondering why I had kept it so long, but even while I wondered, I knew the answer.

As I sat alone in my dry bathtub, fully clothed, I let my mind wander. Velma had presented the plastic bin to me for my birthday, complete with my very own stash of cosmetics. Back then I shared a bedroom with two of my nieces, and at the time, I was proud to have something that belonged solely to me.

But of course, Ansel and Velma's children didn't need labels to make them feel secure in their home. Unlike me. Those four words had given me a sense of ownership, because that bin belonged to me and nobody else in the house. It was mine alone, and I could hide anything in it without fearing the other kids would get it. If they had tampered with *Lynda's Stuff*, they would've had to deal with Velma's wrath.

I shifted in the tub, trying to find a comfortable position, but the seam of my jeans kept digging into my hip. The wind raged outside the house, and occasionally I could hear the siren wailing from downtown. That siren always went off, though, so I didn't get alarmed. After pulling myself from the tub, I scurried to the bedroom, grabbed two pillows and a quilt, and resumed my station in the bathroom. This would be a waste of time.

Right before I left her house, Velma had cornered me about taking cover if the storm got bad, hence the bathroom hangout. No windows. No glass. Interior room. When Ruthie had been young, there were a few storms where we actually pulled her twin mattress into the bathroom on top of us, but I didn't bother this time. Tossing the pillows into the tub, I plopped back down, pleased to discover my backside was a teensy bit more comfortable. I sat on one pillow and leaned back on the other, resting my head against the tile. *Lynda's Makeup and Stuff* caught my eye again.

I suppose I had always had a private box. Even after I married, I kept my trinkets and mementos—and letters—in the firebox, where Hoby wouldn't mess with them. At least I told myself he wouldn't, but looking back I wondered if he had known about them all along ... and if I had added to his insecurity.

Wind shifted through the attic above my head, sounding like air being let out of a tire, and when the lights quietly clicked off, goose bumps tickled across my shoulders like gnats. But it was only darkness. Nothing permanent. I reached over the tub and ran my palms across the cold tile floor, searching for my cell phone, and then I turned on the flashlight app and let its glow warm the room.

A crash of thunder reminded me of the night Clyde took me to see the windmills in the lightning storm, and I wished I were there now instead of stuffed in my tub. The wind in the rafters changed into a howl, matching the eerie shadows created by the dim light, and when a loud crash sounded outside in the yard, my heart raced. The house seemed to be breathing in and out with the storm, the walls creaking as though they might be ripped away from the foundation at any minute. Easing to one hip, I pulled both pillows over my head and squeezed my eyes shut.

This was worse than I'd thought. My family crossed my mind. Velma's house was jam-packed without enough bathtubs or interior closets to protect everyone. And Dodd and Ruthie would be at the church building with Fawn and JohnScott. I gripped the pillows in hardened fists, trying to imagine where they would all take shelter. Dodd's mother didn't live too far from there, so maybe they would go to her house.

And Clyde. He had worked this afternoon. By now he would be at his trailer house, the most dangerous type of structure in high winds. But no, he would be at church with the others. Wouldn't he?

Another blast shook the house, and the wind howled even louder. A sharp crash two feet away rattled my nerves, and I cried out. But it was only the old makeup kit that had fallen from the shelf and scattered across the floor. I shone my light and saw that the kit's dry and hardened plastic had broken in pieces. Just as well.

I hugged a pillow against my chest. My family members were clustered in two separate places, but at least they were together. As usual, I was alone. A cramp tightened my stomach, and I wished I had stayed at Velma's. *Why didn't I?* It was just like me to run off by myself. That's what I preferred ... usually. But this time I felt like it would have been better to be with them, smashed into the little ranch house, surrounded by love.

Squeezing my eyes shut, I tried to block out the vision my imagination had conjured. Clyde crouched in his trailer as it whirled through the air, three hundred feet above the ground. A sob shot from my throat like a volcanic eruption, and I was so caught off guard that I inhaled and sat up straight. Crying wasn't something I did, but at the moment, it seemed like a very good idea. Another crash shook the house, this time seeming to have come from the back, and when I heard breaking glass, I assumed it was my bedroom window.

I inhaled ragged breaths as I feared for my life and the lives of my family. And Clyde. As the storm intensified, I eased back down to lay on my side in the tub. My knees wanted to habitually curl up to my chest, but the sides of the tub wouldn't allow it, so I pulled the pillow down over my ears and began to hum. Not a melody, just notes, sounds, something for my lungs to do besides whimper.

The bathroom door rattled as though a monster wanted in, but I didn't stop humming. Even when the commode gurgled loudly, even when the air seemed to be sucked from the room, even when I could no longer hear the sound of my own vocal cords over the fury of the storm. The oxygen I breathed seemed charged with electricity, and the hairs on my arms stood on end. Then the wind came closer, on the other side of the bathroom wall, as though my bedroom had been opened up and exposed to the rage. My humming turned to crying again, but I no longer held back the tears. My fears had given way to a primal instinct for survival, and I openly sobbed. And prayed.

God, please don't leave me alone. I don't want to die.

Something slammed against the opposite side of the bathroom wall and rang slightly as if it were metallic, and I hunkered down even more. But then, suddenly and eerily, I could hear the siren again, rising and falling on the wind, no longer drowned out by the storm's anger. In fifteen more seconds, the piercing howls had stopped completely, and an unearthly silence fell over the house.

I didn't move. Was it over? Was I safe? A low, rumbling thunder growled in the distance, but it sounded like the beast had been tamed.

The heels of my tennis shoes pressed against one side of the tub, and my elbows shoved against the other. Every muscle was taut as though I could hold myself in that slick-sided tub, just by my own willpower. In the distance I heard the wail of an emergency vehicle.

My fingers were clenched tightly into fists, but slowly I relaxed them and pushed myself up, fumbling for my phone. It wasn't bright enough to calm my nerves, and my hands shook, sending trembling shadows jittering across the walls. On shaky legs I stood and tripped over the edge of the tub, stumbling over makeup and broken plastic.

I paused with my hand on the doorknob, imagining the wind would still be raging on the other side of it. My brain felt foggy, and I blinked to clear my head, but it only made me dizzy. Jerking the door open, I shone the light into the hallway, then stepped toward the living room. A soft breeze came through my bedroom door, sweeping past my ankles like ice water. When I shone the light in there, I could tell the corner of the room was missing, but I couldn't see much else. It gave me the irrational feeling that the house was no longer grounded on earth but up in a tree, or on top of another house, or dangling from a light pole. I hurried to the front door, fearing the whole structure might topple at any moment, burying me alive.

The front door dragged along the hardwood floor, refusing to swing open more than a foot, but I squeezed through to the porch. I staggered down the steps and halfway to the street, where I turned back to peer at my home, fully expecting it to be visibly altered, but it wasn't too bad. The hatchback still sat in the driveway, but the carport had been peeled away like the top of a tin can, and the tree that Clyde had trimmed after the last storm had snapped off at the ground.

My arms and legs felt numb, and my ears seemed to have Styrofoam covering them. Everything I felt and heard was dull and muffled as though I were underwater. Neighbors stumbled from their houses. Someone was moaning. In the distance a child screamed. And through it all, a light smattering of raindrops fell softly, as if Mother Nature was teasing us, claiming the storm had never happened.

I clawed at my cell phone, desperate to check on Velma and Ruthie and the others, but I had no service. Even my flashlight was getting dim, its battery low. I shut it off and stood still in the middle of the sidewalk, not knowing what to do, not knowing if my family was alive or dead, not knowing if I could survive if something had happened. To Clyde.

Headlights came around the corner. A car moving slowly to avoid fallen tree branches and other debris in the street. I squinted when the glare hit my eyes, but then I got a better look at my house as the lights swept across. All I noticed was that the roof slanted to the left, and my groggy brain registered that I shouldn't go back inside. Not safe.

I wrapped my arms around myself, gripping my waist, and started to hum again as I rocked back and forth.

"Lynda." A light pat on my shoulder told me the owner of the car had stopped. She now had her arm around me. She was talking, asking if I was all right, insisting we needed to go to the Dairy Queen.

"The Dairy Queen?" I asked, barely able to form the words for all the questions flooding my mind. Velma and her kids out at the farm. Dodd and Ruthie at the church. But Clyde wasn't at the Dairy Queen. No reason to go there.

"Hurry!" She sounded frantic. "It missed the church building, and Ruthie heard from Velma. Your family is all right. They're safe, but Clyde's in trouble at the Dairy Queen." She tugged on my waist. "Come with me, Lynda."

And then my ears popped, and the Styrofoam fell away, and I was no longer numb, no longer seeing things through a fog. I was alert and adrenaline charged, but my heart tightened into an immovable mass of clay. Clyde was in danger. If something happened to him, I would be alone for the rest of my life.

I yielded to the gentle pulls of those two soft hands. The person who came to get me. The one who knew I belonged with Clyde, and the one who understood what it felt like to be alone for so very, very long.

Susan.

CHAPTER
FORTY-FIVE

Thick darkness wrapped around Clyde like a wool blanket, but it did nothing to shelter him from the cold temperature of the freezer. The metal floor felt like needles of ice poking through his jeans, and his head and shoulders pressed against a wall that reminded him of an igloo. Another box. Another cell. After the storm had banged against the door with ferocity worse than any prison riot, the abrupt silence smothered him. He could hear nothing but Neil's ragged breathing, and after the intense volume of the tornado, the small sound echoed through his head like a bass drum.

"Is it over?" Neil yelled the words, and his voice bounced around the enclosure, ricocheting off the frozen walls. "It sounds like it's over, but there's no way to get out of here!"

A knifing pain sliced across Clyde's thigh, radiating all the way down to his toes, and when he gingerly felt his leg, his fingers came away moist and sticky.

"You idiot." Neil cursed in the darkness, and Clyde could hear him bumbling against shelves and knocking over boxes. "We're going to survive a tornado just to freeze to death. Or suffocate."

"We can get out, man." Clyde felt dizzy. "The door opens from the inside."

"Thank God." Neil clawed for the latch, apparently ready to abandon Clyde in his frenzy to escape.

Clyde didn't care what happened to Neil. If he managed to evade the Texas Rangers, the highway patrol would catch up to him before he made it to Mexico. And even if they didn't, that was fine, too.

Neil pulled the latch, and a sliver of gray appeared against the blackness. "It's stuck." He slammed against the door, grunting like a wild animal, but the sliver of gray only widened to a crack. Neil must have shoved his hands through and gripped the door, because Clyde heard him pulling and shoving in an attempt to free himself.

Clyde wondered if the rest of the building was still standing. Just before the door closed, it had sounded as though the roof was ripped away.

Neil stilled his frantic movements. "Something's wedged against the door, and it won't open more than three inches."

"Is it the grill?" Clyde asked, knowing it didn't make a difference but thinking his voice might calm Neil.

"Feels like the jukebox from out in the dining room, but there's something on top of that. There's debris piled higher than the freezer. I can't tell what it is. Might be a table. Maybe the cash register or something." He cursed again. "We're going to die from this cold."

So they were buried beneath piles of machinery and furniture. "Power's off," Clyde reassured him. "The freezer's not running, so now that you got the door open, it'll warm up in here. We'll be just fine."

"But I've got to get out!"

Clyde tried to push himself up to a seated position, but his palms slipped in thick wetness on the floor, already freezing to a slushy consistency. "I think I'm bleeding." He felt as though a magician were twirling a wand inside his head, and he closed his eyes to still the movement.

Neil scurried toward him, bumping Clyde's sore leg and feeling his way from Clyde's shin to his hip. He moved away momentarily, then pressed something soft against the wound.

Clyde gritted his teeth. "What is that?"

"My shirt. It won't absorb much, but if you hold it tight, the bleeding might stop."

"We need light," Clyde said. "You got a phone?"

"Do you honestly think I wouldn't have already called for help if I had a phone?" His answer burned like acid, but then he sighed helplessly. "I left it in the truck."

Clyde held his hand against his leg, but even through the fabric of Neil's shirt, liquid oozed between his fingers. "You hurt, Neil?"

"Bump on the head." He grunted as though he had touched a wound. "Goose egg. And I feel like I have glass fragments embedded in my skin, but other than that, I'll live."

He would live.

Clyde closed his eyes, wondering who else would live. Fawn and the baby would be with JohnScott, but where was Lynda? The coldness crept farther under his skin, all the way down to his heart. Most likely she would be home alone, holed up by herself, scared.

Father God, please keep her safe.

He felt in his pocket. "I've got matches. If we started a makeshift fire, we would have both light and heat."

"And smoke inhalation," Neil snapped, but in spite of his argument, he groped for Clyde's hand and took the matches.

"If you build it next to the door," Clyde said, "it will vent out."

"What can we burn? Boxes?"

"They wouldn't last long. What else can you find?"

The crack in the door let in just enough light that Clyde could make out Neil's shape as he fumbled around the shelves, mumbling about frozen food, and then the rancher felt around outside the door. "There's a box out there, above my head. I don't know what it is." He grunted. "Can't quite reach it."

Clyde knew Neil wasn't handling the stress well, because he had lost the ability to problem-solve. "Get a couple hamburger crates to stand on."

For the next few minutes, Neil worked, slamming packages of frozen food so he could reach the box just outside the freezer. "I don't even know what's in it."

"Whatever it is, it's not frozen."

Neil reached through the crack again and ripped the box open, and then it sounded as though he pounded his fist against the doorframe. "It's just bags of chips. A lot of good those will do us."

"Fritos?" Clyde chuckled softly. "That'll work." A few seconds of silence followed, and Clyde squinted into the darkness. "Seriously, those things burn like a torch."

"You think you know everything." Neil spoke in a desperate whine. "That doesn't even make sense."

Clyde inhaled deeply, trying to muster the strength to explain, but then he heard the crinkle of a Frito bag and the scraping of a match.

As soon as the flame leaped to life, Clyde could see that Neil was pale, frantic, terrified. But probably not worried about suffocating or freezing to death. Neil Blaylock was trapped with fate spiraling around him.

The fire licked at the corner of the Frito bag, engulfing the yellow plastic. Neil seemed transfixed by the flame, then quickly set it down next to the barely open door as the fire settled into the chips, crackling and popping as it slowly consumed the oil.

Clyde inspected his leg in the dim light and found a deep, gaping wound with blood seeping around the shirt, even when he kept his hand firmly shoved against his thigh. He looked around the small room and pointed at the shelves. "I could use some of that tape."

Neil reached for a box of hamburger patties. Stripping the packing tape from the seams, he knelt by Clyde's side and wrapped the plastic around his leg and the shirt. When he tightened it, the bleeding slowed.

Clyde clenched his fists against the shooting pain. "Thank you."

Neil pushed the burning corn-chip bag with the toe of his loafer. "The smoke seems to be getting out somehow, so maybe we're not in too bad of shape." He dropped to the floor to sit cross-legged, folded over the fire, but his actions seemed a degree off. Even his compassion was out of character, and Clyde hoped if Neil warmed himself by the fire, it would help to settle him.

The blood on Clyde's jeans was turning to ice, and he tried to push himself toward the fire, but he didn't have the strength. Instead, he reached one palm toward the heat.

Neil noticed him, then stood and gripped Clyde by one arm, dragging him to the fire. He dropped him roughly near the door, where a shelf dug into Clyde's shoulder.

Clyde settled against the doorframe and bent his good leg to keep from sliding back down, but his other leg lay lifeless. He motioned to two jackets hanging on a hook and chided himself for not thinking of them sooner.

Neil laid one across Clyde's chest and wrapped the other around his leg, tying the arms tightly. Then he settled back on the floor in front of the fire, fidgeting like a caged tiger. "You think the church got hit?"

The church. Fawn and Nathan would be there. And JohnScott. Clyde wiped his forehead. How could he be sweating in a freezer? "Was Susan at the church building?"

"Without a doubt."

Clyde stared at the flickering firelight. He didn't know the path of the twister, but Velma's ranch was farther from town. Maybe Lynda had been out there and missed the worst of it. Maybe she was safe. Alive. Maybe his world wouldn't be snuffed out.

"What if they're all dead?" Neil's palms covered his head. "What if this is how it ends?"

"How what ends?"

"The nightmare."

Clyde didn't have to ask what he meant. Both of them had been living a twisted nightmare for two decades, and it wouldn't surprise him if it ended like this, with Trapp, Texas, and all its gossip, drama, and lies wiped off the face of the earth. If he and Neil were the only two left alive … that would be just what they deserved.

"Did you always love her?" Neil asked. "Lynda?"

Normally Clyde would have told him it was none of his business, but if having a conversation would keep Neil tethered to reality, Clyde would be honest with him. "Yes, always, but I wasn't going to split up the two of you."

"That's awful sentimental of you." Neil snickered, sounding more like himself. "As if you could have split us up anyway."

Clyde closed his eyes and said softly, "I split you up in the end."

"Was that your intention when you dated Susan?"

"Of course not." Clyde's answer came sure and certain, but he didn't care to go into detail.

Neil leaned forward, his eyes wide as if he were watching a gory movie and enjoying it. "Do you regret being with Susan?"

Suddenly Neil was an annoying inmate, a rookie, stupid and panicky. Clyde felt as though claustrophobia was closing in on him. Twenty years of imprisonment should have made him immune, but blood loss amplified the effects of the tight space and the stress. Not only did he need to keep Neil talking, but he also needed to keep himself conscious. "That's not a yes-or-no question."

Neil leaned back on his palms and stared at the ceiling, watching the smoke swirl and seep out the door. "No, it's not."

"I regret all that happened, and I regret going to prison." Clyde took a deep breath, trying to keep the room from spinning. "But I can't regret Fawn."

"No," Neil said. "I can't regret Fawn. Or Nathan." He shoved another bag of chips on the fire.

"Did you always love Lynda?" Clyde's words slurred.

"No. I loved her in high school. I thought I loved her enough to marry her, but when it came down to it, I guess I didn't. Not that kind of love anyway. My parents—my dad especially—wanted something different for me. He told me that some things were more important than love … and then Susan's family offered me all those things."

Anger sparked at the base of Clyde's spine, but it fizzled instantly from lack of fuel.

"If I had loved her as much as she deserved," Neil said, "I wouldn't have chosen a cattle ranch over her. And a near stranger for a bride." He cackled. "A stranger fat with another man's baby."

A drop of sweat trickled into Clyde's eye, stinging. "You've sure given Lynda a lot of grief over the years."

Neil grunted, and his words became daggers. "When Hoby married her, I thought I would explode. Not just because he had Lynda, but because they were free. They got married because they chose to, and they had Ruthie because they chose to." He hissed. "They had everything."

"You couldn't stand it." Clyde struggled to keep his eyes open.

"I know I drove them mad." Neil stood and shifted his weight from foot to foot. "I was insane with jealousy. As though Satan had thrust his talons deep in my chest and wouldn't let go. And I had so much guilt. For leaving Lynda, for marrying Susan, for not being the dad Fawn needed, for hating Hoby." He pressed his fist against his lips. "For putting you away." His movements stilled, and he wilted. "I wanted to die, Clyde. So many times over, I wanted to die, but I'm too much of a coward."

Above them and to the side, thumps and clanks could be heard, then silence again.

A jolt of energy caused Clyde to open his eyes. "Need to bang. Let them know we're in here."

Neil was already shoving items to the floor, yanking at the shelving, knocking boxes over.

Another muffled sound came from outside.

Clyde leaned his head against the door, spent. "Use your belt buckle."

Neil didn't hear him, and Clyde had to repeat himself, but then the rancher slid off his belt and clanged the shiny buckle against the metal shelves, the walls, the ceiling.

Clyde held his breath, listening for any sound that might indicate the rescuers would help. He thought he might have heard voices calling, but his ears were ringing so badly, he couldn't be sure. He leaned to the side and rested his temple against a box. It was cool and smelled of cardboard, and for a moment he thought of the back room of the Trapp Door, where everything smelled like books. *He couldn't pass out.*

"I heard something!" Neil shoved against the door again, but Clyde didn't move. "I hear a rumble. Probably a tractor pulling this pile of junk off us." Neil put his mouth to the door. "I'm in the freezer! Get me out of here!" He paced a few more times, then threw himself back to the floor. His gaze jerked from the four corners of the enclosure to the crack in the door, and then he rubbed his knuckles.

Undoubtedly Hector Chavez would be out there—if he were still alive—with the Rangers, ready to arrest Neil for Hoby's murder. Clyde thought of Lynda, and a wave of grief washed through his lungs. Lyn had been through so much. She didn't need anything else. Except God. Clyde only hoped he lived long enough to help her see that.

He squinted at Neil. "Why did you turn the church against Lynda?" His voice had become even softer, and he wondered if Neil would hear him. "Why did you want her to leave the congregation?"

Neil didn't answer, and Clyde didn't have the strength to repeat himself. He didn't even have the strength to breathe. He supposed it didn't matter anyway. Even if he bled out and died in the Dairy Queen freezer, what had been done all those years ago could never be undone.

"I didn't just want her to leave the church." Neil tried to snicker again, but it sounded pitiful, as if he was crying inside. "I didn't care so much about that. I wanted her to leave Trapp altogether, but I should have known she wouldn't abandon Ansel and Velma."

Clyde wiped his tongue over dry lips as he pictured Lynda struggling to get by with a child while she fought depression. "Why'd you hate her so much?"

"I didn't hate her." Neil's words blended with the rumble of the distant tractor until Clyde imagined him to be a dragon, growling low and breathing fire-laced threats. "I wanted her for myself so badly, I couldn't think straight, but she wouldn't. Even with Hoby gone, she refused." He sniffled. "And when Hoby died ... I needed her away from Trapp so people would forget him. Stop wondering where he'd gone off to, why he never came back, what could have happened to him." The dragon voice shuddered. "I needed her gone. But she just wouldn't leave."

Clyde watched the pathetic beast. Neil's fingers trembled, and his eyes showed too much white. "But you're not a killer," Clyde said. "Are you?"

Neil looked up in surprise but didn't answer, only shoved another bag of chips to the fire.

They sat in silence, listening to the sounds of liberty and capture coming closer, and Clyde realized the question had calmed both of them.

Neil cleared his throat. "There was a time I hated you so much, I thought I could have killed you."

"Me? Or Hoby?"

"Both of you." His face twisted into a grimace. "But you were safe in prison by then."

"Why me?"

Neil laughed as if Clyde had told a bad joke. "You ruined Susan's life, and after a while, that started to bother me."

Clyde could feel the vibrations of the tractor now as it worked to free them, probably pulling rubble one piece at a time.

"I'm not a killer," Neil growled, "but I might as well be."

Clyde's vision was swimming, but he focused on Neil and the words he was saying. "Tell me what happened."

"He came to my house!" Neil bit into his fist. "Susan saw me leave with him. She probably thinks I killed him."

The room tipped to the left. "Then what?"

"Hoby wanted to know the truth about Lynda and me, whether we had been together." Neil sobbed, but the sob turned into a high-pitched laugh. "He was sober and levelheaded, and he kept asking me, man to man, if Ruthie was his daughter." Neil stared at Clyde as though begging for mercy. "And I lied to him again. I claimed Ruthie as my own because I couldn't bear the thought of Hoby having something I wanted."

"But the gun?"

"We were out at the lake. I took him down there so nobody would see us together." He shrugged. "That's where we used to hang out, you know. It seemed harmless enough, but when we got down there, he got all emotional. One minute he was trying to slug me for taking his wife, and the next minute he was crying and saying he was worthless."

Clyde could feel his consciousness slipping away, and he wondered if he would die. He wondered who would take care of Lynda if he did. She would be all right because she had Velma. And Ruthie and JohnScott ... So many people loved her.

Neil slammed his fist against the floor, jerking Clyde back to the present.

"Did you get your gun out of your glove box?" Clyde asked.

"No," Neil whined. "Hoby got it. He knew it was there, of course. Everybody in town knew. We were arguing. He called me a snake and said something about blowing my head off." Neil's fists gripped his hair. "That's what I thought he said, Clyde! I swear that's what I thought he said!" He stared into the fire before finishing his story with little emotion. "I tried to grab the gun away from him, and it went off." Neil's eyes glistened in the firelight. "But then Hoby fell to the ground ... and that's when I saw it ... a diamondback. It was warm that day and the rattler had come out of hibernation, groggy and slow moving. The thing was no real threat, but that's what Hoby had said to me. He was going to shoot the head off the snake."

"So it was an accident," Clyde whispered hoarsely.

Neil's jaw hardened. "He was killed with my gun, Clyde. In the middle of nowhere. And Lynda knew I had a motive, and she would have told everyone."

"You could have told the truth."

"It's too late for that now." He cackled again, returning to his agitated state. "For God's sake, I dragged his body all the way to Picnic Hollow after I dumped his wrecker in the lake. I filed an insurance claim for a gun I threw in the lake." He shook his head. "No jury will believe a word I say."

A loud scraping sound came from outside the door, and it swung open, causing Clyde to fall hard against the floor. His eyes squinted against bright lights, and he heard voices. Troy. And Lynda. Even Susan.

But then warm darkness seeped through his brain ... and he was gone.

CHAPTER
FORTY-SIX

"It's a fine day for a funeral, Lynda." Tuesday morning Velma stood at the back of the church building, peering through the window at the bright sunshine, and I wondered if my sister was blind to the chaos. Even though the small chapel remained standing, it was one of the few buildings in Trapp that hadn't suffered structural damage. Toothpick-sized splinters had been driven deep into the white-washed siding like so many nails, and the steeple had been hurled into Charlie Mendoza's cotton field as if God himself had thumped it with His index finger. I couldn't help thinking the Big Man had finally gotten fed up with our town and had shaken us by the shoulders to get our attention.

"At least the funeral home wasn't hit." I squinted at the brightness, reminding myself that my cup was half full and not half empty, but still, my heart couldn't muster a happy thought. There was too much destruction, too much death, too much sorrow, and I realized that being alone all those years had its perks. When I sheltered myself from the world—keeping distant from anyone who tried to befriend me—life hadn't hurt this badly. I chuckled, but it tasted sour in my mouth. I thought life hadn't hurt because no one stood close enough to touch me, when actually it hurt tremendously. Because I hadn't been alive.

"It's time." Dodd tapped my elbow, and I joined the slow procession down the aisle. Every pew in the little building was packed to bursting, and folding chairs had been stuffed along the side aisles and in the foyer, but still, the crowd overflowed onto the lawn. As we passed the fifth pew from the back, I glanced at its polished wood and remembered sitting there with Hoby. Ruthie had squirmed on the pew between us, swinging her patent-leather shoes and trying to be quiet. Then one day Hoby was gone. It seemed so long ago, and all that time I never knew I was a widow.

The strong scent of flowers threatened to give me a headache, but their beauty comforted me like one of my momma's lingering hugs. People cared about my family. They cared about our loss. They cared about *me*. Even the Christians showed compassion with their casseroles and sympathy cards. Pamela Sanders had met me in the parking lot just this morning, not wanting me to walk in without a friend by my side. Troy hadn't been with her, but that was to be expected. He would be tending to Clyde at the hospital.

I stopped, and the heels of my shoes dug into the plush carpet while I waited for Ansel's children and grandchildren to file into the first three rows. They packed themselves like sardines, as though their pain would be lessened if they only got closer together. Then I followed Dodd down the fourth row, and Ruthie sat between us, and I was glad her husband wouldn't be preaching the eulogy. Ruthie needed him by her side, and I needed him, too. Over the years I had known family and friends who passed away, but I hadn't been compelled to attend their funerals. Now I wondered why not. Clyde would say it was because of painful memories of my parents, and maybe Clyde was right.

I sighed, wishing he could be with me, holding my hand, letting me hold his finger. He had scared the wits out of me on Sunday night. When they finally pulled his limp body from the rubble at the DQ, I thought he was dead. I thought I had been abandoned yet again, but they whisked him away to the hospital in Lubbock. After a few pints of blood had been administered, Clyde came to, babbling and asking if everyone was all right, and wanting to know about me. *Me.*

My initial reaction had been anger. Of course. After a short visit in his hospital room, I fled to Ruthie's house to sleep off my emotions. That had been yesterday, and today I was dealing with the loss of Ansel. I hadn't yet let myself think about the others in town who hadn't made it through the storm. Maria Fuentes, Quinten Snodgrass, Corky Ledbetter and her youngest child, but I could work through that grief later. I was in no rush.

And I wasn't alone. I never had been.

I peered at the back of Velma's head, her hair more gray now than brown and flattened on one side as though she had lain down for a nap before the service. Her oldest daughter sat by her side, sniffling, and Velma's head lolled to the side without energy.

Velma wasn't alone either.

The preacher from Slaton officiated the service, and even though Buster was a nice man, I had never thought about him as one of my brother-in-law's close friends. It didn't really matter, of course.

Everyone for miles around knew Ansel, and the small building swelled with mourners. The fact that Ansel's was the first funeral following the fatal tornado only packed the place more tightly, because even near strangers needed a release for their pain. Didn't we all.

Toward the end of the service, Dodd stood slowly, and Ruthie looked at him in surprise. When Buster noticed Dodd making his way to the front, he stepped aside.

"Ansel Pickett was a good man," Dodd began. "Lots of people would say he was so good, God wouldn't dare keep him out of the pearly gates, but I want to tell you today that none of us need to make excuses for Ansel. We don't need to bargain with God, or pray real hard, or cross our fingers, because Ansel was right with the Lord." His gaze swept the first rows. "Last week your father called me to come out to the ranch. We sat in his living room and drank lemonade … *and Ansel talked.*"

Dodd's eyes crinkled as he smiled. "He didn't usually have much to say, but that day he almost wore my ears off, saying he had a lot on his mind and he needed to unload." Even though Dodd was grinning, his eyebrows still held a sad slant to them. "And then he asked me to keep it under my hat until today."

A hush fell over the audience, and I felt my burdens lift slightly, eased by the curiosity of what Ansel had said.

"He felt he needed to confess to me, even though I told him most things were between him and God." Dodd swallowed, blinking away a tear. "And then he asked me to baptize him. I can still hear his voice as he said the words. *Dodd, some folks don't adhere to baptism, but my boy JohnScott did it, and he said he felt real clean afterward. I want to feel like that, too. Washed clean.*"

Several of Ansel's daughters leaned forward to look at their brother, who had tears running down his face even though he was laughing quietly.

"So I baptized that stubborn father of yours right there in the bathtub." Dodd's eyes reddened as he smiled. "You all know the size of that tub, so you can imagine it took a few dunks to get all of him wet, but when I helped him to his feet and he gripped his walker again, he was grinning from ear to ear. He was nodding his head. He was laughing out loud. Because he said it worked. He felt clean." Dodd chuckled. "I don't remember his exact words, but I think he said he felt better than a mountain boomer on a sunny day."

Sniffles mixed with giggles erupted from the rows in front of me, and several of my nieces nodded.

"I just want you all to know that I would never use this scenario as a means to pressure you or guilt you into following the Lord." Dodd wiped his eyes with a tissue. "But your dad clearly didn't have the same scruples, and he told me not to breathe a word of this before today. For one, he didn't want all the attention and questions, but more than anything, he didn't want to have to debate it with any of you. He wanted me to stand before you today, at the base of his casket, and tell you these words: *Get yourselves in church.*" Soft laughter erupted from all over the room. "He said now that he got you here, you might as well stay for a spell."

I squirmed on the hard pew, feeling like Ruthie all those years ago and figuring she was thinking about me, too. So many times in the past year and a half, she had said she'd give anything to have me in church with her. But she hadn't meant she'd forfeit her uncle Ansel.

As we crept back up the aisle, my gaze roamed the packed pews, and in the eyes of the congregants and the townspeople, I imagined I saw repentance instead of piety, compassion instead of scorn, forgiveness instead of criticism. But deep down inside, I knew it didn't matter what they said to my face or what they mumbled behind my back, because they were there for me. Maybe they had always been there—*some of them*—waiting to help me whenever I was willing.

We cleared the doorway and walked out beneath a sunny sky, and I squeezed Ruthie's hand before I slipped to the hatchback. Without my saying so, she would understand that I had pushed the limits of my goodwill. Even though I felt a connection that I thought had long since been severed, I needed a time-out. If I was going to the cemetery, I needed a few moments, alone in my car, to process my scattered feelings.

And boy, were they scattered.

Once again I ached to have Clyde by my side, making light of my sadness and lifting me up. After the graveside service, I would make another trip to the hospital in Lubbock and tell him about my morning. He would probably just nod and *hmm* and scratch his chin, but that's all I really needed anyway.

As I watched people move haltingly from the church building to their cars, I evaluated each one of them, remembering the hurts between us but also recognizing—and admitting—the strengths. For years I had scorned the small world where I lived. I had seen only the bad in the people and always, *always* the faults in the church, and I had blamed my problems on my circumstances. And on God, if I was honest.

But as I watched those people console my sister, hug my daughter, and shake my son-in-law's hand, I knew they were not the source of my problems. Sure, they were a gossipy bunch who didn't always say or do the right things, but they were real. They were human.

And they were just like me.

A movement far to the left caught my attention, and I turned to see puffs of gray smoke billowing into the clear sky. For an instant I feared someone else might be trapped or dying, but then my pulse slowed. The smoke was farther away, up on the Cap, where Clyde's old house stood, and I could just make out orange flames flicking into the air.

At that moment, I realized I'd be missing the graveside service after all. It wouldn't be the first time I had avoided a crowd, and it wouldn't be the last, but this time was different. This time the reason was something other than my own discomfort.

That stinker. Not only had Clyde been released from the hospital, but he was up there on the Cap, burning down that silly token of his. And I needed to go to him.

CHAPTER
FORTY-SEVEN

As I rounded the curve in front of Clyde's house, I slowed the hatchback, watching as flames thrashed through the open windows and devoured the roof. The dry wood of the place was going up fast, and the smoke rose straight into the air, unhindered by any sort of breeze. No wind. No weather. Nothing was left of the raging storm of two nights back.

Except mud. Apparently Clyde had asked a neighboring farmer to plow a swath around the house, because the earth had been upturned to create a barrier of moist soil to prevent the fire from spreading to the mesquite trees and cedars and the fields beyond them.

A safe distance from the fire sat a water truck from the volunteer fire department, and Troy Sanders sat atop it, watching the show from the best seat in the house. On the ground at the front bumper stood Clyde.

He must have seen me before I saw him, because he was watching as I eased the hatchback to a stop. When I opened the door, I could feel the heat from the flames, and I stepped to the far side of the car where the air was cooler.

Clyde said something to Troy, who glanced at me and laughed, and I wondered how Clyde had explained the fire to him.

I leaned against the hatchback with my arms on the roof, and Clyde limped across the yard and joined me, bending slightly to rest his elbows next to mine. We watched silently as the roof of the house fell in on itself, temporarily dousing the flames for several seconds before they leaped back up. We stood together as his memories went up in flames, and I wondered if Clyde felt the same release I had felt.

My gaze slid to his elbow, and I noticed his tattoo peeking out from under his sleeve. My fingers wiggled, wanting to pull his sleeve away, wanting to touch the Bible verse branded on his arm, but I kept myself from it. I kept myself from imagining the locations of his other four tattoos.

I forced my gaze back to the house just in time to see the last wall fall. Then the fire slowed and gently gnawed on the remaining timbers.

Finally I got up the nerve to speak, but not about the obvious. "When did you get out of the hospital?"

Clyde looked at me out of the corner of his eye. "Just this morning the doc said I was good to go as long as I went home and rested, but I haven't made it home yet." He looked over his shoulder at the view. "Unless you count this place."

I laced my fingers together, then alternated my thumbs. "And aren't you supposed to keep your leg elevated?"

"Yep. That, too. And I'm supposed to be on crutches for a few weeks."

I rolled my eyes but didn't look at him.

"Troy's got 'em in the tanker." As if hauling crutches in a vehicle would heal his leg just as quickly as walking with them.

Only a few smoldering piles of debris remained where the old shack had been, and Troy called to Clyde, then swept his palm toward the fire like a beautiful girl presenting a Lamborghini at a car show.

Clyde gestured toward the house, a signal for Troy to spray the place down with water. At first the droplets sizzled and steamed, sending a fresh bundle of smoke and soot into the air, but after only a few minutes, the flames stopped fighting.

"I was sorry to miss Ansel's funeral," Clyde said.

"You would have been proud of him." I chuckled. "He left Dodd with instructions to give the family a guilt trip about church."

"Naw." Clyde's jaw dropped open in a grin. "I didn't know he was a believer."

"Just recently, I guess."

Clyde rubbed his chin. "Well, don't that beat all." He faced me then, leaning his side against the car so that he could stare. "What did you think about his challenge, Lyn?"

"It's only been twenty minutes. I haven't had much time to think on it."

He hummed in thought. "If you had to guess, what would you say you'd think about it, once you had time to think?"

I rolled my eyes again. "I might tag along with Velma sometime. She's been talking about it a little."

"You'd go with ... Velma?" His left eyebrow lifted slightly.

Troy called across the yard, and I welcomed the interruption. "You got it from here, Felton?"

"Sure thing. You go on now."

"It was a good burn!" Troy yelled.

As the water truck pulled away, I asked, "A good burn?"

Clyde shrugged. "Burning stuff is fun."

We stood in silence for a few minutes, and then Clyde gazed over the rim of the Cap.

"The town's a mess, I guess," he said. "I haven't been down there yet."

I followed him to the edge of the drop-off, where we looked down on Trapp. The damage showed even more from this perspective, and I could see how the tornado had hopped from street to street, leaving some houses and taking others. I cringed. *So many people were hurt.* "Half the buildings are gone. The grain elevator ... the elementary school ... the United."

"How's your house?"

"There's a chunk out of the backside, and there's no sign of the carport." I shrugged. "But I haven't had anybody look at it yet." *That was Ansel's job.*

"I can take care of it, Lyn." Clyde put emphasis on the first word, and his eyes bored into mine. "If it's not too bad, I can fix it up. With JohnScott's help." He looked away as though it were settled. "Where are you staying?"

"Dodd and Ruthie's house. On the couch." I looked back toward town, my gaze following the path of destruction. "Your trailer's gone."

"Gone?"

"I've seen parts of it all over town, but not any pieces large enough to keep for a souvenir." I shivered. "Good thing you were at the Dairy Queen."

We stood in silence then, looking far below, watching a long line of cars making their way toward the cemetery. The shadow of Ansel's death washed over me again, but I brushed it aside, unable to dwell on the sadness because of my relief. Relief that Clyde had been saved after being buried alive.

"I guess we'll have a few more funerals this week," I said.

"Sorry for those ones."

"Me, too. Maria Fuentes was a friend of Ruthie's." I took a deep breath. "I came here to apologize."

"Apologize?"

"Is that so hard to believe?"

"Naw, it's not that," he said. "It's just that I'm not sure what you're apologizing for."

"Like there are too many things?"

He frowned. "No. Like I'm not sure what you're apologizing for."

I walked away from him, stopping a few yards in front of the car, where I could glare at the mounds of steaming ash. "I'm sorry for giving you a hard time about your grandpappy's house. I'm sorry for turning away from you because of it. I'm sorry for being a basket case."

"Well …"—he studied me from where he stood at the edge of the cliff—"I'm sorry you thought I was dead. I don't plan on ever leaving you again."

"You better not," I called. "I've decided to need you."

"No way."

"And I've decided to let you take care of me."

Laughter boomed from deep in his chest. "Come back over here, Lyn."

"No." I raised my chin. "You come over here."

He did nothing except smile, and his shoulders shook silently.

I pouted, wishing he would come where I was. Wishing I didn't have to go to him. Wishing he would do everything in the world to make my life easier.

He shook his head and held his hands out as he did so often for Nathan, and the action sent my heart into a tailspin. Satin cords pulled me toward his open arms, so ready to shelter me, comfort me, want me. I took three steps and melted into his embrace.

"Thank you for burning your stupid house." I rubbed my cheek against his chest. "I can't believe you did that."

"I got the idea from you."

I started to ask him what he meant, but then I remembered jokingly telling him to tear down the old place. I shuddered. And that night at the diner I said I wouldn't go there with him. I wanted to blot the memories from my mind—along with my selfishness—but that likely wouldn't happen. I hadn't been able to erase any other memories, not completely, but I had been able to let them go. And Clyde would help me.

"I'm a better person with you than I am alone," I said.

"I could say the same thing. We're a team."

He smiled, but he was no longer laughing at me. Instead, he was just happy. Happier than he'd been in years—maybe in his whole life. He held me against his chest and kissed the top of my head. "You don't leave me either, okay?"

I looked up at him. "Not a chance."

EPILOGUE

The following year was full of changes. For starters, Clyde and I got married. We didn't make a fuss, as that wasn't our style. We simply got a license and had Dodd speak a few words before we made our promises. Ruthie and Velma stood by me, and Fawn and JohnScott by Clyde, and Nathan toddled back and forth between us. It was a good day. A healing day. Full of recovery and hope.

Clyde had stayed with Troy and Pam after the storm, making the necessary repairs to my house before we married, and then he quietly moved his things in. Not that he had much to move, because everything he owned—including his sedan—had been destroyed in the tornado. He didn't seem to miss those things, though.

For the first month at least, I hid myself in my bedroom again, but this time with Clyde by my side. It had been built differently than before, with no ghosts or haunts from the past. No clumpy, chipped texture on the walls. It was our room. Mine and Clyde's. I explored his tattoos, and he kissed away my doubts, and we clung to each other as much as possible, trying to convince ourselves that life was real. That happiness was real. That it wasn't going to slip away from us again. After years of turmoil, Clyde and I were finally covered with a veil of peace.

Our little town had its share of lies and secrets, but I got the impression that God—in spite of His infinite love—had grown weary of waiting for the townspeople to acknowledge their faults and had opted instead to blow everything wide open Himself. When that tornado raged through Trapp, it left in its wake a strong group of people dedicated to saving their town. They came together, fighting against the odds, to rebuild and renew, and as they developed a common bond with one another, they gradually began to protect their own with the savage determination of a mother bear.

Clyde, along with the others whose homes were totally destroyed, was showered with food and supplies as well as offers of lodging, transportation, medical care, and anything else he might need. It was as if the storm acted as a great equalizer that leveled the playing field and brought us together.

All of us but one.

Neil had been pulled from the debris at the Dairy Queen and immediately placed in handcuffs and taken away. His trial lasted for months, but according to Hector, there was so much evidence stacked against him, he didn't stand a chance. Even though his gun was never found, they were able to match the bullet in Hoby's skull to two dozen others found in the side of the barn on the Blaylocks' old home place. In the end Neil was convicted of murder and sentenced to life in prison without parole.

Clyde testified in Neil's defense, asserting his innocence and relaying all that Neil had confessed to him that night in the freezer. But it didn't matter. People will believe what they want to believe, regardless of the truth, the jury included. Neil knew that better than anyone. The day Neil's sentence came down and he was sent to prison for a crime he didn't commit, Clyde held me in our bedroom, and we wondered at the irony.

"Things always come back around, don't they?" Clyde said softly.

For some reason I thought of the windmills, spinning constantly round and round, and I nestled closer to my husband. "I guess they do."

Life had a way of repeating itself—sometimes a comfort and sometimes a curse—but because of the predictability, I'd learned to ride out the storm and let the wind die down. No matter what tempest I came up against, eventually the helter-skelter rotations would calm into gentle spirals that I could handle.

"We'll need to visit him," Clyde said.

I nodded reluctantly, not wanting to visit Neil but knowing it needed to be done. "And we need to look out for Susan," I said.

Clyde pulled me closer and kissed the top of my head, and we lay wrapped in each other's arms, staring at the ceiling. Waiting for our world to settle.

And eventually it did.

Once Clyde started making decisions, his confidence snowballed until he was firing off orders left and right. Building a restaurant on the Caprock was the biggest decision he made. A horseshoe-shaped deck filled with tables allowed guests to sit right on the rim while they ate, and those who didn't want to brave the heat and wind could dine inside behind the floor-to-ceiling windows. Clyde and I had more than one debate about which place was the better atmosphere, but even then, I got the feeling he preferred the kitchen.

Every Sunday morning we would set the rolls to rising before we went to worship, and we sneaked out after Dodd's sermon so Clyde could have lunch ready when church let out. Pretty near the entire congregation would show up, along with others who had just crawled out of bed. Clyde's down-home hospitality and good food swiftly became legendary, and after a while he was known for more than just his prison term. Hungry patrons came from surrounding towns, and travelers learned that a detour through Trapp would always be worth the extra time.

"This place is good for us, Lyn," Clyde said one Sunday afternoon. "I'm glad I thought of it."

I dumped a pan of warm buttered rolls into a basket and covered it with a cloth. "That's not exactly the way I remember it."

Nathan ran up to us, bouncing on his tiptoes and stretching his hands above his head. "Clyde! I wanna go up. Up!"

Clyde peered down at the two-year-old. "You know I'm too busy to carry you around." His mouth quivered in a smile.

"I help you, Clyde." Nathan stopped his bouncing and worried his brow as though they were sealing a deal on a major investment.

"Well, in that case ..." Clyde reached down and slowly lifted the child like an elevator going to the top floor while Nathan's Sunday shoes swung back and forth. He nestled the boy in the crook of one arm and picked up the basket of rolls with the other.

"Hand sanitizer," I said, squirting a dollop into Nathan's tiny palm.

As I made my way around the dining room, greeting friends and strangers and offering them menus, I watched my husband with his grandson. Clyde would greet the customers with his booming voice and ask them if they needed a warm-up on their rolls. He held the basket close to Nathan, who would pick up a roll and hand it to the customer. Depending on who was requesting it, Clyde might encourage the boy to pitch it across the table, or keep it to himself, or even take a bite out of it before passing it off.

"You're teaching that kid to be as ornery as you." I tried to frown, but my lips wouldn't cooperate.

"The kid doesn't need teaching, Lyn." Clyde winked at me. "He's a natural."

I followed them out to the deck, where Dodd and Ruthie sat at a table with Fawn and JohnScott. Velma was there as well, and so was Dodd's mother. Nathan scrambled out of Clyde's arms and ran to the side of the deck, where he pressed his palms against the Plexiglas barrier and looked down at the town far below. His long, black curls swished on the breeze.

"Clyde?" JohnScott drawled. "I've been telling Fawn the kid needs a haircut, but she won't listen."

Fawn smiled. "Just because his grandpappy got a haircut doesn't mean Nathan needs one."

"Aw, now," Clyde said. "I don't reckon it matters none."

"He looks like a little girl," Ruthie quipped. "Just the other day at the Walmart in Lubbock, someone asked Fawn how old her daughter was."

"But look at these curls." Fawn reached toward her son and ran her fingers through his hair. "I just can't."

Clyde, still holding the basket of rolls, slipped his arm around my waist. It felt good to be with my family, sharing in their banter, but it felt even better to be standing next to Clyde, saying nothing at all. Gently I shifted my hip to bump his thigh, and he nudged me back.

Velma, sitting at the end of the table, shifted in her chair, and I recognized the look on her face. Obviously she had been waiting for the perfect opportunity to say something that needed to be said, and now that it was here, she wasn't about to miss it. She leveled her gaze at her son. "JohnScott, it's about time you and Fawn had another baby." Her lips curved upward. "And try to make it a girl this time so Fawn can play with ribbons and bows."

My nephew's cheeks flushed red, but his mouth fell open and he laughed loudly, as did everyone else at the table.

The laughter dwindled, and Dodd cleared his throat. "Actually …" He eased to his feet—the preacher could never say much in a seated position—and he looked right at me. "Actually, Ruthie may be able to help with the ribbons and bows."

Two long seconds of silence passed, and then the women at the table squealed. Including me.

More laughter followed, and slaps on the back, and question after question for Ruthie.

And I smiled, realizing I was flooded with happiness. Happiness felt so good. How had I ever thought I could live without it?

Clyde leaned over with his lips next to my ear. "You all right with this news?" His palm slid from my waist to my backside, and he squeezed. *"Granny?"*

"Yes." Raising up on my tiptoes, I giggled but moved toward his tickling instead of away. "I'm just fine with it."

And I was.

I had finally realized it didn't matter if my glass was half full or half empty. That's not what life was about. What mattered was that God stood behind me with a full pitcher, waiting to refill my plastic tumbler … if only I'd let Him. Since I had discovered that fact, my cup hadn't ceased to overflow. Not with material possessions or money. Not with promises of fairy tales and happy endings. Not even with a secure knowledge that I would never be hurt again. *I might*. God simply gave me the hope that I could handle whatever life hurled at me, and then He filled me up with peace, joy, love.

And people.

All the important things.

... a little more ...

When a delightful concert comes to an end,
the orchestra might offer an encore.
When a fine meal comes to an end,
it's always nice to savor a bit of dessert.
When a great story comes to an end,
we think you may want to linger.
And so, we offer ...

AfterWords—just a little something more after you
have finished a David C Cook novel.
We invite you to stay awhile in the story.
Thanks for reading!

Turn the page for ...

NOTE TO THE READER

I hope you enjoyed reading about Trapp, Texas, as much as I enjoyed writing about it. As a child I grew up visiting my grandparents on their ranch in West Texas, and my hazy memories turned up all over *Jilted*, especially at Picnic Hollow. It's a real place, packed with history and nostalgia, but unfortunately, its sandy walls were relocated to the bottom of Lake Alan Henry when the dam was built in 1993. Nevertheless, I couldn't bear to leave it down there. Granted, I took creative liberties in my description of the site, but there are a few details that ring true, like the wagon train … and the rattlesnake.

The geographical inaccuracies don't end there. My version of the wind fields isn't entirely true to Garza and Scurry Counties, because I shortened the distance between the windmills near Fluvanna and those in the cotton fields of Roscoe. I regret this in a way, because one of the things I love about West Texas is the way everything is spread out. On the other hand, Clyde and Lynda simply didn't have time for all that driving.

Even though I already have another story bouncing around my brain, as I finish editing *Jilted*, I'm sad to be completing the Mended Hearts series. Over this three-book journey, the best thing has been the readers I've met along the way. For those of you living with depression and anxiety, I pray Lynda Turner's story will give you strength as you fight the battle. I'd love to hear from you, so feel free

after
words

to contact me through my website, varinadenman.com, or one of the social media hangouts.

Thank you for reading,

Varina

ACKNOWLEDGMENTS

The more I write, the more I appreciate the team of family, friends, and professionals who help make it happen. I owe you all a Texas-sized *thank you*.

To Don, more than anyone, for making it possible for me to write at all. Thank you for your encouragement, your help with laundry and dishes, and for not complaining about all the frozen pizza and ranch dressing we've eaten in the past year.

To my children, Jessica, Drew, Dene, Jillian, and Janae. You guys motivate me more than you know, because I realize someday (far in the distant future), I won't be around to talk to you anymore … but my books will.

To Marci and D'arci for telling me I'm doing it right and for walking arm in arm as we battle our family's version of depression. Lynda Turner called it a beast, and I simply call it Satan. But Satan's a dork. And God is bigger. And we're winning the battle. *Oorah.*

To Mom and Dad for instilling in my heart a love of West Texas. For hauling my siblings and me to the ranch year after year in the old, blue station wagon, for teaching us the difference between cottontails and jackrabbits, and for showing us how a family—even an imperfect one—can love each other deeply.

To Sudona Lombard for reading an early draft of *Jilted* and talking me down off the ledge.

after words

To Linda Wise for proofing the galleys of all three books. Honestly, by that point, I'd read the manuscripts so many times, I couldn't even see the words. Thank you for being my eyes.

To my church family for falling in love with Clyde and Lynda, JohnScott and Fawn, and Dodd and Ruthie. You guys have been a tremendous support and have made this journey even more fun.

To John Boren for loaning me Picnic Hollow and offering to keep it a secret that Clyde and Lynda couldn't actually have hiked there. I'll always consider it an honor to have experienced the satisfaction of standing in the shadow of all those names.

To Ann Montgomery-Moran for advice regarding the legalities of Clyde's registered sex-offender status, Neil's threat of a restraining order, and Hoby's abandonment. You saved me much embarrassment, though I could have avoided a timely rewrite had I contacted you six months earlier. I live and learn.

To John Corp for explaining the basics of wind-farm procedures, the dangers involved for workers, and all the details that brought the turbines up close and personal. I regret not finding a good spot for one of my characters to use a turbine for target practice. That was my favorite detail from all that you told me, so maybe I can use that tidbit in another book someday.

To James M. Childers, PhD, for walking me through the stages of crime scene investigation and allowing me to pick your brain … where I was surprised to find a mother animal scavenging human body parts for her pups, a waterlogged corpse floating to the surface of a lake … and Boy Scouts. I can't make this stuff up.

To my agent, Jessica Kirkland. Thank you for watching the news that day at the lake house. Those two headlines (the car in the lake and the tornado in the small town) supplied me with *Jilted*'s basic plot skeleton (pun intended). And as always, thank you for talking me through the jumble of ideas in my head and helping me figure out my crazy, messed-up characters.

To my developmental editor, Jamie Chavez, not only for cleaning up my story line until it became a sensible plot, but also for teaching me countless secrets of the craft of writing, all while boosting my spirits and counseling me through writer angst. You make an excellent therapist.

To Ingrid Beck, Nick Lee, Helen Macdonald, and Susan Murdock, for turning a mess of typewritten pages into a book. To the marketing people, Lisa Beech, Darren Terpstra, Karla Colonnieves, and Jeane Wynn, who helped put *Jilted* in front of readers. To the copyeditor, Jennifer Lonas, for going over the manuscript with a magnifying glass and remembering miniscule details across all three books. To the cover designer, Amy Konyndyk, for bringing the wind fields to life. And to the folks at David C Cook for taking a chance on a series from a debut author. I will forever be grateful.

BOOK CLUB
DISCUSSION GUIDE

1. *Jilted* opens with Lynda Turner wallowing in bad memories. Have you ever been "stuck" in a pity party for yourself? What steps did Lynda take to pull herself out of her depression? How long did it take?

2. Lynda's depression has been fueled by a lifetime of abandonment. First her parents, then Neil Blaylock, and finally Hoby. How did these abandonments affect Lynda's life in the past and present? Have you ever experienced feelings of abandonment? How did you cope with your feelings?

3. Clyde feels like an outsider at the Trapp congregation. Why do you suppose he feels that way? How could he take actions to change the status quo? What might happen if he did? How else could this problem be remedied? When have you felt like an outsider in your own church? Have you ever inadvertently caused another Christian to feel unwelcome?

4. Lynda's brother-in-law, Ansel Pickett, is like a father to her in many ways. How does his declining health affect Lynda? Explain Ansel's actions near the time of his death. What steps did he take to prepare? Have you ever felt abandoned when a loved one passed? How did Lynda eventually handle his death?

5. Neil Blaylock has caused problems for Clyde and Lynda for years. Have you ever known anyone like him? What motivates his actions? What part of his character can you relate to? How do Clyde and Lynda deal with him? Do you approve of their attitudes? Explain.

6. Clyde and Lynda share a passionate kiss after the football game, but the action is uncharacteristic for both of them. What do you think prompted them to behave in such a way? Were their actions justified? Why or why not? What effect do you think the situation had on Neil? When have you acted rashly because of an emotional reaction?

7. When Hoby's wrecker is found at the lake, some of Lynda's feelings of abandonment shift to grief. What must that have been like for her? How did you feel when she locked herself in her bedroom again? What emotions does she work through as she ponders all that happened when Hoby disappeared and everything that has happened in the years since?

8. Hector Chavez is not only the sheriff but also Lynda's lifelong friend. When he brings news that shakes her world, how does Lynda react? How do you think the truth affected her grieving process? Explain.

9. The author makes gruesome references to Hoby's body, both on land and in the water. Why do you think she included those details? What do the descriptions add to the underlying current of the story? What parallels can you draw about Lynda's depression? Clyde's imprisonment? Neil's bitterness?

10. Clyde enjoys reading. How did this fact influence your opinion of him? What did he learn from books while he was in prison? How did his reading positively influence his post-incarceration syndrome (PICS)? How might this be different for other ex-convicts?

11. Throughout the book, windmills are used as a metaphor. What different ways does the author tie them to Lynda's life? What effect do the turbines have on Lynda? Does Clyde understand this? How do you know? Do you have a special place that gives you peace? Describe it.

12. Neil becomes increasingly unhinged toward the end of the story. How does he attempt to divert the blame from himself? What effect do his actions have on the other characters? What do you think Neil is feeling? Do you think he will ever find peace? Why or why not?

13. Lynda has several "psychological tokens" that she burns on her back porch. Have you ever kept something that reminded you of a painful time in your life? Did it help you? How do you think Lynda's psychological tokens helped or hurt her? What emotions does she feel when she destroys them? How does Clyde's burning his shack on the Caprock bring Lynda's grief full circle? Are psychological tokens always a bad thing? Explain.

14. Lynda deals with two huge losses at the same time—realizing Hoby is dead and losing Ansel. At one point, she says she has too many things distracting her from her grief. When have you had similar times in your life? What helped you to grieve effectively?

15. Clyde and Neil are trapped in a walk-in freezer during the tornado. How do the two men differ in their reactions to this entrapment? What might they have been feeling? Can you relate to either of the men? Both of them? How does your own past affect your outlook on difficult situations?

16. The tornado destroys much of the town, and Lynda wonders if God simply got fed up with the narrow-minded ways of the townspeople. Do you think God would really do something like that? When have you wondered the same thing or been aware of others wondering about it? The town pulled together because of the devastation, but do you think their common bonds will last? What else might need to happen to prevent the citizens from slipping back into their old ways?

17. Neil is eventually imprisoned for a crime he didn't commit. Why is this appropriate? What feelings did you have as you read his verdict? How do you think Neil will manage his imprisonment? What do Clyde and Lynda do to help? Do you think you would have been as compassionate as they are? Why or why not?

18. In the end Lynda and Clyde get their happily ever after. Does Lynda think she will always be happy? What has she discovered about happiness? How have you learned this lesson in your own life? What else has Lynda learned?

ABOUT THE AUTHOR

Varina Denman is a native Texan who lived her high school years in a small Texas town. Now she and her husband live near Fort Worth, where they enjoy spending time with their five mostly grown children. *Jilted* is her third novel. Look for other books in the Mended Hearts series online and in bookstores.

The
Mended Hearts
Series

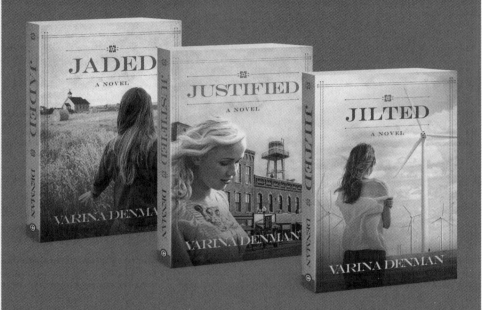

Small Towns Always Hold Big Secrets

The Mended Hearts series captures the rhythm and romance of small-town life. Each intertwined story features a woman searching for hope, whether in the midst of depression, insecurity, or judgmental treatment from the local church.